BLOW-INS

With massive appreciation to my writing group for their constant support, and also huge thanks to Mo Robinson, whose encouragement, and meticulous critical eye, are an essential part of my process.

The characters in this story are all fictitious and any similarity to any real person, living or dead, is probably because I've tried to make them all realistic.

BLOW-INS

Crysse Morrison

HOBNOB PRESS

First published in the United Kingdom
by The Hobnob Press,
8 Lock Warehouse, Severn Road, Gloucester GL1 2GA
www.hobnobpress.co.uk

British Library Cataloguing in Publication Data
A catalogue record for this book is available from the British Library

ISBN 978-1-914407-33-8

Typeset in Adobe Garamond Pro 11/13 pt
Typesetting and origination by John Chandler
Front cover: from a painting by David Moss

Prologue

It's 2000, and people all over the world are celebrating the new millennium arriving without its promised bug: no planes fell from the sky, and the computers of big business continue to function. In the United Kingdom the Prime Minister is Tony Blair, who will be returned in the next election with an even bigger majority. The twin towers in New York City are still an iconic skyline and in London, the Millennium Dome has already been dubbed 'the Ozymandias of its time' by the *Sunday Times*. The 'Gay Plague' is still rampant and much feared, but the Good Friday Agreement has ended the spate of IRA bombs in England. Freddy Mercury has died, and so has Princess Diana, but David Bowie will headline Glastonbury and Coldplay are just about to release their debut album. In Southern England, the M3 is now complete but there are problems with the older roads and much rural rage over the extending trail of phone masts. Yet Somerset and Devon remain immensely popular locations for weekend retreats, with more and more people from the London area moving down.

1   The Kiss

"The Gustav Klimt painting that you probably know is *The Kiss*. As ubiquitous now as Van Gogh's psychotic sunflowers or Seurat's languid river scenes, it is especially popular for greetings cards. Often these show only the heads from this dazzling clinch, focussing on the frisson of incipient passion. The sombre gold surround is trimmed off, the hypnotic magic of the lovers' world sliced away. If you look at the painting in its entirety you may be puzzled by the vast uneasy context of the couple's curious embrace. They are on a flowery bank at the edge, it seems, of the world. Heavy glinting darkness encroaches like a desert storm.

There is no sense of space or movement; this is a breathless moment of such poignant resonance you might think the artist is trying to say that love and need are the same. You can see if you look beneath the flowery caress a reciprocal craving, a rapacious yearning. It begins to look more like life."

Jake reread his final paragraph with satisfaction. He was already late for his deadline so he printed out the full article and faxed it to the obscure art journal that regularly used his series on *The Painter Behind the Hype*. He had rushed this one a bit, but this month, the first of the new millennium, had been unexpectedly busy. All that driving up and down the M3, and the bloody Stonehenge junction a crash lane waiting to happen, and then the exhaustion inevitable after his late Friday evening arrival. Jake's thoughts swayed irresistibly to that arrival and his pulse quickened. His mind filled with images of Fran, waiting, big-eyed and fragrant in something gauzy …he could almost taste her already. Jake snatched up his case and coat, and his massive cellophane pack of hot-house orchids, locked the flat, and hurried down the stairs to the street. In three hours, given a clear-ish road, he would be in another world. The languidly passionate world of Klimt's erotica. Fran's world.

2   Leonora's Plight

Meanwhile, a hundred and twenty miles away, Gwen was having her usual fluster with the taxi-driver, who took her note and pushed off with her change pretending he had mistaken it for a tip. Gwen, flushing, adjusted her expectant stance at the gate to gaze instead at the hot air balloon high above the hills of Bristol. Like a tear drop floating upwards, she thought, and for an absurd but dazzling moment she imagined the distant balloonist could see her too. She put her purse away, blushing slightly. Out of the corner of her eye she thought she saw a man at the far end of the garden, down by the canal, watching her. She turned to look but the silhouette had vanished.

Gwen picked her way down the pebbled path to her mother-in-law's bungalow and announced her arrival with a sharp knock. The door was wedged ajar by the artless but effective device of swollen wood panels and sagging plaster; it yielded, as usual, at her pressure, swinging slowly into the scented recesses of the hall. Like having *Welcome Burglars* written on the mat, Gwen thought, stepping in.

'Only me,' she called, then hesitated, distracted by a shadowy rectangular stain on the wall where on her last visit there had been a framed photograph of a military man with a moustache like a pair of dozing slugs. No oil painting, Gwen reminded herself, but the frame was silver plate. It was very concerning, the way her mother-in-law appeared to be re-allocating her property without any family discussion. Willy-nilly, you could say.

She sighed and tried again. 'Yoohoo Mum? Only me.'

'Come on in. I'm in the bath.' And Leonora was. Gwen stared scandalised as her mother-in-law waved from within the porcelain tub, fortunately not attached to any form of water supply but still in Gwen's view inappropriate in a living room.

Leonora was clad in a batik tabard in tones of claret and

emerald and her hair streamed thinly across her shoulders, brazenly auburn tinted and glinting day-glo orange where sunshine added luminosity to the translucent strands. Gwen decided to put a brave face on. She had a brave face at the ready since it was usually required sooner or later on these Friday afternoon duty visits.

'Now let's get you out of there, shall we?'

Leonora rose, shaky but determined, and stepped onto the bathmat without assistance. 'We? How many of you are there?' as Gwen smiled stoically and reminded herself to avoid the plural form in future pleasantries. Old people can be *tres difficile*.

Gwen pursed her lips into the air close to Leonora's thin cheek and made the slight clucking sound she used to represent a kiss and Leonora closed her eyes briefly with a look of stifled irritation.

Gwen plodded behind her mother-in-law into the kitchen, where Leonora loaded the black-laquered papier-maché tray with Edwardian bone china. A dreadful waste of ornaments, in Gwen's opinion. Leonora, following her guest's glazed gaze to the beaded rim of ants on the honey pot, announced 'Buddhism is a drawback when it comes to housework. I am unable to control the anarchy of ants'

'Actually, I think you'll find that ants are the most disciplined creatures on the planet,' Gwen corrected patiently. 'According to a programme I saw on the television, if they had our stature they could destroy mankind.'

'Precisely. The discipline of ants would thus become indistinguishable from the anarchy of our own species.' Leonora waved the steaming kettle triumphantly.

Gwen waited until she had settled beside the wicker table in the conservatory with the tea-tray before venturing further converse.

'I see you've taken down that photograph from the hallway. Is it going to be reframed?'

'Possibly,' said Leonora, looking inscrutable. Gwen tried another tack.

'I don't really think it's a good idea to leave the front door open, with all your lacquer-ware, Mum' she ventured as Leonora poured the Lapsang. 'Someone could walk straight in.'

'It is the best way to gain access,' Leonora agreed. 'The back door leads only to the garden and the canal.'

'That's another thing –'

'Have a scone. I keep them for the ducks.'

'That's another thing,' said Gwen, placing it casually back on the plate, 'That garden. The canal, the ducks. Surely it's all getting too much for you?'

'The ducks? Oh no. They come and go as they please.'

'It is a big garden,' Gwen persisted.

'I have a man.' Leonora said grandly, and left it at that.

Leonora was eighty now. Until recently she had been a sprightly and skittish late-seventies but this summer, in Gwen's opinion, she was a recalcitrant and confused over-eighty. In short, her mother-in-law was getting doolally. She had tried to tell Neville, but would he listen? She had hinted her anxiety to her sister-in-law Fran, but Fran was on another planet these days since taking up with that louche designer from London. It would all come down on Gwen's shoulders, just like Christmas, which nobody in this family would ever organise if it wasn't for her, though they never seemed noticeably grateful. Gwen, an only child and an orphan throughout her married life, had an unquenchable reverence for families, even a peculiar family like this one.

Gwen's mother had died when she was fifteen, during a Greek island cruise on the day scheduled to visit Rhodes. Her father visited Gwen at her boarding school to break the news. It was a Thursday afternoon and Gwen had to miss hockey practice. 'I'm glad you've taken it so well,' her father said gloomily over strawberry tartlets. Gwen did not like to ask why her mother had been cruising alone so she wiped her mouth discreetly and said nothing. 'What will you do, when you leave school?' he asked her on his final visit. Gwen divined from this enquiry that he did not expect her to return home again. She had hoped to teach needlework but her grades were not encouraging. She opted instead, at her tutor's suggestion, for a retail career, and gained a position in one of the few remaining Department Stores in the nearby town. Those years in Knitwear were the loneliest ones of her life, until she met Neville.

She had on impulse booked an Away Day to Bath and after a tiring tour of the city sights had encountered Leonora by chance at the Pump Room.

'I wouldn't if I were you' came a wry voice as Gwen bent cautiously over the fountain of spa water – 'it tastes like puke.' Gwen straightened up and found herself locked in conversation with a vigorous-looking woman wearing a silk turban and gold hoop earrings. And then the loquacious stranger abruptly announced 'My son,' as Neville arrived with her pack of cocktail sobranies, and as he stood awkwardly smiling Gwen felt a tiny unprecedented frisson. She could see that Neville liked the look of her. He had looked at her and liked what he saw! Gwen fell instantly, gratefully, in love. Neville even in his twenties was burly; he made Gwen – whose previous most cherished approbation had been the day her father called her *bonny* – feel positively petite. He was stoical and slow moving; Gwen began to think of herself as lively and vivacious.

And then, at their wedding two years later, Gwen met Fran for the first time. Until the bombshell phone-call from Leonora to enquire about a bridesmaid's dress *(Nothing serviceable, for god's sake – if it's got to be a church wedding let's at least have a bit of impractical frivolity)* Gwen didn't even know Neville had a sister. How could she have guessed that even the eccentric Leonora could be quite so outrageous as to produce a child at an age when she should have been reminiscing about her menopause. But there was Fran, eight years old, looking like a flower fairy with her big grey eyes and shimmering champagne-blonde long hair. A shy, sly, child who whispered to her brother and turned her face away from his bride. Gwen felt petite no longer; she felt threatened.

But that was a quarter of a century ago, and Leonora's bombastic unreliability had degenerated to more challenging behaviour. Leonora was growing old disgracefully, and as long as she insisted on living in this isolated bungalow outside the town, there was precious little to be done. Gwen had talked and talked to Neville but all she got was 'It's only five minutes as the crow flies' which was really not the point.

Leonora's home was totally impractical. Access, for a start. Two means of entry, each more hazardous than the other! Either the canal tow-path at the bottom of the garden – narrow, damp, slippery, and open to the world and his wife though admittedly rarely used for the first three reasons – or a perilously steep path down from the gate at the top of the garden, with a fence so low that a determined invader could vault it in a trice. And the bungalow itself! The only concession to infirmity was a lack of internal stairs; otherwise the place was as inconvenient as a residence could be. Shallow steps to trip up; awkward corners, narrow shelves, the kitchen cluttered with appliances wedged precariously among painted jugs and buckets of indeterminate functionality. The sitting room had a trellis of flexes connected inscrutably to a red-eyed multi-board balanced on a rather pretty crinoline chair. Secateurs lay on the Queen Anne table by the door, a fruit knife on the settee, and the rug had several inviting toe-sized rips. The whole place was a death trap. And this glass-walled conservatory made the bungalow even more insecure.

'You'll be completely visible' Gwen had said, appalled, but Leonora replied that invisibility was never an ambition of hers. Gwen, who in her early years had very nearly perfected this valuable skill, was silenced. She continued to sip her tea, glancing around apprehensively for barges crammed with staring faces sidling past.

Now, as their conversation lapsed into its usual lull, Gwen patted her mouth with her paper hanky and looked at her watch. Neville left the office early on these Fridays in order to collect his wife and renew a nodding acquaintance with his mother. He was scheduled to pick her up at around five, traffic permitting. She hoped today's traffic would be permissive.

'I am thinking of making a will,' said Leonora unexpectedly after silence had rested in the disorderly room for a while. 'I feel I should mention, so that there will be no later rancour, that I do not intend to leave the bungalow to either of my children.'

Gwen stifled a sharp intake of breath. Not for herself, of course. She and Neville were nicely settled, but that was not the point.

'So, who, who...?' Gwen began, then subsided, feeling like a barn owl.

'I haven't decided,' said Leonora, looking hawkish. Now Gwen felt like a vole. She did not believe Leonora.

Shaking slightly, Gwen took the tray through to the kitchen and rinsed out the cups. There was no tea-towel visible so she flickered her hands a few times and then wiped them against her cardigan. From the doorway Gwen could see that Leonora had settled down to read her library book. She coughed tactfully twice but Leonora remained apparently engrossed. Which would actually be rude, if she wasn't senile, Gwen reflected.

Gwen opened the back door to sigh and survey the long lawn leading down to the canal. The ducks were icing-white blobs almost motionless on the dark water and the trees were quiet in the afternoon sunlight. She thought of her own small patio, bright with bedding plants and Neville's arduously-built intricate rockery with its compact water-feature which they switched on for visitors. She looked at the lush lawn and the pluming grasses scooping into the water's edge. This section was now silted and thick with rushes, so barely used by narrowboats, and the original border seemed to have sunk almost to a wildflower bed. She breathed in until her breath meshed tightly in her chest, and then suddenly she noticed a slight movement in her peripheral vision. There was a man in the greenhouse.

Gwen could see a tough, toffee-brown, naked torso clearly through the window-frames. His arms seemed at first to be bangled, but as he turned from profile to back view she realised that his upper body was decorated heavily with tattoos. Gwen leant on the doorway to try to see his face, and felt a tingling frisson like a tiny electric shock. Static, she thought; how odd. Her hands must be still wet.

'Your gardener doesn't look like a village man,' Gwen said to Leonora as she returned to the conservatory and reseated herself to wait for the sound of Neville's car. She shot a keen look at her mother-in-law, who was still leafing vaguely through her large-print volume.

'He's not.' Leonora conceded, letting her book drop. 'He's from the Convoy. He helped me out, disposing of a few bits and pieces for me,' – Gwen winced visibly – 'and I asked him to stay on after The Eviction, and he did.'

The Eviction had been a major local event. Television pictures had shown a crowd of stern-faced policemen striding into a settlement of vans and trailers while small children and chickens scattered. A uniformed arm wielded a sledgehammer to shatter the windscreen of a gaudy elderly Volkswagen while a thin young man cried wanly *that's my home* and a woman with a baby screamed from within. Gwen, who had watched nightly on the Regional News, found this image rather harrowing though she was naturally relieved to see the authorities taking firm control, as authorities should. She had no idea she was connected to a protagonist.

'A family man?' she said sharply, suppressing her memory of the outstretched arms of the weeping man on the television.

'I doubt it. I have no written provenance, but he was alone and homeless when we met.'

Gwen felt that tiny uncomfortable trickle which the word 'homeless' always gave her. She knew, of course, that no-one need choose such an option these days; there were plenty of comfortable hostels and many of these people came from good families. Only recently such points had been reiterated in a reputable journal. Nevertheless, seeing those urchins on the pavements of the city did make one wonder, a little, why they should choose such lives.

'He had a horse,' Leonora was saying, 'but he had to let that go. I think he was ready for a change,' she added indulgently, as if speaking of a nappied infant.

Gwen felt tense and slightly flustered. She took a nearly-deep breath, as she had in the garden, and said, 'Where is he sleeping?'

Leonora showed no sign of surprise at this tigerish demand.

'He sleeps here of course dear. I have plenty of room.'

The faint benevolent sound of a car horn signalled Neville's imminent arrival. In a moment he would join them, big and safe and sweating slightly from the heat of his drive, his white shirt with the top button undone and sleeves rolled to the elbow, his plump face crinkled in a benign smile, his scalp pink from the sun where his pale hair was beginning to thin. Gwen rose and rushed to the door.

''Fraid I can't stay, car's blocking the road,' Neville advised his mother routinely, adding to his wife, 'Ready, dear?'

'I'll just pop to the little girls' room,' said Gwen.

The rituals complete, they departed. Neville seemed stoical when Gwen declared herself speechless at his mother's most recent acquisition, but she managed to find words before he had changed up to second gear.

'A live-in gardener, can you credit it? Most unsuitable. And when I saw him! How he ever landed the job I do not know – I'm sure she never took up references. Hair like I don't know what and his back all covered with dragons.'

'Dragons?' said Neville, whose mind appeared to be on something else.

'A tattoo. I think they were dragons. Scaly creatures, intertwined. And he had no hair to speak of, except on top where it was all done up like a lacemaking kit.'

'With bobbins?'

'Beads and bits, anyway. Careful, Neville!' Gwen did not drive, but gave advice on manoeuvres when necessary. 'Disposing of a few bits and pieces! I doubt we'll ever again see that photograph of your father that used to hang in the hallway.'

'It's in the boot' said Neville impassively. 'She asked me if I wanted it while you were in the loo. I thought, might as well.'

Gwen felt a clumsy, tender, surge of sentimental bewilderment at the thought of Neville surveying his dead father's face and thinking, might as well. She closed her eyes briefly. 'Did you not think it a little odd, Neville, that she has started dismantling the house and has now invited a total stranger to take up residence?'

'Well he's not a total stranger to her, is he, dear. I suppose she feels that's what counts. And as to dismantling the place, it's hardly the Berlin Wall. In fact I think he's done a bit of repointing.' Gwen closed her eyes again. Pointing was not the point, she felt, although there was no point in saying so since Neville would be bound to snicker. Neither was political history.

'We have to face it, Neville. Your mother is getting beyond mere eccentricity. I am seriously concerned for her safety. I mean, sitting in the bath with all her clothes on! I'm only thankful she wasn't immersed.'

'She was probably trying out that handrail' Neville suggested. He could be very stubborn sometimes. 'She said Social Services was putting one in for her.'

'Well she didn't say anything about it to me. And another thing. D'you know what she wanted to make the tea with? Rose petals! And when I said, ever so nicely, "They look so pretty in the vase, Mum, shall we leave them there?" d'you know what she said? "They are tea roses!".'

Neville snickered. 'Good thing they weren't dog roses, or she might have wanted you to take them for a walk.'

'Not the point, Neville' Gwen said patiently. 'The point is, it's all getting too much for her. And that place being right on the canal's edge, she's on the brink of calamity daily.'

'The bungalow isn't exactly overhanging the water. There is a sizeable garden in between.'

'That's another thing. She wanders about, unsupervised. And not even a Neighbourhood Watch sticker in sight.'

'She's lived there for years, I suppose she feels safe.'

'Well she shouldn't.' Gwen snapped. She had done her best.

Neville cruised the Volvo to a stop outside the garage and Gwen got out.

'And another thing –' she said. She turned the catch on the garage and pushed the big door upwards. It swung slowly and wavered just above the height of the car. Gwen reached within to extract a golf-club and stood wedging the door aloft with it while Neville drove slowly in. When the car was inside she removed the club and the door dropped with dramatic instantaneousness. Gwen waited for a few moments until there was a sharp tap from within and then repeated the lifting-and-wedging procedure on the door-canopy.

'And another thing –' she said,

'I wish you wouldn't let it drop like that,' said Neville. 'You might wait until I'm out.'

'You should fix it.' said Gwen, removing the golf club swiftly so that Neville had to leap the last few feet like a Nintendo street-fighter impelled by joystick thrust '– it's not just the outgoings, Neville, it's her stuff.' She chewed her lip. Was it ignoble to resent the dwindling assets of Leonora? Gwen thought of the gardener rampant among Leonora's effects as the echoes of the garage door's descent rumbled away. 'We have to think of these things. We have to think of Clive.'

'Ah. Clive,' said Neville, and he went inside and stretched out on the settee while Gwen fetched the supper trays.

So it all came down on Gwen's shoulders, as usual, and she said so aloud in her magnolia hallway as she lifted the telephone handset. Neville was on the beige leather settee with his feet up, hugging the remote control like a comfort blanket. Gwen keyed in her sister-in-law's number. While she waited she looked at her reflection in the gilt-framed mirror in the hallway and fiddled with her ends, lifting them up and letting them drop thoughtfully, the way her stylist did.

The ringing tone cut and Fran's rather breathy, ingenuous, voice came on the line. 'This is me, but I'm not here, and neither is Jake...'

Neville surmised the outcome of the phone-call from his wife's air of smothered annoyance as she returned to the living room.

'Fran not answering?'

'I don't know why your sister can't lift the phone on a Friday night,' said Gwen, truthfully. 'They're always in. Jake gets down from London around seven or eight, and they don't go out.'

'Call tomorrow' said Neville taking an Embassy. 'If it's important.'

'It is, Neville. You didn't see him.'

Neville did not reply. Gwen ascended the stairs and groped in her bureau for the solace of her daily diary. *Leonora is becoming a liability* she wrote. *Faith-wise, she has chopped and changed again and now announces herself a follower of Isis. She showed me a flyer. I asked her what ceremonies were involved in this day and age, and she merely laughed.*

The tasselled shade of the side-lamp fell jaggedly across Gwen's page, reminding her curiously of the wild figure of the man in the greenhouse this afternoon. She wanted to write sagely about the inadvisability of old ladies housing tattooed travellers, but the requisite composure for discursive prose eluded her.

Gwen sighed. She chewed her biro fretfully and wrote *Belinda is on heat again, which is tiresome. I have to lock the cat-flap and then there is no end of trouble controlling her comings and goings.* It was going to be the same with Leonora. She would be left to simply run wild unless Gwen got something organised.

Gwen closed her diary unmollified and went downstairs to give Belinda her jellied salmon chunks. 'Is Clive home?' she called but Neville, prone on the sofa, was thinking of something else and did not reply. Gwen wiped the coffee table, shifted the legs to stop them denting the pile of the carpet, and freshed Neville's ashtray.

'It's absurd' she said, aloud.

There was applause on the TV set and Neville opened his eyes.

'Totally inappropriate. A live-in gardener!'

'He's made a nice job of the sweet peas,' said Neville mildly.

'You didn't see the man. Like a tribal warrior. He's probably 'casing the joint' right now.'

'Or rolling it,' suggested Neville, but Gwen did not smile.

'You must talk to Fran,' Gwen said again. 'I think we should drive over there, tomorrow.'

Neville swivelled slowly upright and switched off the television. Gwen plumped herself in the space beside him and he placed a conciliatory arm around her shoulders. 'She might be out,' he said, 'She and Jake sometimes drive into Bath on a Saturday.'

'Then we must meet there. Fran needs to know the situation.'

And by breakfast time Fran did.

3   Decisive Moments

– Breakfast time for Fran and Jake, that is, for Gwen had long since cleared the crumbs from the breakfast bar and washed and dried the grapefruit segmenter.

Fran took the call naked with Jake's hot thigh on hers. Jake watched her making sympathetic noises and widening her eyes, and wondered whether to have another croissant or another fuck. He moved the tray with the cafetiere and coffee cups further down the duvet. 'OK,' Fran was saying. 'Yeah. Well, OK,' Jake slid his hand along her thigh and looked questioningly at her. Fran fractionally widened the knee that was bent and Jake decided instantly against a second croissant. 'Yeah, twelve's fine,' and Fran fingers slipped over the cut-off button on the phone and she uncurled slowly backwards.

Fran and Jake had lived in this cottage for only four months. It was their first home together, selected primarily from Fran's trust of instinctive imperative. They had been lovers since they met the previous summer, on the eve of Fran's thirtieth year.

Until then Fran had managed to remain essentially single, avoiding long-term relationships for essentially the same reasons she had also decided against getting a red setter: commitment, cost, and kennelling. Falling in love with Jake was unplanned. A year on, Fran could recall the first moment she saw him with instant clarity, as if she had had the foresight to video it.

Fran trusted such moments. Fran carefully erased from the canvas of her life the graffiti scribbles of discord, to create instead a pattern that was decorative and beautiful. Jake argued – among other things – that this was not possible. Fran did not argue. She intended her life to be like her own paintings, a glittering canvas of colours and patterns, perfectly controlled.

Fran had gone up to London for an exhibition with her friend

Babette, co-sharer of her staff accommodation on the leafy site of the private school in Bath where Fran taught art. Babette was uninterested in art but keen on a party in Primrose Hill with some people she had met on a life-changing course on a Greek Island. Fran had visited Greek islands too, but not to change her life; Fran's life was fine as it was. Fran was perfectly in control. She saved her salary to explore art galleries throughout Europe. She became knowledgeable, and a friend of the Headteacher asked her to catalogue his collection. Fran, delighted, had spent long fascinated evenings researching each piece, and was elated by the cheque she received in return. She would have done it for a tenth of the sum.

'You were ripped off' said Jake, standing just outside her conversation at the party.

Fran was not accustomed to put-downs. While she was deciding a reply of sufficient indifference, she looked again at the dark-haired man with pirate's eyes and realised with a potent sensation of thrill and apprehension that she was in love.

Jake was a highly successful free-lance graphic designer. He did not get ripped off. It was not his style, however, to discuss fiscal matters, even to art teachers up from the country, and so Jake allowed his comment to remain unexplained and instead invited Fran back to his flat.

Fran had never before gone to bed with a man after only half a conversation. It seemed important to establish some structure of intimacy, however fragile – perhaps share some confidences during their hasty mutual undressing. Jake discouraged this.

'Don't tell me anything about yourself' he said, kneeling before her naked body, kissing her belly-button, 'People are all essentially unknowable.' What Jake meant, Fran realised later, was that as he expected this to be a one-night stand there was little point in wasting time and energy. But she had taken Jake at his word, on this and on every other point.(Later, when he was deeply, jealously, in love, Jake would become angry with Fran for her reticence. He saw it as coolly, calculatingly, inscrutable. Fran of course was only being obedient. So perhaps Jake was right the first time, and people are all unknowable.)

Within a few weeks Fran was in London again. Going up on the train she decided against attempting to contact Jake. By Sunday's journey home they had spent thirty hours inseparable and pledged the next weekend together. Within two months they were planning to live together. They found the cottage in the autumn.

There were sensible reasons to buy, although the Surveyor's Report was not one of them. Fran needed somewhere accessible to the school, and this was only a short drive away. Bath was expensive, and this way Jake didn't need to sell his studio flat in Ealing. He could work from there during the week and make the fast drive home on Fridays in his testosterone-red Porsche 911.

They found the cottage at the end of a long Sunday spent driving round with a wad of Estate Agent's details. Fran made pencil notes of Jake's comments against each as they eliminated them.

'This one's impossible' said Jake, as the rutted track turned once again, now several miles from the edge of town. There was something in the quiet speculative tone he used, combined with the long delay on this expected comment, that gave Fran a tang of excitement. He knows too, she thought. This is it.

The lane turned again, and there was the cottage; honey-stoned, clung around with winter jasmine, all in one sharp intake of breath. Beside it a tiny stream, gold speckled on black in the late afternoon sunlight, trickled past the gate and disappeared in the bracken of woods beyond. A sycamore tree glowed golden in the fading sun, littering the path with fallen leaves like gilded stars.

'I suppose this is the *space to park*' said Jake ironically, bringing the Porsche stickily to a halt on the damp leaves of the widened bit of the track. Fran said nothing.

Jake sighed, and stretched his arm along the passenger seat. Fran leaned silently against it. He touched her hair gently.

'It's utterly out of the question,' said Jake. 'It'll be a mudtrap here in winter. The damp will be unbelievable.' They both knew, in the taut excitement of their arrival, that the decision had already been made.

Jake wound his window fully down and they sat silently. Bird song tweaked the still air.

'Smell that mint,' said Fran at length. Jake lifted her soft thick hair and breathed deeply into her neck. He kissed gently into her throat. Fran tingled like static electricity.

'OK darling,' said Jake, 'let's see what we're letting ourselves in for.' Jake, usually so sure-footed in business deals, had simply submitted, as if this place like their passionate affair had the imperative of authentic inevitability.

They moved to the cottage in the late Spring, when the forsythia was vibrant and peachy roses scented the doorway. Fran spent her solitary evenings longing and decorating. Now the cottage was full of light and colour, the bedroom full of paintings of their love. Not all were Fran's. In the hallway, opposite the front door, hung a reproduction of Gustav Klimt's painting entitled *THE KISS*. The lovers in the picture are swirled in golden garments on a field jewelled with tiny flowers. A golden cape surrounds them like a husk, a sheath, a shroud. He is leaning over her, his flushed and ardent face half-hidden. Her recipient cheek is smooth and calm. You might think she is ignoring his intense embrace until you see the tautness in her body and her gripping hands. *It's us*, Jake whispered. He had the picture expensively framed in broad copper with art nouveau lilies in elegant relief.

Fran's weekends were absorbed by Jake's arrival, and planning for those weekends absorbed the rest of her life. Fran hardly went out at all in the evenings now, and she had not visited her mother much lately, either. Was that tart comment of Gwen on the phone about 'leaving Leonora to fend for herself' justified?

'Maybe I should see Mum more,' Fran murmured ruefully. (Leonora's children both referred to her as Mum though they addressed her, according to her preference, by her given name. Gwen tended to reverse this strategy.) Jake emerged from other contemplations.

'You could go after work, instead of jogging,' he suggested. Fran said nothing. This was fragile ice. She had folded up her social life for him and now rarely went out without Jake except to run.

Jake was unhappy about the running. 'I always run alone, Jakey,' Fran had reassured him, surmising correctly that Jake's opposition was symbiotically linked to images of men with beefy calves and sweaty underarms jogging powerfully beside her. But actually, he explained, this was precisely his objection. Alone! Strange men may meet her – accost her, frighten her. Rape her. 'It's not being neurotic to think of this,' he said, 'it's stubborn and very silly not to.'

'If I'm not frightened of strange men I don't see why you should be,' Fran had replied. 'Most rapists aren't strangers anyway. They are someone the woman knows and trusts.'

'Fran, there is always the exception. You are a very beautiful woman, you know.'

'Rape is nothing to do with looks.' Fran spoke quietly, unassertively. Lovers do not argue. Her calm irritated Jake; irritation made him feel guilty. Jake did not want to feel these uncomfortable emotions – he had not intended them. It must be Fran's fault. Jake felt aggrieved and unappreciated. Fran worked hard each weekend to convince Jake how much he was appreciated, to keep in her grasp that magical flush of loving rapport. Sometimes she was almost glad, in an exhausted, dreamy, kind of way, when it was Monday again and she could relax and look forward to next Friday night.

Fran no longer worked at the school in Bath. She had a new job in the nearby town, on the editorial team at a printing firm specialising in art books and part-works. Her new job took her into a world full of men. This was deeply distressing to Jake, and Fran worked hard to reassure him that she was not to blame for this. The world outside the art room of a Private School *is* full of men. And it was Jake's idea anyway, although this didn't add much oil to the salad.

'You made an awfully good job of that catalogue,' Don Glossop had said over the tepid white wine at an exhibition in the local gallery: 'Would you like to join my Management Trainee scheme? On a salary, of course. I'm developing a Design Section.'

Don Glossop owned a local printing firm. Fran had laughed.

'What an absurd idea,' she said, but she was sufficiently pleased to go straight over to tell Jake.

'It's a very good idea,' he said. 'You're surely not intending to spend the rest of your life teaching little boys?' He contrived to make the final phrase sound like some fastidious but slightly tacky euphemism for youthful genitalia. Fran blushed. Before they left she located Don Glossop again to ask for an interview.

It turned out then that what Jake really meant was that such jobs are a very good idea in principle, not that she should have been singled out by Mr Glossop to initiate his Design Section – this was not a very good idea at all. And leaving the school was not such a good idea, at this moment in time. She would lose the holidays, for one thing. 'The long summer holiday,' he said, wheedling, as if it were the only soft centre left in the box.

'You don't get school holidays,' Fran pointed out, but Jake felt this was irrelevant. He did not need them. She did. There was still much to be done around the house and garden; the plans he had meticulously sketched needed implementing – they needed Fran's practical flair. And there was also the matter of the men. It took one wine-sodden weekend to assure him that everyone called Mr Glossop 'Don' and she had not had an affair with him, and a further two to establish that she would not have an affair with him, not ever, not even if the opportunity repeatedly contrived to arise.

Fran found Jake's jealousy bewildering and irrational. 'Why is it' she asked, gently but with a glint of irony, 'when you say *How was work?* you only want to know if I met any men? Isn't that a tad mistrustful?' Jake thought not. It was the consequence of his passionate love for her, he explained; she was to him always desirable, hence always desired by others, hence always potentially naked in other men's arms. Fran found his logic more silly than sinister. 'But Jake, that's absurd. You don't seize every woman you take a fancy to, do you? Well then.'

Jake seemed to have lost the mood of the moment. He rolled onto his stomach and closed his eyes. Fran began to press his toes gently, individually, on the fleshy part underneath.

'Don't, it'll tickle' said Jake unhelpfully, but Fran ignored him. She pressed delicately, pushing her fingers between each toe. Jake did not object again, and gradually his breathing became slower and more audible as his feet relaxed. Fran progressed to the underbelly of his foot, delicately, pressing her fingertips like a cat softening a cushion. Jake said nothing. Fran drew her fingertips across his sole and made tiny taps around his ankle. She stroked his calves gently, pushing her hand just a little way up towards his thighs. Jake lay still, his face averted, breathing deeply. After a little while Jake moved, turning over and pushing her down on the bed in one smooth decided movement. His face was slightly flushed and his eyes glittered darkly; his mouth taut and teeth slightly parted. His face became a primitive erotic mask as he pushed himself inside her, and Fran heard a thin scream deep within her. Or perhaps, she could not tell, aloud. Jake remained above her, staring as though he saw but did not know her; unsmiling he beat down on her and Fran felt herself swooning into a vague rotating darkness. For a tiny moment there was nothing but a breathless dark sheath clinging around them, and then a kind of frail gasping sobbing, around which the spinning particles of Fran gradually coalesced. And then there was Fran, on the bed, very sticky round the thighs and absurdly shakily happy, and Jake, serenely beautiful, whispering passionate, vulgar, rhapsodic, endearments. In this disarray they both slept for a while.

'Remember we're meeting Gwen,' said Jake, rousing Fran with tea. He kissed her nipples and put her sleepy fingers round the cup as Fran sat up.

'Jake,' said Fran.

'What?'

'Nothing. Just, I know we can make it. With that kind of magic, we can make it together.'

'So what happens when we can't?' said Jake. He stroked her hair and stared into her eyes. He was joking, perhaps. Fran could never tell. 'On the first day we don't make magic, when the time comes when I can't and you don't want to? Do we self-destruct?'

'We always will. At least, we'll always want to.'

'Nobody always wants to make love,' said Jake. 'Old people

don't care.'

Fran sipped her tea and looked down at her arms, stretching and twisting. She tried to imagine them thinned by the passing of years, pale, the flesh loose. She thought how her waist was beginning to look just a little creased when she undressed, the first tiny intimations of a kind of softness that would one day wrinkle all over her body. She would not then be able to touch Jake naked in such perfect confidence of her desirability.

'Won't you want me when I'm old and ugly,' she said, laughing, pretending the agony was only a tease.

'I'll be older too. I'll be paunchy, and my hair will grizzle and fall, and one day you won't want to lick the sweat from under my armpits any more. Will that be the end of our love?'

Fran tried to imagine Jake less strong, less desirable, less vividly present, and she failed. She tried to visualise his face soured with age, that irresistible mouth steadied into an old man's pout, his heavy eyelids creased and yellowed.

'I'd love you whatever way you looked. If you got a beer belly or if you shrivelled away, I'd still want you.' But Fran could not envisage any of it. It was so much a part of this colossal love that they were both beautiful animals.

'And when I can't make you any more,' Jake pursued, still in that light, slightly serious, tone, 'one day when we're threshing around, and its just sticky and sweaty and uncomfortable and we're trying to remember why we used to enjoy it – what then?' He held her down, kissing her hair.

'It won't happen, Jake.'

'Of course it will. One day, it will. Even Krishna can't get a hard on every time.'

Fran closed her eyes to his consoling kisses. But she felt obliquely warned. I must not be too demanding, she thought. But how can I be less ardent without changing the pattern of this erotic passion which is the way we know each other?

She turned, very slightly, from the overwhelming closeness of his embrace. The moment held them, dispassionately, and then released them to the day.

4   Babette's Baby

Babette was seated in the branches of the big oak tree listening to the sound of the leaves. She rubbed the coarse bark and snapped off an embryonic acorn. The tree was in the school grounds on the far side beyond the staff houses and since term had ended there was no-one else around. The drop to the ground was about thirteen feet but Babette felt secure. Secure to the point of being wedged, if she was honest. She had climbed up the fraying rope ladder to the abandoned tree house on impulse but found the musty smell and lack of view uninspiring. A slow cautious crawl along one of the thicker branches had provided this forked perch and here Babette sat, secluded from the afternoon sun, thinking of this and that. She nibbled at a tiny acorn absently and quickly spat the sour scraps away.

Tom crouched quietly within her, subsisting like a little gasp at the end of every breath, and she forgot sometimes that no-one now in her life knew about her son. She had given him up deliberately, and there was nothing she really cared to say about the matter. It was so long since she had familiarised herself with that sense of unspeakable failure, accepted the others' view that she was impatient with him, disorganised, not maternal at all. It was obvious he would be better off in the commune with the other children than going with her when she left. Indeed, everyone behaved as though her own leaving was merely the not-very-important exercise of free choice, but to take Tom would he iniquitous, a kind of theft. His security was at stake. His roots. Her fragile child not ready yet for pricking out. Perhaps Babette had believed that too. The communal philosophy hadn't worked for her, but she still believed Tom would have a better life there, running free and playing in the long and sunny grasses. And the commune was so far away, and when it broke up it was months before they had written – now in a council house and naming their wedding day – to tell her. There was never any question of custody; the word was not mentioned on the Christmas card that told her of these changes. "Hope you're glad for us!" And a picture of Tom in his school uniform. Long fringe and a red tie, slightly awry of course, to tug more rigorously on her heart strings. Tom no longer free-range, perhaps in no better a battery than she could have provided.

It could not be thought about. It was part of her now, the small and shuddering dread when the motoring flash came on the radio *due to a bad accident* or on the news that *a boy was swept over and drowned when a freak wave hit...* He did not write any more. That at least was a comfort. There is absolutely nothing in the world so screamingly unbearable as an envelope addressed in the round-handed print of a child.

She had overheard some friends, once, talking about her. 'She could have got a solicitor, even then' she heard, and the indolent reply, 'Of course she could, if she'd wanted him.' It had never occurred to Babette that the law could help her. Solicitors belonged like mortgages and life assurance policies to a world she had no way of attaining. Yet she accepted the indifferent overheard, judgment completely. She must have allowed it to happen, or it would never have happened. The logic was unanswerable. Our fate lies not in our stars but in our flaws.

And yet, she hadn't given up entirely, had she? She had believed for years there would be another chance – another child to love. And this one would bloody well be the best-loved kid ever in world history, Babette knew that for certain. But perhaps her body was frightened of such responsibility – or perhaps, as Babette feared deep in her wary heart, her body no longer trusted her with the care of anything so precious as a child. She would be wild with excitement at another late period, then bedridden with grief and pain only a few weeks later. She'd tried talking to Rupert, her co-worker at the School House, but his determined empathy had irritated her into a series of misstatements and wild claims simply to stop his sentimental speculations. She did not want anyone to tell her they knew how she felt, offering self-indulgent evidence in lieu of a little bit of quiet listening but hey, Babette reminded herself – people go into care work because they need care themselves – as she also frequently reminded her colleagues.

So an occasional sojourn in the tree house was quite a good idea all round, Babette reckoned.

She had disciplined herself as the years passed not to picture Tom. There was no other way. Once, coming home with strawberries, she had allowed herself to pretend briefly they were for Tom. He used to love strawberries. It was calamitous. Before she had even reached the door, a four-litre saloon had shot from the corner of her mind and knocked him senseless. Screaming and sobbing she fled to him, and tried to hold him. He was floppy like a jelly boy, his head a jammy mush like pulped strawberries. *I'm sorry mummy*, he said as the blood trickled in dark threads from his ears, *I'm sorry mummy*. She had never cared much for strawberries since.

5   Pleasant Surroundings

When Gwen telephoned Fran for a family conference about Leonora she had suggested a rendezvous outside the Pump Room in central Bath purely as a notional start. Her idea was that they would then find somewhere more secluded for their discussion. But Neville had problems parking and by the time they arrived Fran and Jake were already sitting at one of the open-air tables drinking iced coffee and watching the buskers. Fran waved as they approached, and Jake looked up without removing his sunglasses.

Jake was wearing jeans and a pale silk shirt with a gaudy waistcoat which Gwen considered absurd on a man of his age. He must be forty at least, she thought, looking at the undone waistcoat points arrowing down to his crotch. Fly buttons, she noted. They seemed slightly obscene, and inexplicable in these days of nylon zip fasteners.

Jake pulled off his shades and looked at her with heavy lidded eyes for a moment before he smiled. Fran and Neville clasped each other's wrists briefly in greeting. They were not demonstrative siblings.

'You look well,' Neville said as he pulled over two chairs.

'She's beautiful,' said Jake proprietorially and slightly too loudly. He put his hand on Fran's thigh. Gwen looked away.

'Two coffees please,' Neville was saying to the nonchalant waiter.

'Cappuccino? Filter?'

'Frappuccino here is nice,' said Fran, and in the small skirmish of their order Gwen realised the dynamic of her meeting was slipping nonchalantly away.

'How's work?' Neville said, by way of general enquiry as they waited for their order. Gwen fidgeted, feeling forlorn, while the other three chatted.

'How's the Oxfam shop?' Fran asked eventually, and Gwen corrected her quickly 'The Heart shop. It's a British charity. Very nicely, thank-you.' She would have said more but at that moment the waiter returned, and Jake decided to order again, and then Fran slid her loose top off revealing a tiny-strapped teeshirt and no bra, and Jake bit her shoulder softly and longingly right there in front of everyone, and Fran did not stop him. Instead she ruffled his thick dark hair and whispered something that caused him to half-groan, half-purr. Gwen, turning sharply away, caught Neville smiling at them.

'I did want to talk about something rather important,' said Gwen.

Neville sucked the froth off his teaspoon and said benignly 'Fire ahead.' The encouraging words disassociated him instantly. Gwen's shoulders drooped. This was going to be Boxing Day all over again.

A small crowd was gathering around them at the open-air tables. Gwen half-turned, and saw they were forming an audience for the juggling busker, who was now lighting up his firebrands. She turned back to the matter in hand.

'It's Leonora,' she said firmly. 'I don't think she can be left in that house for much longer. She's erratic and unsteady, and she is vulnerable.'

At last she had their attention. Fran looked immediately troubled.

'She needs a live-in companion,' said Jake decisively.

Gwen resented Jake making decisive comments. He'd only been around the family for five minutes, and hardly knew Leonora at all.

'That's part of the problem,' she said primly. 'She has taken someone on, and he is not a proper person, nor indeed a person one would wish to see in the house at all.'

Gwen reached her denouement triumphantly and awaited their anxious questioning. There was a murmuring sound from behind her, like a small crowd watching something excellent occurring, and Gwen realised that the eyes of her listeners were no longer on her. They had all been lured to gaze over her head at the antics of the busker beyond. Fran and Jake rose in unison and after a moment Neville stood up too. 'I say, do look,' he appealed, 'this fellow is extraordinarily clever.'

Gwen tightened her lips and drank her coffee.

Fran and Jake had clasped hands and Fran's eyes were wide. Jake pulled her hair away from her face so he could whisper in her ear. Fran giggled. Neville was staring with a very slight smile and eventually, when she had finished the last of her coffee, Gwen yielded and stood and turned to look at the busker.

He was clearly visible above the crowd as he juggled his blazing clubs, poised on a unicycle and pedalling vigorously to retain his balance. The major focus of audience appreciation was not the busker's poise nor his hand-eye co-ordination but his minimalist attire: an immensely swollen sliver of black lycra clinging tightly to his gleaming dark-ochre body.

Gwen took a breath and looked around the crowd. Women were staring and smiling, men were grinning and nudging. No-one seemed to object. One woman in a romper-suit put her hand on her breast and mimed panting. Gwen wanted to sit down but feared to make herself conspicuous. She watched the busker blow out his firebrands and throw them down. He called to someone to hold the unicycle steady and then executed an exquisite handstand onto the slim saddle. Women squealed as the busker's muscular thighs vibrated with the effort of holding himself rigidly upright upside-down. He executed a slow circle so that the onlookers had a full display of the shiny black sack which bulged alarmingly. Gwen closed her eyes.

The small crowd continued cheering and the busker had jumped down. He picked up a hat and ran round the group as it began gradually to disperse, still with laughter and applause. Jake threw a couple of pounds in while Neville fumbled.

'What about a drink?' Jake said cheerfully, checking the bill and putting down a note which more than covered all their coffees.

Neville brightened. His expression suggested that the afternoon was looking up despite a thin start.

'We haven't decided anything,' Gwen lamented. Jake put his

hand on her arm.

'At the pub,' he said. Gwen pulled away.

'I don't think that's the place.'

Fran took pity on her sister-in-law. 'You guys go on. We'll have a stroll and talk and meet you there in half an hour. Will that be OK, Gwen?'

Gwen nodded glumly. It wasn't much, but it would have to do.

6   Desirable Residents

'Well she couldn't really come here,' said Fran, 'could she, Jakey?'

Fran was tossing the salad in French dressing with slow judicious movements, wearing nothing except one of Jake's shirts with the sleeves rolled up to her elbows. Her hair was loose on her shoulders and crowned with a daisy-chain Jake had made her. 'It should be forget-me-nots, really,' Jake said, 'but the stems split.'

Jake had wanted her to wear the golden shirt and blue flowers in her hair to recreate their favourite picture, the Klimt painting of the lovers' kiss that hung in the hallway. Now he decided Fran would look even better with nothing on at all and he put down his wine glass to disrobe her with both hands. Fran held the olive wood servers aloft docilely, one in each hand, while he lifted the shirt over her head as a magician plucks at chiffon.

Fran was beginning to find Jake's attentions irksome. She had been waiting for a suitable moment to talk about her mother and the odd conversation with Gwen in the precinct. By tacit agreement neither of them talked further of Leonora's Plight, as Gwen called it, after meeting up with their men in the pub. In the car on the drive home it had been difficult to distract Jake from his preoccupation with the notion of Gwen's Heart shop.

'It's hilarious,' he said, chuckling as corroborative emphasis, 'I can just picture her, sizing a customer up for fit. *I think that heart is a little too generous for you, we have one here which is rather more ironic. Or this doleful heart, reduced for a quick sale?* Jake had assumed a falsetto voice which amused him immensely. He continued to smile imperturbably through Fran's account of her discussion, and offered his own summary with a laugh that was only a hair's breadth from a snigger.

'So according to Gwen, this extraordinary character, part-totter part-Bluebeard, has got his feet under your mother's table and will inherit everything he hasn't already stolen?'

Fran, who only drove the Porsche if Jake had been drinking, was concentrating on the traffic and did not smile. 'I don't know. But Gwen seems to think we need to act. Or at least be prepared.' She conceded a small smile but she was beginning to feel frustrated. Jake clearly considered the problem existed entirely in Gwen's imagination. It was true that Gwen had been reluctant to specify precisely in what way she felt Leonora at risk from the man. *As a woman alone*, she had emphasised. *Do you mean he might attack her?* Fran had asked, but Gwen did not seem to mean quite that. Some other kind of deeper female vulnerability.

Now as Fran put the supper things ready on the tray, she tried to return to the subject while Jake poured them both a cook's glass from the chilled bottle.

'I'll go and see her, of course, but I don't know what Gwen thinks I ought to do. It's up to Mum who she employs. Gwen's been worrying for ages about whether she can manage on her own. If she's not capable of choosing her helpers, then maybe she should leave the bungalow.'

'I can't see Gwen welcoming her at their place. She hasn't even got rid of Clive yet.'

Fran nipped her lip with her front teeth, a habit Jake found irresistible.

'Don't start on about Gwen and Clive again. Jake, no, that tickles. She worries about him, that's all. Mums do worry about adolescents, especially when they're not sure what they want from life.'

'She disapproves of him, Fran. Mind you, she seems to disapprove of everyone. She is the most uptight woman I've ever met. It's a mystery to me how she ever conceived a child in the first place. What Gwen needs is a good shag.'

'You're disgustingly sexist when you're boozed, Jakey,' Fran said calmly, but she was not pleased with Jake. She did not like the suggestion that her gentle brother was inadequate. 'Could we talk about my mother, please? And not your favourite hobby.'

Jake caressed her shoulder with his lips. 'Talk,' he suggested between purring breaths.

Fran hesitated. The moment now somehow did not seem right. Difficult emotions were lurching in the shadows, menacing the golden pattern planned for Saturday night with Jake. Fran had erased the messy colours of her childhood deliberately and calmly. She had painted her life with glowing precision. She had chosen love – not the nurturing parental love she used to seek, but the absolute passion of a man who adored her. Ultimate love, thought Fran. She bit her lip and the guilt bit back.

'Well she couldn't really come here,' said Fran again.

Jake put his glass down, spilling drips from the brimming rim. 'Of course she can't come here. She's got twenty years in her yet. She'll outlive us all – she'd drive us crackers.'

Fran laughed uncertainly. He kissed her ear.

'And we don't even know if we'll stay here.'

Fran stiffened, forced herself to relax. She smiled. 'It's ready. Shall we eat?'

'Then again, we might need the room for a baby.'

This was all getting out of control. Everything they had never discussed – family loyalties, long-term commitment, children – was suddenly slithering across the kitchen like some unappeasable python. 'Supper?' said Fran, pleadingly. Jake concluded his spiralling kisses and took another bottle of white from the fridge.

'I'm not hungry yet.'

'It's trout,' said Fran. She tried not to sound peeved. It was an awful rush on Thursday evenings to get the shopping after work and she always planned his favourite meals. Now she found she was feeling almost cross as she covered the cooked dish again and said flatly, 'We can have it cold, later, if you want.'

Jake became more serious. He placed both refilled glasses on the side and took her arm solicitously, as if offering escort across a hazardous junction.

'I'm not being heartless, Fran. Think about what you're saying. She's 'not safe' in a bungalow, so bring her to an ancient three-storey cottage? She's 'isolated' a couple of miles out of town, so bring her further away?'

'Further from Bath, but only a few miles to town the other way.'

'To a different town – one she doesn't even know – and too far for her to walk. She's only two minutes from the bus route where she is, five minutes from the pub and the Spar.'

'Ten, I'd say.'

'She's spry. It keeps her fit. She'd deteriorate stuck here, away from her friends.'

'Mum has no friends. That's one of the problems.'

'She has all the company she wants. You know she's anti-social in normal terms, Fran, she won't make new friends here and more to the point, she doesn't want to leave.'

Jake was right, Fran reassured herself. Jake was being sensible.

'This is all in Gwen's head,' said Jake, lifting his drink to toast the trouncing of Fran's protests. 'Don't let a neurotic woman get you in a flap too.'

This was not quite the way Fran saw her cogitations.

'Well, maybe it's not about moving Mum out. Maybe it's about getting her more help. Some kind of companion.'

'She has help. She has a companion.'

Fran picked at the lollo rosso edgily. 'Oh we're just going round in circles. It's the companion that worries Gwen.'

'Yes, and you know why? Sheer prejudice. It's because he's from the Convoy.'

'We haven't even seen him, Jake. Maybe Gwen has her reasons.' Jake shrugged and restarted the jazz CD. 'What Gwen needs is a big dick.'

'Oh Jake. Not that again.'

'It's true. That's why she's so uptight about this. She needs a good shag.'

How can sensitive Jake say these crude things? His reassuring hand still stroked her shoulders; he had the same delightful smile and his delicious eyes were still intent and sulphurous blue.

She stepped away. 'You're disgusting when you're boozed, Jake.'

Jake saw her unhappy lips. His arm swung away.

'So I have to be PC in my own kitchen, now?'

Fran snatched up her shirt and struggled into it. Arguing naked had been a bad idea. It's not about bloody political correctness, she wanted to say. It's about my mother, and you're not listening.

'If you're not hungry yet, I'm going for a run,' she said flatly, emerging from the neckline.

Avoiding Jake's silence Fran fetched her denim cutoffs, pulled on her old trainers without bothering to find socks, tied the shirt loosely round her, and managed a small enchanting smile before she left. They had only just celebrated their nearly-a-year-since-we-met anniversary. Fran didn't want a first-row anniversary, not ever. She started to jog up the lane.

Fran's circular running route took only about half an hour, a good length for an evening run. The track from the cottage joined the lane which passed the fringe of the town beside the printing factory where she worked. Here a broad grassy verge spread between the pavement and the road, with a wooden bench where the same man often sat. He had longish light hair and a palomino-pale coat and he looked up as Fran passed.

Fran gave the familiar figure a vague wave. She was thinking about Leonora. To be more accurate she was thinking about today's unsatisfactory conversation with Jake, which Leonora had caused. Not a row, of course. Fran would not row with Jake, not ever. And especially not on Saturday evening when the bright dusk was sensuous with birdsong and the table on the patio laid to dine al fresco, the bread rolls warm and the white wine chill. And yet somehow the placid and passionate intimacy of the evening had soured. Jake had not said the right things. Something had gone wrong around the time Fran said *she couldn't really come here* and Jake had agreed.

She has no friends. That's one of the problems. Fran had surprised and saddened herself with this sudden realisation. Where had everyone gone? Her childhood had been raucous with the noisy voices of Leonora's causes. Leonora had campaigned, sometimes in official positions but mostly in loose quarrelsome assemblies, for a miscellany of just causes throughout Fran's childhood. Fran had accepted her mother's vigorous enthusiasms docilely, and trusted the rest of the world would too until the day a friend asked innocently *where's your mother?* and Fran heard an ironic voice answer on her behalf *Liberating Chad.* And then general laughter. In adulthood she had been able to share the memory with Neville. *Has Mum liberated Chad yet?* they would ask each other. *No, still busy at it.*

But now maybe Chad was free enough for Leonora. She still snipped cuttings from the Sunday papers, she still wrote occasional letters, but the multi-faced, multi-faceted urgency had gone. Her overflowing world was smaller now. Fran thought, it's years since I've seen anyone else at the bungalow apart from us. What does Leonora *do* all day?

At the cottage Jake was feeling hungry. He picked at the cooling trout and wondered sorrowfully why Fran had abandoned him supperless. He planned ways to enquire which would reproach without renewing their differences. Acrimony is not aphrodisiac. Right now Jake just wanted Fran. He jettisoned reproach for readiness: he laid two places, and picked a bosomy scented rose. The rose made him think of Fran. He poured another glass of wine, and the way the light swirled and slopped in the pale liquid made him think of Fran, and the sweetness on his hand as he licked the drips made him think of Fran, and the silvery saxophone notes slipping from the jazz on the radio made him think of Fran. He sighed, and the slight sibilant sound of his breath made him think of Fran. He groaned.

He wandered moodily to the door and stood looking down the lane.

The evening air was pale but still bright and the heavy-blossomed white rose hedge was almost luminous. A woman was travelling slowly up the lane on a moped. Her enormous bulk was comprised, Jake realised as she neared the gate, of multi-layered clothing and at least two coats. Two bulging cases strapped behind her slithered visibly nearer the ground as she wobbled bumpily over the muddy ruts. She saw him and waved erratically. Her mop of curling hair massed around her like ancient candy floss, in tones of sliced salami streaked intermittently with pure raspberry sorbet.

'Remember me?' said Babette.

Jake regarded her as a vegan might look at an abattoir. He remembered Babette. *That woman's an emotional mess – how did she ever get to be Housemother at that school?* was one of the first questions he had ever asked Fran. *It's a notional title,* Fran had explained, *she's care staff really.*

'I've just left Rupert.' said Babette.

'Who's Rupert?' said Jake.

Babette alighted and slapped him on the back. Jake's wine sloshed. 'You know, Rupert. After you swiped my housemate, Rupert moved in. He teaches computers, or art, or something. Both, I think.

'Does Rupert know you've left him?' said Jake, after a thoughtful pause during which Babette divested herself of jackets in a purposeful manner which struck him as distinctly sinister.

'He watched me go saying *I don't believe it, I don't believe it,* but I expect he does now. There's nothing so concrete as absence.'

The pile of packaging on the ground mounted and Babette arrived at a grubby teeshirt announcing A WOMANS PLACE IS IN THE STRUGGLE beneath which there were clearly no more sartorial options. Jake closed his eyes.

'I left him a note,' Babette said. 'Knowing how much Rupert admires ephemeral art, I iced it on a special farewell cake. I used the fine rosette nozzle and rather a lot of cochineal. It came out perfect, all crispy squiggles. GOODBYE RUPERT.' She scrolled in the air. Jake thought of snow signatures with pee in long gone wintry days.

'Fran not here?' suggested Babette as Jake remained in front of the cottage like a small child awaiting the return of his mother.

An appalling thought was beginning to arise in Jake's mind, like some bathyphilus bubble. 'Was Fran expecting you tonight?'

'Oh, no. Well, not really. She knew how things were...'

Did Fran invite you? No, Jake decided. Unwise. He did not want to think of such treachery. He would be unable to believe Babette anyway.

'Perhaps you'd like to eat,' said Jake ungraciously. 'We haven't had our supper yet.' Babette said no, but she wouldn't mind a drink.

She followed Jake inside and surveyed the decor ostentatiously with arms akimbo. Jake surmised this pantomime was designed to imply she had never visited before. He indicated the wine bottle unspeakingly and Babette fetched a tumbler. 'Rupert and I should never have got together,' she said by way of a toast.

'So why did you?' said Jake. Rudely. Babette plonked herself on the pouffe.

'Insufficient procrastination,' she said. 'It's always been my problem. The Head asked if I minded who shared the house. The only stipulation I made was non-smoker.'

Jake fought curiosity with silent belligerence, then said, 'You smoke, don't you?'

Babette nodded. 'I hate people scrounging my fags.'

'Babette, I have seen that staff house, don't forget. It's only shared accommodation. You didn't have to share a bed.'

Babette sighed and topped her tumbler.

'Insufficient procrastination,' she said again, in that indifferent, slow, irritating way, almost as though she found perverse satisfaction in random contiguity.

She fiddled with the stereo, moving the setting so the sultry saxophone instrumental was abruptly replaced by a local radio station phone-in. A mealy-mouthed man was maundering on about a proposed hostel for the mentally ill. 'We'll be turning in our beds,' the droning voice prophesied morosely.

'And murdered in our graves, too,' said Jake. He felt glad to have someone to be angry with at last.

Jake turned the radio off and poured himself another glass.

'Cheers,' said Babette cheerlessly.

Jake acknowledged the salutation with a brief reluctant movement. He leaned back. He pushed a hand through his hair and wished Fran would come home. Missing her made him feel sexy and wanting her made him feel restless and restlessness made him feel angry.

'So, you're coming to stay?'

Babette looked a little less glum. 'I was beginning to think that wasn't an option.'

'You don't seem to have any other. There's a sofabed in the

study.' Jake fetched in the final haversack and threw it on the floor.

'Is this all your stuff?'

'Mostly. I'll go back for the rest tomorrow. Who's that?' Babette indicated a photograph of a little girl with a precision-cut fringe feeding pigeons in Trafalgar Square.

'Cassie. My daughter. Fran got an enlargement.'

Babette scrutinised the picture then replaced it. She said inscrutably, 'Yeah, Fran believes in daughters.'

Jake leaned back and stared at Babette.

'How did you get to be a friend of Fran's?' he wondered aloud, incuriously. The question was clearly rhetorical but Babette answered anyway.

'Fran tends to see the best in people.'

Jake regarded her warily. This might be an oblique criticism of himself, and anyway he didn't want to discuss Fran with Babette. Babette had a you-started-it look in her eye so he said nothing.

'She's one of those optimists who always sees some drink left in the glass,' Babette went on, smirking glacially. 'I think that's part of her enchanting appeal, for people like us .'

Jake let the implication pass. It was all beginning to feel faintly, but not unpleasantly, conspiratorial.

'That you?' said Babette, pointing to Fran's most recent portrait of Jake still on the easel. His heavy-lidded eyes were watchful and sultry; she had captured the delicate sensuality of his slim mouth and the insouciance of his long-lashed gaze. The hair, dark and slightly curled at the nape of the neck, was tactile in its exactness. Fran had rubbed soft crayon into the charcoal drawing, blue for the shirt line, and flecking the dazzling eyes; pale ochre to suggest skin tones. Colours of desert sand and sky.

'It's a likeness,' Babette conceded, as Jake stared back at her without answering. 'Naturalistically, it's a good likeness. Not the essential you, though, is it? All sugared almonds and not a scrap of gothic.'

Jake started to bristle loyally and then thought how absolutely aptly Babette had put it, and subsided into silence.

Babette leaned back in her chair. Through some trick of the

evening light she looked larger than ever, despite her extensive disrobing, as if the thin air around her was shrinking away from her voluptuous intensity. Jake shook off an uncanny sensation that she was swelling slowly like a vast membrane as Babette continued talking about art. Like that Klimt picture you've got in the hall, she was saying, '– glitzy, erotic, and utterly irrelevant. The real message is in the chaotic fragmented surround, the embrace is pure fantasy.' Jake, not really listening, heard the word *erotic* and thought about Fran's slender golden body and her thick soft tawny hair.

Babette's brash lollipop mop glowed in the low evening sun. She smelled of sweet scent and dry wine and woman.

Jake stared into his glass. He loved Fran totally. He disliked and mistrusted and slightly feared Babette. He had made an eternal contract with Fran. But Babette had walked through the door into their private idyll, and Fran had gone out running.

Fran had let Jake down. She persuaded him to believe in imperatives, to forget that everything is accidental.

Fran had completed her loop and started on her homeward run. The man on the bench had gone. The bench was there, and the trees, and the starry-eyed daisies, dense and glittering white and gold. Fran ran on, pressing the petals at the grassy rim of the path. She thought of the picture in her hallway and she smiled as she ran. She had got over her anger with Jake now. She was ready to give him all her attention and all her love.

As if I do not have enough to worry about with Clive, Gwen wrote in her diary that night, and then scratched out the last two words. She put down her pen and buffed her pale fingernails for a few moments before returning to the task of defining the preoccupations of the day.

Clive still has no proper job. Gwen wrote. He has bought a pair of boots that look designed for walking in the Himalayas, I should think any employer would find them most off-putting. I shudder to think how much they cost him. Gwen brooded for a moment and then deleted *him* and replaced it with irked emphasis by *his father.*

Neville should never have agreed to Clive leaving school without A levels.

'What can we do? We can't manacle him to the school gates,' Neville had said, but Gwen felt that was not the point. It was a question of attitude. Clive did not have the right attitude and frankly, neither did his teacher. 'We can't give very good predictions for Clive,' she'd said, 'and the way he feels about school quite honestly I should let him leave and find his own niche in the real world.'

'But there are no niches for the unqualified,' Gwen had objected. She was ready to take up cudgels there and then at the parents evening, but Neville had just nodded and shaken the teacher's hand and said, of all things, 'Thanks'.

And had Clive found his niche? Of course not. Unless you count – which Gwen did not – a few mornings work at the Health Food shop, which she only found out about last week when she went in for *Quiet Life* and found her son squatting in a green apron bagging up mung beans. Vegetables! As far as Gwen knew, Clive still thought purple sprouting broccoli was something she bought for flower arrangements. Gwen hardly knew whether she was pleased or put out. Part-time packaging delivers no diplomas. And that band was hardly niche material – not even a proper ensemble, just a lot of drums and a didgeridoo. Neville was no help with that either. 'A band is almost obligatory for boys that age,' he said, 'They're warriors. If they weren't battling with the sound barrier it would be in cider bars, or football terraces.'

'Did you fight, Neville, at that age?' Gwen had enquired, arching her eyebrows ironically. Neville blinked. 'I was in the scouts,' he said evasively, adding with a nostalgic smile, 'Got pushed around a lot, but all good fun.' Which really wasn't the point.

And now Leonora. Fran was most uncooperative when I mooted the notion of a Home. She said, We can't make decisions like that behind her back. Her back in my view is hardly the point. We have to know the options ourselves or it will all be done in a panic. It is only sensible to make a few enquiries, to test the waters at least.

Gwen began her water-testing activities immediately after the aborted family conference by beseeching Neville to accompany her to the Social Services office. As luck would have it Leonora's social worker was Duty Officer that afternoon, though Mandy Mells may not have shared Gwen's satisfaction at this serendipitous coincidence. Mandy smiled in a terminally anxious way at Gwen and looked warily at the phone on her desk. She was waiting for more complaint calls about the proposed new halfway hostel for people with mental illnesses.

'We are really overstretched, I'm afraid, and spread rather thin,' she told Gwen. Gwen thought Mandy was spread rather thin herself. Tomboy haircut and eyes like spiders snagged in fishnet. 'It's really up to the family,' Mandy added, and Gwen, sitting primly on the edge of her chair, found her eyes following Mandy's mesmerised gaze to the phone. She pursed her lips and waited.

'We can't offer any more funding, at the present time.' Mandy emphasised the end of her sentence optimistically as though another load of funding was expected any Wednesday now. 'Was that what you wanted to know?'

'No' said Gwen. 'I – the family merely wants to know what

the options are. We are thinking along the lines of respite care...'

'Respite?' Now that the tricky query of funding was clarified Mandy's brow had unfurrowed slightly and she looked less peaky. 'For whom?"

Gwen hesitated. Respite care seemed a useful phrase. It had a functional sound yet with soothingly temporary overtones. Gwen realised that the 'respite' in question strictly speaking referred to whoever normally had the burden of care, making the concept ambiguous in Leonora's case. Her mother-in-law was managing an independent life. In whose interests would they be acting? A respite for Leonora from her own haphazard self-management, or for the inscrutable gardener?

'Well, for a short time. A trial period. So that my mother-in-law can make her own decision about her longer-term future.'

'Care in the private sector can be very, adequate,' Mandy said, almost enthusiastically, and she started looking in the files for brochures.

The phone rang. Mandy stopped rummaging and started looking anxious again. The phone stopped. Then the phone rang again and Mandy picked it up quickly and said 'Just a minute please.' Gwen could hear faint hurdy-gurdy music pinging away to the unknown caller while Mandy told her, 'I feel it's really a decision for the family – Mum of course, but you too, as the carers. Mum can probably see some benefits, particularly for the future, but she may need a bit of persuading. Or, you can take other steps. You can come back to me of course, if you feel you need more support.'

Gwen took the proffered brochure, thanked Mandy, buttoned her jacket, gathered her bag, and left the office.

We have to be proactive Gwen wrote sagely. Proactive was another useful word like respite. Contemporary, positive, words, brimming with valuable insight. In fact proactive was even better because its pronunciation is unequivocal (respite has that inherently tricky second syllable; is it spit or spite? Gwen was never certain) and because it sounds just a little like Prozac. Pros and cons, thought Gwen, doodling in the journal margin. Profess, confess. Probe, proboscis, procreate.

She scratched out these irrelevancies and wrote firmly *Someone has to think about these things and though it should of course be the daughter, there is no way I will turn my back on family responsibilities even if Fran is heedless of her mother's needs. The bungalow is unsuitable for a geriatric, even without* – Gwen paused in mute contemplation of the invading dragon boy and found her thoughts sliding bizarrely to the juggling busker – *other dangers,* Gwen concluded. Why on earth Leonora persisted in living in a mildewed place of pre-war construction was a mystery only her mother-in-law's stubbornness could explain.

Gwen and Neville had managed to find quite a new house when they married, even though it was situated in a part of Bath largely Georgian. Gwen knew that older houses had more character but felt that coping with peoples' characters was arduous enough; she did not want a house with quirks of its own. The rooms in Gwen's house were docile and sanitary – she could have leased them unaltered to advertise any desirable domestic product. The bathroom looked like one of those spotless bathrooms where muscular cleansers terrorise the germs away. The kitchen looked like the best half of one of those kitchens sliced to show the superior power of the more efficient cleanser. The dining-room was pledged to the shine of glossy spray polishes. The bedroom was tidy and floral like one of those magazine bedrooms where sleepily smiling women are woken with trays of mis-made breakfast by their impish children – though this was not an event Gwen had ever encouraged. The lounge was more difficult. Even in product advertisements people seemed to sprawl about in living rooms. They spread themselves carelessly and indulged in messy activities, like reading newspapers. Clive had been forever wanting to paint. 'Can't you do that in your room?' Gwen had urged, because boys' rooms can be, well, boyish. 'The light's no good there,' was his stock response. The light was certainly no good there now, since Clive had painted the walls and ceiling black. And Neville had let him get away with it! Gwen's lounge, however, was satisfactory, with muted colour-scheme. Visitors commented on what a restful room it was. Neville certainly seemed to find it restful; he often spent much of the evening there asleep.

The tiny back garden was immaculate too. Its borders were meticulously edge-trimmed, with phostrogen-bright bedding-plants spaced neatly on the dark earth. All a tribute to Gwen's conscientious industry. The rockery however was Neville's realm. Gwen was not convinced about the rockery. The pond was alright, and the fountain – a nice feature with water bubbling over a stone, not one of those peeing cherubs – but the surround remained devoid of alpines despite her reminders. Neville seemed simply to like rearranging the chunks of stone. He knew these elements intimately; he was on first name terms with them. The granite. The quartz. The Italian marble, the Galway slate. He rearranged them assiduously, heaving at the bigger ones, making imperceptible alterations which he contemplated for long periods, but he never seemed quite ready to add any plants.

But on the whole the garden was satisfactory. And the house was a shrine to good taste – except for Clive's room which positively shrieked for a makeover. Clive was resisting, of course, but dispiritedly. He was turning out sadly dispirited, Gwen felt. Adolescence had stolen her pale, intent, sweet-natured child, and left a pallid, listless, moody changeling who answered sporadically and accused her of interference when she tried to tidy up. Recently these attempts had become so contentious that Gwen crept in only when Clive was out.

Clive was out now. Gwen topped her pen and made a tidying sortie, fine-tuned now to a feisty raid on abandoned clothes and a gloomy look around the room for non-contentious trash. Much of what appeared to be indubitably bin-able rubbish had, in the past, become vehemently disputed trove. Gwen's disapproving gaze ranged the room and locked on the Magic Eye picture opposite Clive's bed.

Deciphering Magic Eye pictures had never been one of Gwen's achievements. You have to relax, Clive told her when he first blue-tacked it up. Gwen knew about relaxing. She had been to classes to learn how to do it by breathing and lying in a special way. Relaxation was a technique, something scientific. It was not just this sloppy way of flopping around that Clive and his father seemed to think. Nevertheless, she had not yet despite several breathing sessions managed to see anything in the poster except a fizzle of yellow speckles.

Gwen reunited two estranged socks by folding the ankles together in a love knot and frowned at the Magic Eye poster. She measured an arm's length from the patterned image and stared at the golden slivers of pattern scattered densely across the glossy surface. Her mind slid slowly to her last visit to Leonora's bungalow. From the frazzled fragments in front of her, abruptly, her mother-in-law's gardener emerged, crawling on all fours through the undergrowth. Gwen blinked. It was not exactly the dragon boy, but certainly a male figure, and there was someone else in the picture too, fallen perhaps. She couldn't quite work out what the crawling figure was doing with his third arm, no, third leg, no – oh my goodness. The figures in the picture twined and reared as Gwen stared. She felt the heat of a blush racing up her neck and down her forehead. Wasn't this sort of thing against the Commandments? No, that was graven images, not seedy Karma Sutra postures. Perhaps they ought to have been included – perhaps they would have been if Moses had known.

Gwen returned to her bedroom and unclicked her diary. *Magic Eye indeed!* she wrote, *just a way of hiding smutty pictures.* The words looked unsatisfactory and faintly risible, like some wavering voice chiding her from long forgotten school days. Gwen crossed out *smutty* and replaced it with *risqué*. French words are always more tart. She twiddled with her hair ends and stared at her reflection in the mirror. That anti-wrinkle cream was not what it was cracked up to be.

On impulse Gwen donned the embroidered kimono Neville gave her for Christmas, rarely worn as silk is so tricky to clean, and went downstairs to see what her husband was doing.

Neville was eating marshmallows and watching the late-night movie. He looked perfectly happy. Gwen nearly said routinely, 'You'll get fat,' but instead went over to the settee and wedged herself beside him.

'Can't sleep, pudding?' Neville asked kindly, making room. Gwen's shoulders drooped. He makes me feel like a marmalade sponge soggied over with custard, she thought.

Gwen attempted to convey with raised eyebrow that Leonora's plight practically demanded insomnia, but Neville wasn't looking. She got up and went into the kitchen for the colour brochure that Mandy had given her, collecting the biscuit barrel on the way back.

'Peace of mind in pleasant surroundings,' read Gwen enticingly, crunching a pecan cookie.

'Piece of whose mind?' said Neville, as Patrick Swayze gyrated exotically to a samba rhythm. Gwen paused, briefly distracted, then continued to peruse the page. 'Pleasant individual rooms. They look enchanting, Neville. Even a bedside phone. With benefit of astounding views. You can see right over the city.'

Neville caught her drift. He dipped his hand in the marshmallow bag again. 'Mum may prefer her present views. You can see right over the countryside.'

Gwen crunched undeterred. 'And look at that magnolia!' she coaxed, 'Little short of sumptuous.'

Neville sighed stickily.

'Tea dances on the first Wednesday of each month,' Gwen said after a few more moments scrutiny. She licked her finger and pressed it onto a straying chocolate chip.

'Good-oh,' said Neville.

'Immediate placement beds always available on doctor's recommendation.' Gwen folded the brochure and placed it beside Neville on the settee. 'You should visit, Neville.'

'It's Mother who should visit,' Neville said, but mildly.

'At least consult her doctor,' Gwen urged. 'Test the waters, at least.'

'I'll phone on Monday,' Neville promised. Gwen put the top back on the cookie barrel and patted his knee approvingly.

Neville, surprised, with half a pink marshmallow between his lips, leaned towards her indicating with his eyebrows that she should relieve him of the extruding soft plumpness. Gwen started to put out her hand, then moved her face forward and bit firmly into the pink marshmallow. It pulled slowly away. Sugar fell softly between them. Gwen ate her pirated piece of sweetmeat slowly thinking, 'This is probably the sort of thing that Fran does with Jake.' The notion was delicious.

Next morning Gwen discovered she was pouring milk. She had the jug poised above the cup and she tilted it to watch the creamy white liquid descending. It looked extraordinarily thick, more like cream than her usual semi-skimmed. The milk jetted and cascaded, spraying huge droplets which bounced from the rising surface within the cup. She poured and poured.

Gwen remembered that she did not drink milk. 'Would anybody like a cup of milk?' she said aloud, her voice sudden and brash in the bedroom silence.

Gwen woke, embarrassed. She was often embarrassed by her dreams. Luckily today she was alone, Neville had gone downstairs to make French toast with Ravel on the radio. Sometimes he did the wash-up afterwards too, though on those days Gwen wiped the kitchen surfaces and checked the non-stick pan for those tiny eggy spangles that tend to survive cursory male attention, and to muse aloud on the usefulness of dishwashers.

This morning she padded to the bureau and fetched her diary and wrote *I dreamed that I was pouring milk. Neville and I had been enjoying breakfast in bed. It was all quite delicious. Neville licked honey off my fingers and I licked the honey off my knife and all the sticky tissues dropped to the floor as though the frilly-lined waste-paper-basket were simply unimportant.* Gwen had read once in a magazine that it is a good idea to write one's dreams first thing in the morning without thinking about them, but she sometimes found herself writing the oddest things. She mused for a while and then concluded her morning entry briskly: *Clive threatens to acquire a whippet. I hope he does not plan to make a career of dawdling the streets with a dog on a twine. I have in any event put my foot down.*

Gwen closed the diary and clipped the clasp. Standing by the window she watched Belinda prowl across the lawn and pause significantly on its pristine turf. She tapped on the glass and Belinda hurried away.

Gwen pulled the curtains closed to practice her yoga stretches.

She breathed in deeply, leaning backwards. She exhaled slowly, leaning forwards. I wonder how many yoga positions it's possible to make love in, Gwen found herself thinking, unexpectedly, at the limit of her stretch. She slid pensively into the cobra and sighed.

Gwen concluded her routine and selected her underwear from the neat drawer. She fingered her midriff. *City of jewels*, her yoga teacher called this area. Gwen wondered if hers was becoming rather too precious. *'Life is too short to diet'* Gwen had quipped to Leonora last week, having read this philosophy ascribed to various meaty celebrities. *'Nonsense. Life's too short to spend it guzzling synthetic cream from penis substitutes,'* her mother-in-law had retorted, and Gwen had consumed the remains of her penis substitute pinkly and in silence.

Now, half dressed, she studied her undulations in the bedroom mirror. Perhaps she was one of these women who sees their reflection distorted, mistakenly imagining a enlarged version of reality. Perhaps in truth her thighs were taut and coltish with a triangle of space where they met below her panties, and her stomach was slender as a silver birch. She looked doubtfully down. Her blouse, gaping very slightly, beamed back up at her, its pearly-toothed buttons glinting squintily. Gwen put on her skirt and tugged the zip up to the waist, then held her breath in while she slid the fastening round to the side. The lining didn't seem to have slid as far as the rest of the skirt. Gwen hitched up the hem and fished about, jiggling and fidgeting until the creases were smoothed. She clipped on her earrings and went downstairs.

Neville was standing on the patio gazing with an expression of indefinable excitement at a white scar of vapour trail dissecting the cerulean sky. He lit an Embassy. His crockery he had already placed dutifully beside the sink. Gwen stared at the skin from his milky coffee, lowered like a shroud into the ashtray. Housework is something women do and men help with, she thought. That's what sharing the housework means.

She filled the bowl with sudsy water and washed Neville's breakfast cup and cereal bowl and the ashtray with its drape of congealed coffee-skin. Perhaps, she thought, it's an endless rebuke from God after Martha's moaning about wanting a bit of help. A bit of help, that's exactly what we get. She wiped the crockery and cutlery and put it away.

Neville finished his cigarette and came back inside, closing the patio doors politely behind him.

'Any plans for today?' Gwen enquired, with no particular interest. Neville's plans for Sunday generally follow stolidly Taoist principles of musing inactivity.

'I thought I might have a look at the spare room. In case Mother needs somewhere to stay.'

'Stay? Here, Neville? But that is my sewing room. I machined all our curtains and drapes in there – I might well need it again.'

Neville looked enquiringly at the satin-finish honeysuckle flounces and Gwen's excuses faltered. 'But, you are the son,' she exhorted him, 'Surely, it should be the daughter...'

Neville said 'Well, perhaps we should be ready to bear some of the brunt.'

Gwen flushed. Leonora in Lear-like procession from Fran's house to hers, sitting about, wanting feeding, wanting walks. Needing constant attention.

'It was your idea,' Neville was saying with infuriating composure. 'You seemed so very sure, yesterday, that she can't go on as she is.'

Gwen pressed her lips tight again and refolded the tea-towel. This was not her idea. Her idea was that Neville and Fran – especially Fran – should recognise the need for involving relevant agencies, that professional advice should be sought and appropriate action taken. Not that Leonora should come here, filling Gwen's tidy rooms with her devastating elderliness, that was not what she meant at all.

'But, a Home, Neville, with companions her own age, is far more suitable,' she pleaded. 'Leonora can afford it, surely?'

'My mother has never relished the company of her contemporaries.'

'But this place looks so charming!' Gwen snatched the brochure from the letter rack and riffled through it at speed as she continued: 'The decor – the amenities. Constant care. We should ask her doctor's opinion. Telephone him, Neville, do!'

'It's Sunday, dear,' Neville said reasonably. He opened the fridge door and looked lyrically at the left-over chocolate mousse.

'As a friend, Neville. Just to talk it over. You play golf together.'

'With George. George is not her doctor.'

'It's the same practice. Neville, please. When Fran telephones we need to know what the options are.'

But George, when Neville eventually conceded, failed to share Gwen's cavalier view of patient confidentiality, and to console his disconsolate spouse Neville suggested a visit to the American Gardens outside Bath. 'Nothing else we can do about Mother until we hear from Fran', he pointed out. 'She's popping over today, so let's just stop worrying, eh, pudding?'

'As long as you phone the doctor tomorrow, Neville. Test the waters, at least – no matter what Fran says.'

8   The Gateway

Fran had more than her mother on her mind by the time she got around to visiting Leonora on Sunday. The day had almost been swallowed by the maelstrom of Babette's arrival.

Fran had arrived back from her run on Saturday evening to find Babette in the bath and Jake in a state of agitation. He grabbed her in the hallway and clung to her with the fervour of a drowning man, kissing her ardently, and then pulled away and whispered fiercely 'Did you tell her she could come here?' Fran, recognising the purple haversack on the floor, felt flooded by a sinking sense of the ruination of some fragile part of their passion. She knew how Jake deplored Babette. 'Honestly, darling, I had no idea,' she said – 'I would have told you. Jake, let go my arm, you're hurting. Is she stopping?'

She was. Jake had already opened out the futon in the study – 'I thought I ought to, I thought you had practically invited her.' Fran was touched at his reluctant compassion. 'I didn't, darling, and I wouldn't, not without talking to you,' she said. 'But you're right, once she was on our doorstep I would have done the same. Anyway, it can't be for long, can it? She'll have to resolve things one way or another before September, because she's got to be back for the Autumn term.'

So when Babette emerged from her ablutions lobstery pink and shiny, Fran hugged her and agreed that of course she could stay until she'd sorted herself out. Babette pulled Fran's oyster-gold satin robe around her and knotted the tasselled cord, nodding.

'I'll fetch some more stuff tomorrow, then,' she said, adding mysteriously, 'I'm making a Hanging for Peace.'

Babette's arrival, though unexpected had at least solved one concern for Fran. With the futon in the study now fully occupied there was no possibility of installing her mother at the cottage, even on a short-term basis to assess her future needs. Fran felt guilty at her selfish relief, but relieved none the less. Perhaps, Fran thought, she could talk it through more positively with Babette, away from Jake's flippancy and Gwen's dramatic over-statement.

'Alzheimer's can strike at any age,' said Babette. 'It destroys the personality totally, eats away at it like acid.'

Then again, perhaps not.

'She's wacky, but she isn't senile,' Fran tried to explain – 'I may have to face that one day, but not now.'

'Then what's the problem?' Babette wanted to know, pouring the last drops from the cafetière. Brunch was over; Jake had disappeared with his laptop and Babette was girding herself up for what she was now calling – worryingly for supporters of reconciliation – a raid on Rupert's rooms. Fran stacked the coffee cups by the sink and looked out at the fragrant roses wavering close to the open window. She would rather be lying in the garden with bluesy jazz breathing from the CD player than driving through the afternoon heat on a Sunday visit.

'It's the gardener Gwen's bothered about,' she explained. 'She feels that old people are vulnerable to a friendly face.' *Especially old people whose daughters have been too passionately preoccupied to visit.* Fran suppressed the irksome self-reproach. 'We've never talked much, her and me – not in a mother-daughter sort of way. I can't start now. And Mum doesn't really want to.'

Babette belted her scooter jacket and picked up her helmet. 'Nothing you can do. It's her choice.'

Was Babette's ruling a comfort? Fran didn't really know. She had said something similar to Jake earlier and he had been similarly succinct.

'Has she ever given a flying fart about your needs? Well then.'

But Fran was not comfortable with indifference or resentment. She had privately valued the freedom which that lack of any strong motherly bond had given her, and she had never begrudged Leonora her non-maternal eccentricities. There was a far bigger age-gap between them than for most mother-daughters, for one thing, and Fran could empathise with the frustration Leonora, already nudging into her fifties, must have felt to discover her body was not having a menopause, but was instead having a last fling.

Fran drove through the quiet lanes feeling pensive. She found her mother in the kitchen casting runes when she arrived at the bungalow at around three.

'You have started the cycle of self-transformation. You are on the threshold but the gateway is not yet open to you,' Leonora intoned to her companion, a lively-eyed young man in cutoff denims.

'On the threshold again?' Fran bent to kiss the top of her mother's head. She looked discreetly around for signs of disarray and doolally-ness. The kitchen was unusually tidy and smelt enticingly of cinnamon toast. The only difference Fran noticed was a crystal hanging from a long slender thread like some exotic sparkling spider.

Leonora raised her bangled right arm to grasp her daughter's wrist without turning round from her stance at the table. They held the tableau momentarily.

'The Gateway Reversed is a very common reading,' said Leonora. 'Most people are blocked. Meet Polo.'

The gardener was seated beside Leonora scrutinising the stones she had laid out for him. He looked up at Fran and nodded. His heavily beaded hair was bound in a mane and strands of pink and gold flopped across his forehead. He looks like My Little Pony, Fran thought tenderly.

'I got the elk,' said Polo with apparent pride. 'Protection.'

'You are my protector,' Leonora interpreted 'and don't fiddle, you'll put it in reverse and that's no good at all.'

'I'm sorry I haven't been round for a while,' Fran said, 'One of our friends has had a bit of a crisis.' Leonora nodded. 'How is Jake?' she enquired, without looking up.

'He's fine.'

'Are you two still not talking?'

'What on earth do you mean? We've never not talked. We talk all the time.'

Leonora pulled her cotton stole around her like a ruffled owlet and looked sceptical. 'Love is a meadow that needs setaside to thrive,' she murmured, after a pause. It was unclear to Fran whether this was a message from the runes or another of her mother's inscrutable theories.

A light breeze from the window twirled the crystal on its thread, and snatches of rainbow coloured light flickered round the room. 'Like butterflies,' said Fran, watching the dancing prisms on the walls which, she realised now, seemed spacier than usual. Almost as if they had been denuded.

'Weren't there shelves over there?'

'The seed of the new lies in the shell of the old. All that is no longer needed must be stripped away to allow the harvest.' Leonora was definitely now addressing not her but Polo as she concluded her reading. Polo nodded enigmatically and went to the sink to fill the kettle. Fran tried to decide if this was suspiciously proprietorial or merely friendly and helpful. He had a certain swagger about him, but this seemed to be a natural style rather than anything sinisterly Svengali-ish.

'Blood siblings,' said Leonora as she collected up the runes and replaced them in their silk pouch. She pointed theatrically between Fran and Polo. 'I have Romany blood, you know. My family descended from Fair Rosamund, the mistress of Edward the Second, whose bastard line became the Rosoman guild of Goldsmiths in medieval times.'

'I know,' said Fran, 'you told me.' She watched Polo intently: he was shaking his head slowly but his smile suggested affection rather than dissent.

'I brought a carrot cake,' Fran said, unboxing.

'GM free?' enquired Leonora, sniffing as if she could scent baked modified genes at ten paces.

'Yeah, I checked,' Fran fibbed quickly.

'Looks good,' said Polo. He gave Fran a sibling grin and unsheathed his knife.

'My daughter is a painter,' Leonora informed him as they sat around the table munching, 'or at least she will be, when she has suffered a little more.' Fran smiled wryly.

'That's a bit of a cliché. Is suffering essential for creativity?'

'Of course it is. You are a very good draughtsman dear, but slick. Your best painting by far is that one in your hall.'

Fran pressed her finger onto some stray icing and licked it unperturbed.

'That's a Klimt reproduction, Leonora. As you very well know.'

'Is it? That painting of a phallus with faces?'

Fran ignored her. Leonora's eyesight was not that bad.

'So this is what you do all day,' she said serenely as Polo poured the tea. Both Leonora and Polo looked at her indulgently but neither commented. Fran decided on a more direct approach.

'What do you actually do, these days, Leonora?' she asked, reaching for the last walnut on the sticky yoghurt topping to make the enquiry sound more casual.

'I write, I sketch, I muse. Theoretically, at least. In reality, the minutiae of living takes most of my time. Unwinding dental floss from the loofah, redirecting junk mail. Colour-coding empties for the bottle bank – finding a tea strainer not clogged with spinach. I expect you find your life much the same.'

'She keeps busy,' supported Polo, speaking with his mouth full.

'I'd hate to think of you just sitting and staring at day-time TV.'

Leonora shook crumbs vigorously from the fringe of her stole. 'Nothing wrong with that. You learn a lot from those afternoon programmes. History for Schools has been tackling the last three decades, which I found most informative.'

'Leonora, you lived it!'

'Precisely. A clump of grass is no way to measure the meadow. This must be the first generation to actually comprehend their past. The old used to say, *Ah but you don't know, you weren't there.* Now the young can tell their elders, *You don't know, you didn't see the documentary.* Context is all.'

Fran hesitated. Jake had only last night reminded her, in a discussion about local fury at mobile phone masts devastating the region, that context could only arrive from complete perspective. It had sounded totally convincing when Jake said it but when Fran ventured the view, it seemed less conclusive than she had hoped. She looked across at Polo who watching them both impassively.

'Context requires pragmatic compassion,' Leonora corrected calmly. 'Certain Icelandic tribes, I'm told, used to rewrite their history routinely in order to strengthen current friendships.'

'That was probably for trading. Economic forces, Leonora, not compassion.' Fran collected the plates. Her mother had not lost the capacity to crusade for meaningless causes, it appeared. Leonora merely shrugged and said, 'It seems a very sensible arrangement.'

'But, history – I mean, what actually happened – is at the root and heart of understanding what's happening now, surely you can see that? The past shapes the present.'

'Very probably. Which makes it all the more useful to have a little flexibility. And now, dear, I am going to the bathroom, so that you two can talk about me.' Leonora gave an ostentatious wink and Fran laughed dutifully, feeling outwitted yet relieved. She would feel even more relieved when her visit was safely anecdotal. Love is always easier in the comfort of distance. Proximity is the tricky bit.

Fran tried to think of something she could usefully ask Polo but she was distracted by the sunlight and the dancing prisms from the crystal in the window, fluttering on the walls like tiny flags of freedom. She picked a stone out of Leonora's silky pouch and twisted it round in her hand. 'Which way up should this one be?'

'Doesn't matter,' said Polo. 'That's elemental disruption, it's always the wrong way up whatever way you hold it.'

'My life's going to be disrupted?'

'Elementally.' He was smiling now.

'Oh. Well if a squiggle on a piece of stone says so, it must be true.'

Fran smiled back but she felt that curious frisson which she termed imperative insight, almost as if she were not really in this moment but already a long way distant, looking back and watching it race towards her from a long time ago.

9   Meanwhile. . .

At the American Museum, Gwen was sniffing a bed of scented lovage outside the exhibition hall. Signs to the tea room were reminding Neville he had quite a thirst but Gwen decided to continue alone in order to view the display before embarking on refreshments. She soon found herself surrounded by ancient quilts dangling between notices requesting the public not to touch. Gwen lingered in front of a few, then looked at her watch and wondered how long she should stay before joining Neville.

A little girl materialised at her side in that odd way little girls do, and inquired, 'Which do you like best?' Gwen looked around for the child's chaperone but could see no-one who might be responsible. 'I like this one,' the child confided, pointing to the richly patterned fabric ahead. 'It's got my name' she said blithely and, in defiance of all the surrounding instructions, she leant forward to press her lips against the appliquéd letters G R A C E in a lingering kiss.

Gwen's eyes moistened. She did not approve of precocious little girls and the action was unhygienic as well as disobedient. But there was something extraordinarily moving about the child's impulse. To have such rapport with herself, so that her natural instinct was to touch her name approvingly, lovingly. Gwen was flooded with piquant envy.

Gwen's misty eyes cleared and she found the child had metamorphosed into a uniformed male reminding her that the fabric was old and must not be handled. Gwen nodded numbly. The attendant appeared to realise she had no responsibility for the vanished miscreant, for he relaxed and began to talk about the embroidered flowers on the lavish irregular patches of the hanging. 'Look at the time that must have taken,' he urged; 'They had time, in those days. In today's world this would be an anachronism.'

Gwen wondered if this was something to do with spiders and leaned forward uncertainly to scrutinise the embroidery.

'A portière like that tells us a lot about the lives of those women,' the attendant was saying, and Gwen remembered that an anachronism was something out of time. A straggling recollection assailed her as the attendant explained that this was not constructed like a true quilt – the memory of a doctor's words, long ago, when she was trying for Clive. 'Too much to do, too little time – that's the modern malaise,' the doctor had said. Gwen flushed again now, as she had then, at his self-assured diagnosis of her long unconsummated wait. Gwen had never been infected with the busy virus. In the fashionable stress of late twentieth-century living Gwen, who only ever wanted to be normal, found herself once again out of step. Everything she had dutifully absorbed in her solitary teens about womanly duties had become dramatically outdated. No-one balanced encyclopaedias like primal water pots on their head anymore; nowadays people got out of cars any way they damn well pleased. The graces Gwen had studied and cherished were now a synonym for arcane absurdity. Other women her age had careers and went on management courses. Gwen pottered about in a charity shop like some risible neighbour in a television sitcom. I am an anachronism, thought Gwen forlornly, looking at the dangling portière in its museum splendour.

She joined Neville in the tea gardens and announced the visit had inspired her to use her spare time constructively and create a wall hanging from scraps of fabric. 'Not a patchwork, a collage. Collage is an undervalued skill, Neville,' Gwen explained as he looked at her with bemusement, 'Women's art usually is.' Neville continued to look doubtful as he poured her cup of tea. Gwen's carpets had hitherto been allergic to scraps of any description.

But it was not purely the exhibition which had sparked this quest for creativity in Gwen. Neither was it, although Neville may have suspected otherwise, merely the desire to put the spare room to swift use. Gwen could not stop thinking about that little girl's unexpected kiss. She found herself absently humming *Amazing Grace* while Neville nibbled his Connecticut snickerdoodle.

Tea finished, they walked in the shady arboretum, pausing at the fence to gaze across the sun-dappled valley where the river meanders all the way to Bath and beyond, looping close to the canal and Leonora's bungalow. Neville hoped this would not cause Gwen to recall her concerns about her mother-in-law, but Gwen's geography was flaky and her head was full of her planned collage.

'A woman came into the Heart shop last week looking for fabrics,' she told him as they strolled back past the Italian roses. 'She is creating a Hanging for Peace – an embroidered rural scene, I believe. She gave me a number for contact. I still have it.' Gwen delved into her bag for corroborative evidence. Neville looked at the proffered piece of paper and turned it over twice.

'That's Fran's number, dear.'

'It can't be. Look, it's got her name beneath.'

Babette read Neville. 'Babette who? Well, it's Fran's number all right. Perhaps you've got the digits reversed.'

'She wrote it herself. She told me she was on the move but this would get her throughout the summer. She must be a friend of your sister, Neville.'

One of them clearly had to say *Small world*, so Neville did. 'There was a teacher at that school called Babette,' he recalled. 'Fran used to knock around with her a bit.'

Gwen, distracted by the notion of Neville's sorbet-cool sister knocking around with anyone, frowned fractionally. She did not usually approve of coincidences. Events should be separately discernible, not mixed up together like painted dots with hidden connections. Then she recalled the encounter in the shop and remembered that actually there was something about Babette she had liked on sight. That something was her size. Gwen had liked Babette's bigness. Not as a connoisseur of flesh might, or a feminist, or a fetishist. but because it was decisive. Gwen generally encountered other women warily: was she or was she not the fatter party? Sometimes an affirmative was discouragingly easy to elicit. At other times, decision was more difficult. Layers had to be evaluated, jumpers appraised, underpinnings envisaged and assessed. Sometimes it was touch and go for the advantage.

Occasionally a tiny detail (hair usually – growing-out perms so girth-giving) swung it. But with Babette, Gwen had no such dilemma. Babette was big. Babette made Gwen feel neat and compact. Her comparative diminuity made her feel suave and confident.

Gwen was remembering that feeling as she and Neville sauntered through the arboretum. Sunshine soaked her shoulders through her pale pink acrylic cardigan. Gwen unbuttoned and discarded the garment. For a moment she had an extraordinary fantasy of stripping off her blouse too, and her bra, and standing naked to the waist like a mermaid.

'I shall telephone Babette,' Gwen decided, 'I shall make a panel for her Peace Hanging.'

Meanwhile, Fran was on her mobile to Jake, to give him her verdict before setting off for home.

'The gardener guy seems OK. Mum likes him, and he is keeping an eye on her, but I don't know how long he'll stay. She does seem to be getting a little bit scatty, though. He's put in a smoke alarm, because she's got a habit of forgetting to turn off the hob on the cooker. It does glow red, but in the sunlight you can't always tell, and then of course she puts stuff down on it, not realising. He's looking out for things like that, but he's cool about it all.'

'So why is Gwen in such a state about him?"

'I don't really know. He is a bit alternative, a non-conformist maybe, but he's no crustie. He's from Cornwall originally, though you wouldn't know from his accent. We talked about Celtic myths. Mum thinks she's got a bloodline there, of course. One thing that does bothers me a bit, though, I don't think she's paying him properly. She seems to have no idea of money these days. I did ask her, but she just said grandly "London rates," and he sort of raised his eyebrows at me and smiled. He said "It'll do to the end of the month." I don't know if that was a joke or not.'

Jake seized on the notion of London rates in a range of services and the conversation shifted to other topics. 'I'm missing you so much!' Fran whispered in reply, and it was true. It was almost delicious how true it was. Sometimes her passion for Jake seemed at its emotional peak during these sizzling phone calls.

Eventually she said 'I'd better go, Jakey. I'll be home soon. Is Babette back yet?' and Jake seemed oddly uncertain but then said, yes, she was.

10   Art Therapy

Fran peeped into the room that had until recently been her study. It now resembled the collection point for some international recycling campaign. The floor was covered with embroidered fabric surrounded by scraps of velvet and felt, reels of cotton and silk, needles, pins and all the paraphernalia of a major undertaking.

'The Hanging,' Babette introduced.

'It's exquisite,' said Fran, surprised. She had expected patchwork, with the traditional hexagonal templates, but Babette's Hanging was a collage elaborately constructed from illustrated scenes oversewn with careful detail into panels of varying sizes. Those already tacked into positions showed a vivid map of the landscape of the south-west.

'All art is therapy,' said Babette offhandedly.

'It's enormous. This will need a huge wall, Babette. It's already too big for this room.'

'Yup. The exhibition is going all round the country. They're going to be auctioned for World Peace.'

Fran, examining the appliquéd narrative, had already noticed recurrent symbolic motifs.

'I like the wire-cutting crew at Hinkley Point – clever, the way you've used that netting for the perimeter fence! You've got a few road protesters in there, too, I see.'

'There's other panels, only I haven't finished connecting them.' Babette heaved the heavy carpet of cloth to reveal startling images of war-torn streets. Fran examined a Guernica in felts and bold stitching.

'It's really effective.'

Babette agreed. 'And if you've got any CND badges knocking around, or peace poppies, I need some for this border.'

'Leonora will have stuff like that, almost certainly. We could go over one night next week, maybe.' Fran thought suddenly how different the evenings would be now she was no longer alone, and felt anxious and nostalgic for the golden pattern of her days when all she had to think about was how much she loved Jake. Now there was Leonora to be concerned about and Babette to cope with. Perhaps combining two such feisty personalities was not a good idea. 'On the other hand,' she added casually 'she's a little under the weather at the moment, so maybe we should wait a while.'

And now too there was the matter of the Hanging for Fran to worry about. She foresaw at a glance it would antagonise Jake. Some pairings simply don't work, she thought. Babette at a WI meeting. Gwen at a reggae club. Jake and a massive embroidered protest banner, Fran felt, might be another such conceptual oxymoron.

'It's part of an Arts Peace Project,' Fran told him as she unleashed a glimpse through the doorway. She anticipated a cascade of scorn. Surprisingly, Jake was not scornful. Although irritated that Babette's pacifism like her person was obtruding a bulky presence in their cottage, he seemed appreciative of its purpose.

'I thought you would be scathing, Jakey,' Fran told him almost shyly.

'Why?'

'Well, you know. Sewing as a subversive activity!'

'At least it's positive action, and it's creative – and it's more than our leaders are doing. Conflicts happen in a context of ignorance and indifference. If art can shift that to awareness and concern, it's a step forward.'

'I see' said Fran, puzzled. *I wonder why I never saw it that way?* she thought. *I just thought, Hey ho, Babette taking centre stage again. Striding into war zones with the biggest banner in the world, a Joan of Arc for militant peace.*

'I think we should leave Babette stitching for this very worthy cause and get an early night,' Jake continued, caressing her arm and sounding much more like himself,

The bedroom was not yet dark, full of a gloaming pallor

and the scent of musk roses. Quietness intensified sensation as they touched with mouths and hands and moved together in a breathless silent groaning. Next door the floorboards creaked and there was a small farting sound. Fran choked on swallowed giggles.

'What's the matter?' whispered Jake from the cushion of Fran's warm and slowly breathing belly. His hand caressed and curled her hairs.

'Nothing.'

Jake knelt up and gently straddled her.

'I wish you had come with me to see Leonora today,' Fran murmured. 'You'd have known what to say.'

'I'm sure everything is fine.' He stroked her breasts and gazed down at her. Fran's eyes closed. Leonora seemed a long way away.

An enormous crash followed by a tinkling thud resounded down the stairwell. Fran heard Babette say *Fuck* and hurried to the door – naked, because Babette still had her silk robe. Her coffee-stained silk robe, she noted, as Babette arose, switched on the light, and rubbed her butt.

'Just going to the loo,' she said '– should have counted the steps when I could see properly. I'll clear up the bits tomorrow.'

Jake was sitting up with a cigarette by the time she got back.

Fran opened the window. This did not feel like a good time to remind Jake they had an agreement about him not smoking in the bedroom. She gazed out of the window at the deepening dusk of the garden and watched the roses glimmering with that curious luminosity of white flowers in dark air. Next door Babette had put on the radio and phone-in voices mumbled half-audibly through the wall. *'This so-called halfway hostel…'* Fran heard, and then *'people we aren't allowed to call mental any more.'* Nat King Cole's voice intruded soothingly. Fran recognised the song. *Sitting on the dock of the bay.* Sometimes, and this was one of them, Fran had a floating sense of deja vu when she heard a quiet voiced man singing. Nothing distinct, just a feeling of being held, and perhaps cherished.

Jake waited until both the women had left the house next day before he turned on his computer to write his next *Deconstructing Famous Paintings* piece. The day was already hot, and he was already tired. Making up with Fran had been a piece of cake, avoiding Babette more stressful. He couldn't be bothered to drag out his portfolio of lecture notes, so he flipped through his mind's eye and settled on *The Blue Boy*. He had detested this ever since his art teacher told the class it was Gainsborough's inspired preemptive vision of master Jake defiantly refusing to produce his homework. Everyone had laughed and there were blue bows on his desk next morning. Weasely little shit, thought Jake, still unamused despite the passing years. However the painting was now 230 years old, and the art teacher was probably dead and had certainly said it out of repressed homosexual yearning so perhaps now was time for a reappraisal. He wrote quickly.

When Gainsborough created the most popular boy in middle class history aside from Peter Pan, he chose his dandy blue attire deliberately to annoy Joshua Reynolds, founder of the Royal Academy and darling of the London critics. Reynolds was known for his rigid insistence that blue in paintings was for accents and highlight: his own portrait of a young boy, Master Bunbury, gives the child a rich damson red velvet jacket. This was painted three years after his rival's swaggering Blue Boy, and the younger child faces the viewer in the same insouciant straight-on way, in a similar background of nondescript foliage. Some rivalries are so deep they never die.

He'd gone off point now – he needed to chuck in something about Prussian blue being the first artificially manufactured colour, and the kid's outfit being over a hundred years out of date because of Gainsborough's obsession with Van Dyck, and blah de blah. It was all on Wikipedia now, why was he bothering? Computers were making pontificating art history magazines redundant now – soon every home and school would have one. Every adult. Every child, for heavens sake. Jake's reflections continued irritably as he looked through his notes to find Van Dyck's dates. The ending of the Net Book Agreement controlling retail prices three years ago had let the foxes loose in the publishing henhouse, and supermarket check-out bins of paperbacks at less than the price of eggs would kill the chances of new authors, but probably even that kind of book reading would become an elite occupation practised only in small groups and clubs. Pretty soon, Jake thought, the shit will hit the fan for our culture, and we won't even understand why.

Jake wandered to the window to watch the red and pink hollyhocks swaying above those odd blue primroses – he must ask Fran what they were – and thought how sultry the city would be today. Pavements positively sticky, and hot dust shimmering everywhere. Difficult, he thought, in this Country Garden calendar landscape, not to miss that gritty city heat.

11   A Week is a Long Time

Fran telephoned Neville on Monday. His answerphone took her message, and later in the morning her brother called her back.

'Fran!' said Neville genially, 'We must do lunch together sometime. I hardly see you now you've changed jobs.' The pleasant fallacy existed between them that when Fran had worked in Bath they were able to meet frequently, whereas now she worked in a town ten miles away this sadly was no longer possible. In fact Fran and Neville had never met up during the working day, but Fran knew what he meant. She too had found comfort in potential proximity.

'Sure. Well, check your diary next time you're near it. Why are you never at your desk these days?'

'Oh, you know. Open-plan. Not so good when you need to think quietly.' Fran did not know, but she could imagine. Inactivity tends to swell when noticed. Jests are made, and become folklore. Negative perceptions cling, like the smell of other people's cigarettes.

She came to the point of her call.

'What do you think about what Gwen's saying, about Mum?'

'You know Gwen,' said Neville evasively. 'And Mum is getting on a bit. Eighty is no spring chicken.'

Fran sighed.

'Neville you're telling me absolutely nothing. She seems exactly the same to me, but according to Gwen there's a major crisis brewing. I don't know whether to notify Age Concern or the Fraud Squad.'

'Oh don't do that,' said Neville hastily.

'Which?'

'Neither. Don't do either. Actually, Gwen has some thoughts about that place on the hill, as a future possibility.'

'You're not seriously thinking about putting Mum in a

Home?'

'Obviously, nothing would be done without her consent. The doctor supports us on that.' The doctor had actually said little other than to reiterate patient confidentiality as paramount, though he had at one point murmured the useful information that degenerative cognition would of course need monitoring. There was a surreptitious rustling sound as Neville unwrapped a Twix with one hand while Fran's silence deepened. Since she could think of nothing else to say about Gwen's plot she asked, more gently, 'How's Clive?'

'Clive?' said Neville vaguely, as though he had once known someone of that name but long since lost touch – 'Oh, Clive. He's fine.'

'No luck with a job, yet, then?'

'Well, you know Clive,' said Neville. 'He probably talks more to you than he does to us,' he added with unexpected perceptiveness.

'He always seems fine to me,' Fran said quickly. After the call had ended she sat quietly worrying about her brother and her nephew. Then she worried about Babette and how long Jake's frail tolerance would last and whether she should remind her to clean round the bath or just do it herself. Then she remembered she hadn't yet worried about Leonora. 'Shit,' said Fran aloud and she went to the machine to get herself a coffee. Don Glossop on the printing line below looked up from a disputed magenta bias and waved.

'Pleased?' he called.

Fran was bewildered. Don was doing a thumbs up sign, and the men around him were laughing. Don pointed behind her and Fran turned to look. No longer did butterscotch-coloured breasts bulge over an unrestrainingly-laced bodice beside the coffee machine. The pin-up calendar had been removed.

'Oh, that,' said Fran. 'So you do read my memos.'

'It's down the other end now,' said Don, 'I knew you'd be pleased."

'I'm ecstatic.' said Fran.

She collected her plastic cup and went back to her office. Her amended design for the new logo had come back with a scribbled note from Don which read 'have to leave this for a while – toner crisis not yet resolved.' Fran filed the folder resignedly.

Fran's appointment was Don's first step in creating a Design Section, and Don believed in taking things a step at a time. His next step was to study Fran's suggestions noncommittally until she had produced a draft in which the Manager retained all those aspects of design which Don liked doing and the Design Section did the rest. Fran, coming from a world where things were explained twice and then written out for homework, took some weeks to comprehend that it would be that simple. Her task as Head of – and sole member of – the Design Section had now refined itself into a simple process of elimination in order to discover which elements Don disdained sufficiently to surrender. So far Fran's list included definitely a website and – sometimes – a new logo. In addition to these tasks and her equally slippery Gender Watch role, Fran spent a good deal of her time on cover for more substantial work while other people were away on holiday. 'Best way to learn the business!' Don said. He didn't actually mention the savings to the Temporary Agency – Fran found that out for herself while on cover in Accounts.

It would be easier to think about a Home for Leonora, Fran felt, if she were less anxious about her own. It wasn't just the overflowing study and the '70s songs seeping from the radio, there was the problem of the kitchen. Fran regarded food preparation as a weekend activity. She remembered from their house-sharing days how Babette's grazing had spread constantly across the open pasture of the kitchen. Bags bulging with baguettes, their crusty sides picked raw. Camembert weeping openly on the work surface. Tubs of raspberry pavlova ice-cream trailing stickily. Babette never seemed to actually start or finish a meal but always to be in a process of mastication. And now Babette was her guest.

When Jake had left for London on Monday morning, Fran decided to set some ground rules for their first night alone.

'Shall I fix us a salad?' she offered.

'Let's see what you've got,' said Babette.

Fran watched her friend construct a sardine and avocado

omelette with croutons of grilled goats cheese. It was nice, Fran conceded aloud, while grumpily reflecting that the lettuce and chives would be no good next day.

'When did you start that collage?' she asked Babette now, as she popped the pan and grill in the sink to soak.

'After you left. With your paintings gone the room looked a bit empty, and it started as a splash of colour for the walls. I kept thinking of other ideas for panels, and the whole project just grew. I know collage has got this 'craft' tag, but what's so good about 'art' anyway? Look at that – what's that about?' Babette leant back in her chair to indicate the golden Klimt, glittering in the hallway like sunlight on a deep pool. Fran knew that it was about tenderness and passion, about the essential energy of erotic love, but in the face of Babette's laconic belligerence she did not like to say. There was a more pressing topic anyway.

'Have you talked to Rupert yet?' Fran asked Babette, casually wiping the slug trails of olive oil off the counter.

Babette shook her head in lieu of speech.

'Will you be a referee for me?' she asked, instead. Fran, startled, pictured Babette in a tiger skin leotard leaping into a boxing ring with Rupert, herself nervously poised with a whistle. The image vaporised at Babette's next words.

'I thought I'd apply for that proof reading job that's going at your place.'

'Proof reading?'

'You said they don't bother advertising because people apply as soon as the word gets round. So, I thought I'd apply.'

Babette picked at a peppercorn fragment which had lodged between her teeth and spat it neatly sideways.

'But you know nothing about proof reading,' Fran said, surprised into candour.

'Reading proofs, isn't it? I can do that.'

'It's quite a bit more than that, actually. They're not manuscripts, for one thing. Most of the text is on disc, and you have to know the systems, and how to set in the edit commands and, oh I don't know, but it's more technical than just reading.'

'I've got to do something. I can read. Here's a job for a reader.

Are you saying you won't put in a word for me?'

'Well... what about the school, Babette? You've got a good job there. They'll give you a different accommodation – what was the problem with Rupert, anyway?'

'He was always teaching. I can't stand teachers.'

'Well, it is his job, Babette.' Fran laughed, uncomfortably. She was until quite recently a teacher herself.

'Yeah, but he never stops teaching. To Rupert, an intimate conversation is a one-to-one tutorial. Go for a walk and he'll summarise the flora and fauna. Watch a sunset and he'll explain solar physics, or maybe if there's a nice pink-grapefruit tinge to the clouds you might get theory of climatic change. Watch a movie and you're in for a lecture on the director or the genre or some other fuckit-what-d'you-m'call-it. Get the picture?'

Fran nodded, conceding.

'But, if you don't want to carry on sharing with Rupert, won't they give you alternative accommodation?'

'Not just like that, they won't. I'd have to explain why I left, and I don't want to talk about it.'

'Well, yes, I suppose they might think objecting to a teacher a rather odd reason to walk out. Especially from a school house.'

Babette half-closed her eyes in a gesture of exasperation.

'Do you want to know the real truth?'

It occurred to Fran for the first time that her friend might actually have had serious reason for flight. Babette's grim humour had distracted her; Jake's aversion had infected her. 'Why can't you go back, Babette? What happened?'

'I got pregnant.'

'Babette! Why didn't you say?' Fran touched her friends arm, concerned. 'Did... does Rupert know?'

'He wanted me to have an abortion.'

Fran thought how terrible to be Babette, having a baby by a partner who didn't want it. Then she thought, well, Babette got herself into this situation. Then she thought she ought not to be judgmental, and it was nice that Babette could confide in her. Then she thought her cottage wasn't really the place for a lot of messy emotions like this. Then she felt shallow and selfish, and started missing Jake. He would know what they ought to feel.

'What will you do?' she said.

'Nothing. It aborted.'

So Babette was not pregnant after all, and the problem was solved. How odd, and how typically Babette, to fudge her explanations with a sly half-lie. But she would not be judgmental, and Babette, although relieved, had probably felt awful. Like after a really bad period. So Fran held her friend's sleeve and stroked it, staring worriedly down. At length she said, 'Why didn't you tell me before?'

'It doesn't matter now.'

Babette seemed quite breezy, so she must be over it.

'We're still friends, of course. But we do seem to have grown apart,' Fran told Don Glossop on Wednesday. She had decided not to tell Jake on the phone about Babette's baby. She didn't want to trail endless traumas into their precious time together. The uncertainty over Leonora was still unresolved so Fran was anxious to avoid any further disagreements at home. And anyway she felt uneasy about Babette's tale.

'There's something about the whole notion of pregnancy and babies that makes me freeze,' she confided to Don over lunch in the canteen.

Don lifted the top slice from his sandwich and peered at the blotched disordered mess below. 'Pastrami and deli relish?' suggested Fran, who acted as advisor on these occasions.

Don nodded, apparently satisfied, replacing the slice and taking a bite. He looked encouragingly at Fran so she continued.

'It's not that I'm not sympathetic. I hope I am, anyway.'

'Gwas myarr,' agreed Don decisively, continuing more coherently after swallowing, 'Of course you are sympathetic, that's obvious from your Gender Watch reports.' He smiled wolfishly. Fran smiled back, sheepishly.

Gender Watch had been explained to her by Don Glossop as keeping an eye out for Equal Opportunities inequalities and reporting them to the Management. 'Then we pat you on the head and say *Good Girl* and do nothing about it,' Don had said.

The droll summary was proving on the whole more accurate than self-satirising. Wearing her Gender Watch Hat, Fran devised a questionnaire for the women on the packing line – the only part of the factory open to unskilled labour – about creche facilities. Most had been assertively negative. Reasons, where stated, were discouragingly convincing. 'Better off with their Gran,' was the most common; Polly Busby had scrawled frankly 'With all this paper dust? You must be joking'. That had been in her first month; since then Fran had modified her interpretation to a more reactive role. Her Watch reports tended to the pacifist side of the Gender War. So now Fran discreetly ignored the reference and returned to her personal theme. 'Babette seems different these days.'

Don took another bite. 'Grrfmby dllass' he said, repeating more helpfully after a few moments, 'Probably jealous of you.'

Fran shrugged disclaimingly, a little continental moué which caused Don to cease chewing and look charmed. She conceded, 'I suppose she could be jealous now that her relationship with Rupert has collapsed.'

Don was shaking his head. He continued his mastication for a few moments before clarifying 'Not jealous of Jake that way. For taking you from her. A perfectly understandable reaction. For anyone.'

Fran smiled primly and ate her apple silently. Babette, Jake, and jealousy was definitely too dangerous a cocktail to contemplate.

'You realise Jake is jealous of me,' said Babette on Thursday as she sat on the living-room floor feather-stitching the borders of the Peace Hanging, now officially too big for the study. 'He'll tell you to get rid of me. All men are jealous of anything without a penis. They can't understand the attraction.'

Fran paused in her careful pencil drawing. She had learnt to be wary of sentences beginning with either 'If you could replace any of your existing windows free of charge,' and 'All men.'

'I might go anyway,' said Babette, still concentrating on her stitching.

Fran suppressed her sigh of relief. 'Back to the school house?'

she asked casually. Babette grinned.

'Remember the Wollery?' Fran nodded, bewildered. The Wollery was a sturdy tree-house which had been created in the school grounds on a Duke of Edinburgh Award Scheme a couple of years previously and used enthusiastically for a while before safety regulations and PTA recommendations prevailed and it was decreed out of bounds. 'I thought about staying there,' said Babette, 'since we're having such a good summer. Weather-wise, I mean.'

Fran stared. 'In a tree house? But why?'

'Why not? Lots of people do. You must have seen them on the telly.'

Fran recalled the wild grimy faces of the protesters, the cheers as buckets of provisions were hoisted to them, the screams as bailiffs invaded. She looked at Babette, a boisterous mermaid in her self-constructed ocean of creative embroidery. She laughed uncertainly. 'I never know when you're telling fibs,' she said lightly. Babette stitched on, smiling inscrutably.

I'm glad it's nearly Friday, Fran thought, but with a heavy slothful feeling like a cushion of uneasy dread.

The fine weather continued, and Fran prepared supper al fresco on Friday night. She and Jake would be alone. Babette had promised to spend the evening at the cinema: her moped phutted off down the lane an hour before his Porsche cruised in.

The evening air was pale but still bright and the heavy-blossomed white roses were almost luminous. Fran was slicing fruit for sangria. She held a mango, carefully peeling back the luscious red skin to cut into moist golden flesh. Large slices, glittering like fish, slithered into the jug. Ice chinked encouragingly as Fran stirred. Smells of mint and marjoram mingled with the heady fruit scents and the air was still.

Jake stood for a moment, watching from the back door. He whispered *bliss*, and then almost swayed, unsteadied by unexpected dismay. Fran caught the movement in her peripheral vision.

'What's the matter?'

'Nothing. Déja-vu.' He tried to laugh.

But it was not déja-vu, not exactly: more like a poignant premonition.

She was looking at him, troubled.

'You,' said Jake, 'You make me weak.'

'Hunger, more like. We really should eat first,' Fran decided. Now was not the time to talk about Babette or to discuss what should be done about Leonora.

Fran sat with Jake on the grass in the garden and he showered her hair with fallen rose petals. The evening sun was still strong: she could see slight stains of moisture on his shirt, and a fine sheen on his neck where the collar was open. Fran longed to lick the tiny salty beads away. He leaned back, his arms crossed behind his head, and she let her hair become a slowly enclosing curtain as she kissed him.

'You may not like this, Jakey,' said Fran, 'But I think we should visit Mum on Sunday.'

Jake agreed without hesitation. Leonora was a wonderful woman, he said. Witty and eccentric – a delight. Leonora was the least of their problems. No, Fran must sit up again and listen. It was about Babette.

'Babette?' said Fran. She shivered. 'She was very tactful about going out tonight'.

Jake kissed her quickly, fiercely. 'You've got to get rid of Babette,' he said. 'She's dangerous. Please, Fran, believe me.'

'Has she been coming on to you?' Fran's heart was hammering. I didn't know hearts really did that, she thought, I imagined it was a cliché. But something was thumping and hurting her breathing – it must be her heart. She tried to laugh, she pushed her head against Jake's chest so he would kiss her hair, breathing slowly and warmly until his lips touch her neck and his breath is hot against her. Jealousy, thought Fran, although it was not a word she usually used. But who was jealous of who? She remembered Don Glossop and the file called Sexual Harassment which contained all her memos and nothing much else. What was Jake trying to tell her?

'You shouldn't be so irresistible, Jakey. You can stand up to her, can't you?'

Jake sat upright, lit a fag and drew on it. 'Fran, I'm not joking. She could split us up.'

Fran did not believe him.

'Nothing can split us up,' she said, 'but if you don't like her being here when you're home, I'll ask her to find somewhere else for the weekends.'

Jake held her tenderly, kissed her with tiny kisses all along her arms, all along her legs. As he reached her quim he whispered, 'Not just weekends. Send her away, Fran. She's poison.'

I can't do that, thought Fran. Babette is my friend. Jake invited her himself – he can't ask me to chuck her out. Can he?

'Fuckinell, can't you two even wait till after supper?' demanded a crash-helmeted figure towering over them. Babette had returned.

'Lips like scatter cushions,' Jake muttered as their lodger sauntered into the cottage. Fran bit back an involuntary giggle. There was something stuffed and satiny about Babette's smooth curvaceous smile. Jake took encouragement from the absence of reproach. 'And that florid taste of Sweetheart candy,' he said. Fran smiled again but doubtfully. 'Scent, I mean,' Jake corrected himself, 'That smell that's so sugary you feel you can almost taste it.'

Jake was right, Babette as a lodger was beginning to pall. Fran realised it next morning. She was not quite sure why. It was not the crusty spoon in the sugar bowl, or the CDs left out of their cases; it was not even ubiquitous curly hairs embedded in the soap, although these things did not help. It was something more indefinable. A feeling, diaphanous as a dragonfly's wing, of... Fran did not like the word *suspicion*. It was not a word she used about her friends.

'Trust is vanity,' said Babette, and she laughed.

Fran heard her, behind the softly closed door as she went into the back kitchen to take the washing from the machine on Saturday morning. Why did Babette say that to Jake, over the breakfast croissants?

Fran was pegging the washing out in the garden, spinning

the circular line a little with each peg. A maypole of white and gold. Fran's underclothes lacy white, her strappy top marigold. A crisp white shirt of Jake's. A bright yellow teeshirt. Oh, and these pinko-grey socks must be Babette's. Babette unlike Fran did not meticulously check her settings. Babette put everything in on hot; her whites emerged porridge-coloured and wriggling with elastic worms. 'I'll ask Babette not to use the machine,' Fran told Jake, returning to the back door to find him standing with arms folded, watching her. 'She will.' was all he muttered.

'Look, I can't tell her to go with you here. She'll know it was your idea, and you know Babette – there'll be a row.'

'Anyone else for more coffee?' yelled Babette over the explosive sound of grinding beans. Jake winced. Fran kissed him, dropping the washing bowl so she could enfold him in her arms, clasping around his neck and pulling him towards her. 'I promise, Jake. I'll talk to her during the week, and next time you come home she'll be gone. She must have other friends.'

'D'you wanna bet?'

'Well, maybe she can sort it out with Rupert. Maybe he'll ask her back.'

'Is it likely that anyone would ask anyone back who eats icing sugar out of the bag with a tablespoon?' But Jake had relaxed now he had her promise. He cupped her face in his hand and looked deep into her eyes. She knew that worshipping, lustful, gaze so well. She closed her eyes for his kiss.

And Fran decided she was right not to say anything to Jake about Babette's crazy proposal about the tree house in the school grounds. Babette was teasing her, maybe boasting about some kind of perverse moral strength. People don't go and live in trees unless they have something to protest about. And even then, surely not alone, like a solitary bird in a nest with no eggs. Fran had a fleeting image of Babette birdlike, darting her head around with that half-plucked look of fledglings. Her curious mental picture intensified: in the nest, under this big-baby bird's wing, she pictured other bodies, tiny and crushed. Fran thought, she is killing them. She's a cuckoo.

But Saturday night, with Babette fortuitously meeting some mates in the pub and phoning to brag a party and a stopover there, had been everything she could have wanted. In the bliss of her absence, she and Jake had celebrated their re-ownership of the cottage by caressing in every room, even the domain of the Hanging ('Jake stop it!' Fran giggled, near-hysterical with a sense of outrageous liberation as he mimed opening the door and hose-pipe pissing within) and had eventually cuddled together entwined – like in the old days, Fran thought, just before sleep.

On Sunday the phone rang early. Gwen, persisting in her opposition to the regime at the bungalow, could wait no longer to talk about finding more appropriate provision. She had a Place In Mind. Fran erased a bizarre thought of Leonora perched in a tree and spoke firmly. 'I'm sorry Gwen,' she said, 'but I think you're being alarmist. Mum has a perfectly adequate support system. She has a live-in companion, for f-goodness sake.' Fran, aware of her sister-in-law's views on language, checked her emphasis, but Gwen had heard.

'She can't rely on a gardener,' Gwen wailed.

'He's more than a gardener. He does work for her around the house, like the smoke alarm he's put in. And anyway, she values her garden. Gardening is creative – therapeutic, too. You should try it, Gwen.' She wondered if she was being rude. Gwen appeared to be wondering that too.

'I too have a garden,' she said frostily, 'I do realise the benefits. And I have plans for a creative project of my own.'

Gwen ended the call and Fran decided penitently that she probably had been rude. Her sister-in-law had certainly taken offence, anyway. Ten minutes later the phone rang again, and Fran prepared to apologise and prevaricate more politely when she recognised Gwen's voice. Neither strategy was required.

'Babette –' Fran called, surprised. 'It's for you.'

Another curious pairing. Gwen had explained this was a charity matter, but the thought of a liaison between this odd couple made Fran smile as she curled back in the warm nest of Sunday morning. She feels sorry for women with no urgent, passionate, delightful reason to curtail telephone calls and linger in bed, women who need worthy causes in order to connect. She pities poor Babette, poor Gwen.

12 If T'were Done, T'were Well T'were Done Quickly. . .

I'm afraid that Fran is rather missing the point, Gwen wrote irritably in her diary. *The problem is not that this man can't stay there permanently, it's that he is there at all.* She pictured the dragon boy strolling about the house, picking things up and putting them down. She imagined his brown hand dipping into Leonora's biscuit barrel. She thought of him walking naked in the house at night. *A smoke alarm is neither here nor there,* scribbled Gwen fiercely, and then she did some alternate nostril breathing.

No-one understood her sensible concern. Fran's indifference to her mother's wellbeing was simply breathtaking. Neville was still vacillating, though he had eventually consented to telephone Leonora's doctor. And precious little help that proved.

'Your mother would prefer to stay in her own home,' the doctor had insisted. Neville nodded with a mouthful of digestive biscuit.

'My wife's been talking to social services,' he said after a brief pause filled with the gritty sound of munching. 'They seem to feel a Home's a good idea.'

'Her home,' the doctor repeated.

'Hill House Home,' Neville said. 'The one on the hill.'

'Frankly, I can't see her there.'

'The brochure says you could.' Neville sounded puzzled. The doctor sighed.

'Mr Forth, I feel we should meet and talk. Can you not attend my surgery?'

'My wife has been dealing with this, on the whole,' said Neville. 'Women, you know. They feel more comfortable with another woman.'

There was a further sigh.

'I'll talk to my wife again' said Neville. 'Put your point. Better off staying put, you feel. See what she says.' He replaced the receiver delicately avoiding Gwen's eye.

By Sunday night they all knew that Polo was right about one thing at least, the smoke alarm was both here and there and was indeed a point, but by then it was too late. Leonora had set fire to the bungalow.

The most irritating thing to Gwen, as she deleted her previous diary entry, was that Leonora completely lacked contrition and merely said gaily 'The Runes foretold radical change!' as though she had successfully predicted sunny days from seaweed. *I realise laissez faire is the modern trend, but that social worker Mandy is incompetent to the point of conspiracy. When I asked about alternative accommodation while the bungalow is repaired and redecorated, she merely laughed and said 'Let's not panic.'*

'Let's not panic,' said Mandy, who luckily was on week-end call when news of the conflagration was relayed to her. Any more luck like this and I'll be a nervous wreck, Mandy was thinking as she drove out at midnight in response to a call from the Emergency Services, wondering why Leonora had elected to name her as next of kin. 'Enough ups and downs to be going on with.'

'But she nearly torched the house!' scolded Gwen. She and Neville had rushed to the scene of the disaster with blankets and chocolate but Leonora had spurned both although the firemen appreciated the mint thins.

'Well, actually, a corner of the kitchen,' Mandy corrected soothingly. 'No substantial damage, really. Mrs Forth's lodger worked wonders with wet towels.'

Gwen imagined the dragon boy leaping into the flames like a dervish. She perspired slightly and appealed to Neville.

Neville was stalling again. 'Only decent to let her get over the shock,' he suggested, 'and anyway, the injection made her a bit groggy, apparently.'

Gwen's eyes widened. She had missed something here, it seemed. Injection! There must be more. And there was.

Leonora has twisted her ankle in the fracas of this unfortunate debacle, Gwen chronicled jubilantly. *There is no way That Man can act as nursemaid as well as his other dubious duties. She must now admit that intervention is essential. Neville has promised to phone the doctor tomorrow. With his agreement we can get her Placed next week. She has sufficient funds, at present, in the accoutrements of her house alone, I am sure this will be the right thing.* She wasn't sure if she had the right word for furniture and knick-knacks, but she was pretty sure if they had to be sold, it should be by the family and for a worthwhile reason.

'It was only a small fire, as fires go,' Neville told Fran when he phoned with the news next morning. 'Unfortunately there's a bit of roof damage which will have to be made good.'

'Roof damage – it got that bad?'

'With it being a single storey, when the polystyrene ceiling tiles melted they made a bit of a mess.'

Fran shuddered. She imagined Leonora trapped in smoke as smouldering beams collapsed and barred her way. She envisaged the dripping ceiling a surreal scene of blistering stalactites, with sizzling wires sparkling like fireworks, every surface scorching. Unlike Gwen she did not picture the gallant gardener leaping to the rescue: in Fran's scenario her mother stumbled choking and unaided. Feelings of grey guilt like a tired army of ants trudged routinely out. Why had she and Jake not stayed longer on Sunday? She should have lingered all evening playing Mahjong, not sneaked off to the pub like that, avoiding Babette with the pretext of her mother and then selfishly deserting Leonora. Her sense of guilt was followed, inevitable as a shadow, by resentment. *Why does Mum do these things? Is it just to make me feel bad? I am the child, she should be protecting me.*

'Well she was fine while we were there,' Fran now said grimly. She hoped Neville didn't realise how cursory their visit had been. She hoped Gwen believed they had visited at all.

'She's still fine,' Neville assured his sister. 'I've contacted the Insurers already. Don't worry, I'll do any phone calls necessary.'

Neville's next necessary call was to the doctor.

'Mr Forth, I have known Mrs Forth for some time now and

I have the greatest respect for her rugged individualism,' said the doctor firmly. Neville was baffled for a moment until he realised that the doctor was referring not to his spouse but to his mother. He quickly concurred, before continuing cautiously,

'The thing is, it's a safety matter. Can you assure us, categorically, that she's completely physically safe in her present environment?'

'Of course I can't.' said the doctor crossly, 'I can't even say that for myself, or you for that matter, with a hundred percent certainty.'

'What percent? Ninety? Seventy-five? What's the lowest margin of safety we should accept, doctor, in your professional view?' Neville was blushing; he felt uncomfortable bullying but Gwen had left him little choice.

Glumly the doctor conceded that a Home would be able to offer Leonora immediate medication for any pain from her leg, and that a short stay placement would not be detrimental to her general physical care.

At lunchtime Neville returned to report the successful outcome of his mission. Gwen was washing celery. She pulled off her Marigold gloves with brisk satisfaction and turned off the radio quiz. Clive overheard the plotters and came traipsing down from his room with a furrowed brow and loose laces.

'You can't do that to Gran,' he said, and Gwen jumped back startled.

'It's only while she heals.'

'I'll go and stay,' suggested Clive.

'No' said Gwen firmly. 'She needs qualified attention. A Physio.'

'Oh come on, Mum,' said Clive, 'those people can call in, every day if necessary.'

'Don't tell your mother to *come on* as if she were a recalcitrant Pekingese,' said Neville, and Clive, after a pungent look at each of his parents, slouched back upstairs and turned up the volume on Hole.

Fran was preparing to drive over to visit her mother after work when Neville phoned to update her and propose a combined visit. 'Bit of support, you know,' he explained, '– for mother, I mean.' Neville's suggested meeting at the bungalow gave her just enough time for a run, so Fran pulled on her trainers and set off along the familiar route.

Self-reproaches jostled in her head as she ran. When she had finished nagging herself, Fran worried about her mother's smouldering emotions and whether arson was a subconscious metaphor for rage. Leonora hated becoming old, of course. It was burning her up, she was blazing. Was Leonora aware of this impulse to self-combustion, and privately terrified? Fran ran quickly, letting the thoughts roar through her like a wild fire in a forest. Leonora, Babette, Jake, a tangle of responsibilities jumbled up in her head like the mess of coloured skeins currently strewn on the carpets at the cottage. Fran ached for some decisive moment of certainty – one of those clear and certain insights which would bring the necessary impetus for action. Gwen seemed to be so sure what was right. But suppose it wasn't? A small anxious voice in her head kept insisting *We're trying to decide something important before we're ready.* Fran felt a small bleak premonition, as she clicked the gate, of invisible doors closing.

'Gwen sends her love,' Neville reassured his mother by way of greeting when he and Fran arrived at the bungalow that evening, 'and these.' Leonora surveyed a packet of Scotch pancakes unenthusiastically. 'It's no wonder you two are porky,' she said unkindly. 'That wife of yours displaces all her emotions into comestibles.'

Fran hovered, looking anxious. 'Shall I make us a cup of tea?' she said. 'We've brought a brochure we'd like you to look at. Oh, I forgot, you've got no way to heat water. We should have brought a thermos, Neville.'

'Polo has arranged everything,' said Leonora. She waved her stick at a small camping stove connected to a Calor gas bottle standing in the tiled hearth. There was a tin kettle on the single ring, and Leonora's brown glazed teapot had been placed close by on the floor. Leaning heavily on her stick, Leonora rose and began to make her way slowly to the broad-seated crinoline chair beside a low table with a tea tray ready laid. Fran lifted her eyes to meet Neville's. He shook his head almost imperceptibly. They both sat down.

'Have a look at the brochure, anyway.'

'Urge it no more, my Lord Northumberland,' said Leonora with unexpected vigour. She turned the knob carefully with fragile fingers and lit the gas below the kettle.

They sat for a while in silence like conspirators. Leonora was glancing sideways at the brochure on the floor. Hill House had an imposing aspect. Sunlight gilded its Georgian front; flowers rimmed the long lawn.

'A couple of weeks. You could see it as a holiday,' coaxed Neville.

'It's just that you've got no cooker until the wiring's fixed and the new one comes,' said Fran.

The tin kettle on the little camping cooker began to wheeze, strengthening to a querulous protracted shriek. Leonora stretched out her hand to the kettle handle and recoiled at the contact. Fran and Neville exchanged shamefaced looks. Fran quickly handed her mother an oven mitt and with scalding dignity Leonora filled the teapot. An aroma of lapsang infused the air. Fran and Neville waited. Leonora picked up the pot and leaned forward. The cups on the table were slightly beyond her reach. She looked up. Her eyes glared like an ancient animal cornered.

'It's OK, Leonora' said Fran, close to tears. 'I know when there's only you and Polo you can manage –'

'You have made your point. Polo is not a crutch, and it appears I am a cripple.'

'Only till your ankle's better,' said Fran.

'Merely a short-stay measure, while the house is being repaired' said Neville.

And Leonora had capitulated. Neville would drive her to Hill House in the Volvo the next day. *I am sure we have all done the right thing,* Gwen wrote virtuously in her diary. She went over with Neville in the morning to help Leonora pack a suitcase, and encountered a final burst of unexpected opposition.

'As you are paid monthly, I hardly think Mrs Forth's absence will affect you,' Gwen said coldly to the gardener.

She had gone into the damaged kitchen to sort out some of Leonora's bits and pieces, as she terms the contents of the Aladdin washing basket. Gwen had just removed the fragile load – a slip, a nightie, and several pairs of knickers – when the gardener accosted her.

'I'll do them,' he said, nodding to her armful.

Gwen stared at the dragon boy's brown chest and firm, knotty, arms. She was staggered at his impropriety. *You should not be touching her knickers* was the thought that stung her, but it was impossible to utter in the face of his cool laconic stare. To say the word for those intimate items which had pressed on Leonora's buttocks would be like displaying her own.

He took the clothes from her. She watched him stroll to the washing machine and toss them in, pushing the door closed with a raggy-frayed knee.

'Cool,' he said, nodding slowly and profoundly. 'Done it before.'

Gwen licked her lips and looked away. His next words shocked her all over again. 'You shouldn't be putting her away. She's happy here.'

This time Gwen found her voice. 'I beg your pardon! My husband's mother has sustained a fracture. I think a medical decision is required, not a horticultural one.' Gwen felt this was rather good, and was pleased it came to her there and then, and not on the way home.

The dragon boy seemed amused. It was hard to tell if he was actually smiling because he showed no teeth and his eyes did not crinkle up like Neville's, but a sense of something benign hovered around that exquisitely mobile mouth. His eyes are the most amazing turquoise blue, Gwen thought. His hair colour was harder to ascertain, shaven as it was at the sides and embellished with beaded braiding, but she thought it was dark. Or possibly a kind of ashy blonde.

Gwen averted her eyes from the dangling jewelled pigtails and found she was looking at the dark-haired orifice of his umbilicus. Something silver was glinting there, like a magic eye. The dragon boy suddenly contracted his stomach ever so slightly and his leather-belted cut-offs slithered down another few centimetres.

Gwen stared at the lean brown muscles that groped down into the denim thighs of his jeans.

'Doctor's on her side,' he was saying stubbornly.

'It's not a question of sides,' said Gwen, 'It's a very sensible first step. She can't manage alone forever, and rather than deteriorate pitifully on her own, this gives her an opportunity to find out what the Home is like. Just a short-term stay. A trial fortnight.'

She said the same to Neville as he loaded the boot with his mother's belongings. She said the same to Leonora as her mother-in-law emerged dressed in black, apart from the terracotta bandana and blue suede shoes. Polo hugged Leonora while Neville held the car door open. Leonora sank wordlessly into the passenger seat and Gwen scrambled into the back.

'Just for the fortnight!' said Gwen as she waved from the gravel drive of Hill House. Leonora, seated on the sunny terrace of the Home, did not respond. Other staring faces smiled back at Gwen, other frail hands wavered in the air. Matron had said best not fuss her while she's settling, and Gwen, anxious to obey, hurried away. Neville, with his hands in his suit pockets, sweating slightly, had already reached the car and was rooting in the glove compartment for the nutty toffees.

'I suppose we have done the right thing,' he said dubiously, and he thumped the steering wheel vaguely several times before setting off for home. Gwen nodded. It was almost as if he had read her diary.

In fact he had not. Sometimes Neville did read Gwen's diary, but not if he had any other reading material to hand; he found his wife's Pooteresque style faintly dispiriting.

At least she is out of the clutches of that man, Gwen wrote that night. She buffed her nails and looked out of the window at the dark daisy-starry lawn. Those heads need lopping off, she mused, I'll get the Flymo out tomorrow. She recalled with irritation Fran's patronising comment about the therapy of gardening, and thought about the raggle-taggle grasses by the water's edge at the bungalow, merging with reeds and yellow irises. *I am sure he had some kind of hold over her, what with her strange spiritual beliefs*, she penned virtuously. Although of course Isis is essentially female but nevertheless... A goddess of unrestrained passions and abundant love.

Gwen started to think, as she often did in private moments, about the dead Princess Diana. She remembered the morning the news broke, and the aftermath of grieving. Knowing that other people too had walked about for a week dazed and red-eyed made Gwen feel less alone and clumsy in her ordinary Gwen-ness. In weeping for the lost princess, Gwen had found tears for her own long-gone mother too. Almost as though sorrow could be gathered up in a garland and made beautiful. Watching the television that funeral day, all day, Gwen thought she had never seen anything more beautiful than that sea of flowers all the way to Diana's grave. It was the saddest and happiest day of her life. Then afterwards clever men and women on the radio had derided it all and Gwen had sunk back into her usual sense of being faintly risible. But that exquisite sense of shared emotion had been something pure and lovely while it lasted. Strange that the image of that flawed but somehow perfect Princess came into Gwen's mind when Leonora spoke of Isis. A sound of sobbing and a scent of flowers.

I can see that he could be a very compelling person, Gwen wrote, half abstractedly. *Self-assured beyond his years. I imagine he could arouse powerful passions. He is certainly strong. In every sense of the word. His chest muscles are amazing. And his thighs. I imagine they would be rock hard to touch.* Gwen noticed her speculations had shifted subtly from the rescue of Leonora. Those last few comments were not really the point. She scratched through them several times, and then fetched the Tippex from downstairs to whiten the entry away entirely.

Something else was awry, too. Gwen realised with a shock

that the fountain in the garden was still on, a tiny gurgling sound invisible in the night air. She went quickly to rebuke Neville who was supine on the settee watching Discovery.

'Just coming, dear,' he said, 'I only want to see the bit about Mont Blanc.' Bloody Mont Blanc, thought Gwen as she retired to bed alone. Solitary in the narrow light of the side lamp Gwen concluded her nightly chronicle: *I wish that Neville and I could travel in France. Even for a short holiday. I picture us motoring through Monet's landscape, stopping here and there for a glass of local wine. Perhaps we would find a new rapport in such peaceful moments.* She closed the book and lay back with her finger cautiously seeking the place where she put her tampon. She wished she had a tampon in there tonight.

13   Visiting Times

Babette called into the Heart Shop the following afternoon.

Since the day of her epiphany in the American Museum, apart from her tetchy boast to Fran, Gwen had not done much towards her intended collage project. She had spoken on the phone to Babette, reminding her of their meeting and expressing her interest, but Babette had been offhand. It was material rather than assistants she wanted, she said, as she was doing all the design herself. She might need help to put the bits together, she conceded. Yes, probably quite soon. And lots of squares hemmed up for the backing.

'A sewing bee?' Gwen hazarded hopefully, and Babette agreed. And then Leonora's antics had swept Gwen's head of other matters. And now –

'Remember me? The Peace Hanging?' Babette enquired by way of greeting as she strode in. Gwen was alone in the shop tweaking a cerise basque to give it enhanced hanger appeal. She agreed. 'Still up for the sewing bee?' Babette asked, and again Gwen agreed. With Leonora safely settled Gwen felt the time was ripe. She liked the idea of a group of nimble-fingered women plying their womanly craft.

'I suppose Fran will be helping, too?' she said, but Babette demurred. It appeared Babette would no longer be staying with Fran. She intended to move to an accommodation called Tree House, where the premises were unsuited to embroidery. 'Can I leave it at your place while we finish it off?' Babette asked, though somewhat glumly. She seemed to expect a polite refusal.

Polite refusal hovered on Gwen's lips. She puckered them judiciously, as if weighing possibilities, as if contemplating the rival attractions of on the one hand an orderly status quo, on the other a large stranger with disorderly hair squatting in her spare room with an enormous collage. Into this brief pause Babette said, in the same grimly bombastic tone, 'It won't actually bring World Peace overnight of course, but we got to do something, for our children's sake,' and Gwen's reluctance wobbled. She thought of Clive in his big boots trudging the road with sunlight fondling his arms, and a few minutes later Babette was in possession of a sketch map and a pleased smile. The Sewing Bee was set to start that very afternoon, at Gwen's house.

Fran left work early to visit her mother and found Neville already at Hill House car park waiting for her.

'What was all that about Northumberland?' he greeted her.

'What?' Fran had expected some discomfort from her brother but this enquiry puzzled her.

'My Lord Northumberland, she called me.'

'Oh, that. He was one of the lords who plotted against Richard II.'

'Oh. Was he the hunchback?'

'No. That was Richard III.'

'Ah.'

Neville did a little nod and Fran gave a little grin, as their shared connective memory became solved and thus unimportant. Fran was relieved that sorting out the monarchs in Shakespearean drama had deflected from the very obvious inference that their mother saw them both as traitors and herself as wrongly deprived of her realm.

They signed in at the door and followed the signs to the recreation room where Leonora was ensconced in front of a television set. The radiators were on and fusty heat stifled the air.

Leonora nodded at her children curtly as they hesitated around her. There were several empty arm chairs, all set in a circle facing the television. One was occupied by a woman in grey murmuring *It's cold, it's cold.* A carer with a pleasant face and ruby hair tucked her cardigan around her and helped her sip at a cup of tea.

'That woman with the dyed hair is kind,' Leonora identified audibly, pointing with her stick. Neville flinched and coughed. 'The one with the dyed red hair, not the one with the dyed black hair. She is not kind at all,' Leonora persisted undeterred.

'And who is the lady over there?' Neville enquired after pause while Fran fidgeted. Leonora said she didn't know and the kind woman called across that this was Pansy.

'Hello, Pansy,' said Neville. Fran echoed the greeting in a whisper.

'Say hello, Pansy,' the carer suggested.

'It's cold,' muttered Pansy, nibbling her hanky.

'Oh, I know,' said the kind carer kindly.

'Senile,' said Leonora briskly.

'Better than rude,' Neville suggested tactfully.

'No dear,' said Leonora. 'Rudeness can be entertaining. Senility is simply sad.'

Neville made no further comment. The room was quiet apart from Pansy's rhythmic sobbing and the soothing voice of the kind carer. 'I know, dear, I know.'

'So, how's the ankle today?' Neville enquired. 'Better?' His mother smiled wanly and shook her head. 'On the mend, anyhow,' persisted Neville. 'Less pain? Recovering?' He seemed to feel that bullish questioning would somehow precipitate a positive outcome, as though his mother were a small flotation on the stock market of life.

'I've often noticed that minor injury magnifies flaws in the personality,' Leonora said. Her children started murmuring denials and Leonora clarified 'Not the personality of the injured. But visitors can be rather trying.' They lapsed into silence.

Fran stepped across to the window and parted the heavy curtains. Mellow afternoon sun slanted across magnolia walls. 'It's a nice room,' she said.

'There are no butterflies in the kitchen.' said Leonora sadly.

'Muddled,' mouthed the kind carer kindly. 'It often happens, when they first come in. Something in the mind seems to switch off.' Hope, thought Fran.

'I suppose they pick up?' Neville said encouragingly. The kind carer smiled.

'We'll pop in again tomorrow, then,' Neville told his mother, and they sidled out .

'I'm not at all sure that this is a good idea' said Fran as they headed for the car-park. Neville was looking unhappy. 'It's only until the bungalow is repaired' he quoted loyally. 'She seems to be settling in.'

'Does she?'

An elderly lady ran from the door and stretched her arms out towards Fran. 'Mummy,' she whimpered as she was gently led away.

'I suppose we should give her a chance, to settle in I mean,' Fran said uncertainly. She scraped her toe along the gravel.

'Let's leave it till tomorrow, and see then,' suggested Neville. They stood for a moment together before stepping into their separate cars to drive away.

'It's not that she doesn't fit in,' Fran told Jake on her mobile before setting off, 'She isn't out of place, anyway.'

'You mean they're all crackers?'

'It's just that I don't think she's very happy.'

'It's what she chose. Nobody sectioned her or strapped her in.'

'We didn't really leave her much of a choice.'

'Darling, nobody has much of a choice where they live at her age. It's the Babettes of this world who need to get their acts together.'

Fran didn't want to start talking about Babette again. She wasn't finding it easy talking to Jake about Leonora, either. Jake said encouraging things like 'She knows you love her and you're doing your best,' and 'However old she gets she's still your mother, she'll understand.' Jake seemed to have extraordinary faith in the wisdom of old women, Fran thought, remembering the frail childlike arms of the old lady in the doorway.

Yes, Leonora is my mother, Fran thought as she drove away down the broad gravel path. But something happened to the umbilical cord, maybe it was cut too soon and the motherly nourishment dribbled away unseen. That subtle connection of energy, which should remain as an invisible strand between us, somehow never made a complete connection. We bustle across the surface of the world like ants, she and I, looking for something that is not each other. And whatever the bond was or should have been, I lost it a long time ago when I was a tiny child.

On the way home Fran suddenly remembered the butterflies. Of course, butterflies in the kitchen: the sun shining through the magic crystal, flickering colours of azure and pink and gold around the walls. Leonora was not losing her marbles after all, Leonora was simply pining for the sunshine and the colour that had gone from her life. So that was all right.

Cold Pansy was counting on her fingers in the foyer when Fran arrived next time.

'That's right,' said the cheery carer, 'Count the days to Christmas!'

No dementia, Mrs Milsom the manager had said, quite definitely. 'We cannot admit dementia here. However, if some of our ladies and gentlemen get slightly fuddled once they are settled, we wouldn't then put them out. Not when we've got to know their little ways.' Fran, stepping nervously past Pansy on the ramp that led to the day room, began to understand something of Gwen's absurd and hectic urgency. Perhaps Gwen was right. Maybe in her clumsy officious way Gwen had somehow barged into the truth. And perhaps, Fran thought, I've been blocking the notion of Leonora ancient and irresponsible not out of pity for her but because of my own stuff. Fran was starting to recognise that she didn't want to be responsible for the child in her mother when her mother never answered the needs of the child in her.

'What ho,' said Neville, coming along the corridor with Gwen. 'Been here long?'

'Just arrived' said Fran brightly. They went into the day room together.

Leonora seemed more cheerful today. She was looking at some photographs in an old album. She introduced the album's owner as Madge and continued with her perusal.

'That's my brother Wally,' said Madge sentimentally. The picture showed a wedding, with a very much younger Madge on the arm of a dapper groom. 'I can't remember who that weaselly looking man was,' Madge admitted. Leonora bent over the picture helpfully.

'Looks more like a stoat than a weasel to me,' she opined. She turned the image sideways. 'I wonder what it's like to be a stoat. A stoat or an eagle.'

'They're not the same, Mum,' Gwen explained, righting the album. 'One's a bird.'

'They are unified in their diversity,' said Leonora haughtily. 'Predator and prey. Both part of the eternal reciprocity of suffering.'

'That's Wally,' Madge reminded her happily.

'He looks drunk.'

Madge studied the snap. 'He didn't have much of a head for drink,' she conceded.

'A head he may not have,' said Leonora, 'but he certainly has the stomach. Dear me, look at that belly. A glimpse of that naked would put you off soft boiled eggs for a week.'

'What's started all this speculation about male flesh?' Fran whispered to Neville.

'I blame the gardener,' said Gwen, tugging her taupe top firmly down over her hips.

Neville pursed his lips and closed his eyes. Fran found herself imagining her brother naked to the waist, not potbellied like the derided Wally but big and pale and palpable. His shoulders were broad but soft and sloping. Fran preferred shoulders that were broad and straight, like Jake's. Her thoughts slid lasciviously to Jake. She thought of the mobile phone in her car, throbbing with latent contact, and her gaze flickered to the open doorway. The sunlight darkened as a large figure filled the doorframe and then advanced.

'Babette, how extraordinary,' said Fran, 'What are you doing here?'

'Came with Gwendolyn said Babette laconically.

Fran had never heard her sister-in-law called Gwendolyn before and it took her a few moments to make the necessary connection. Even then the trisyllabic word sounded rather like a name for an esoteric musical instrument, but Gwen accepted both the appellation and the arrival without surprise. 'I've had a nice piece of petersham in,' she told Babette, *sotto voce.*

Fran became worried that her mother now had rather too many visitors. She seemed to be going vague from time to time and occasionally, most untypically, paused searchingly in her sentences. 'The worst thing is losing... What is that P word?' said Leonora. 'The heat in here is simply dreadful. It's making me forget everything.'

'Painkiller?' suggested Neville, 'Panadol?' Leonora shook her head. 'The vital thing...' she muttered.

'Paintings?'

'It's not eye-spy, Fran. She's talking about something important.'

'Peace?' Gwen proffered.

'Privacy?' proposed Babette.

'Perhaps it's a name' Fran suggested. Leonora sank back into her chair, her eyes bright and brimming. 'Tip of my tongue' she said testily, 'What is that word?'

'Never mind, Mum. It doesn't matter.'

'Yes Gwen, it does. You're only as good as your words – I don't like losing them.'

Gwen tactfully changed the subject back to the hanging which, surprisingly, Leonora appeared to find intriguing. It seemed ironic, but encouraging, to Gwen that the most successful exchange of conversation she had ever had with her mother-in-law should occur after their battle of wills had ended in Leonora's rout.

'Have you sorted things out with Rupert now?' Fran asked Babette as Neville jingled his car keys hopefully and Gwen gathered up her jacket. Babette got up too and bridled herself into her shoulder-purse, nodding nonchalantly.

'Oh, I am glad... for you.' Babette gave her a lupine look and Fran's fib collapsed. 'Well, I'm glad for me, too. I didn't want to have to choose.'

Babette nodded. 'No hard feelings,' she said quietly.

Fran remembered Friday night, and flushed.

'Babette, did you overhear anything that made you feel you're not wanted? Because I'm really sorry if...' Babette interrupted with a sharp, self-consciously scornful, laugh.

'Hear? I hear everything. You talk to me in your pauses, Fran. You are not quite transparent but you are translucent.'

Neville stooped to kiss his mother goodbye. Leonora turned her paper-fine cheek to receive his dry-lipped pressure. Babette gave Fran an ironic salutation and followed the others out.

Fran lingered for a while after her brother's entourage had gone. She wanted to see how Leonora was coping with the passage-way between the day room and her bedroom. Her mother seemed nimble enough, though lethargic.

'I like that friend of Gwen's' Leonora said unexpectedly as they reached her room. 'A touch of the tar-brush there, I fancy,' she added approvingly.

'Babette?' Fran was too surprised even to flinch at the wording of Leonora's surmise.

'That hair.'

'It's a perm, I think.' It seemed difficult to blame any single process for Babette's coiffure.

'I went to the very first Glastonbury with a man who had hair like that, and he had African ancestors. Don't you remember?

'Leonora, I was two.'

'You were nearly three. You were on my shoulder when Marc Bolan sang. I thought you might remember that.'

'I'm sorry.'

'Running around in the long grass? While I strummed and sang by the glowing embers of the fire?'

That could have been many occasions in her infancy so Fran conceded and Leonora smiled and crooned *Ride a White Swan* for a while in a wavering ducklike voice. 'A perfect childhood,' she added in her normal speaking voice.

'I'm sorry?' said Fran, startled from reverie.

'Always so many people around you, to care for you and love you. You were everybody's child.'

Everybody's child is nobody's child, thought Fran.

'So,' said Fran as silence caressed the echo of her mother's song, 'are you going to be Sewing for Peace too?'

'Certainly not. These hands are beyond needles. However, I

can still manage to crochet. I shall make squares for the backing.'

'Do you want me to bring you some wool?'

'I do not. There is plenty of wool in the recreation room – it's easier to find a ball of wool than a sensible conversation.'

'As long as you've got things to do,' Fran said limply. She looked round the immaculate bedroom. There was a pack of patience cards on the bedside table and a magazine on a shelf.

'I could bring you some books?'

'I am sure I can make my own entertainment.'

Fran stifled a yawn. The heat in the room was making her weary. She put out a hand to the radiator and was amazed to find it warm. 'Why on earth do they have these on in this weather?'

'They are drying us out,' said Leonora.

'I'll do your hair before I go,' suggested Fran. Leonora frowned at the implication of need, but did not resist. Fran stroked the fine strands into a tail and twisted them in a black velvet scrunch at the back of her mother's head.

'Is that a style?' enquired Leonora disparagingly.

'Very much so. You'll start a trend here I expect.'

Leonora nodded. She looked out of the big picture window and sighed. 'Yes, I'm all the rage,' she said, but without her usual acerbic edge.

Babette returned to the cottage that evening to collect the rest of her things (apart from the fudgy razor in the bathroom), entering without knocking because she still had the spare key. Fran heard the front door slamming as Babette left, and put down her pastels to run outside and wave her off. She had hoped for a better leave-taking.

'Anything you want us to store?' Fran called.

'Nope.'

'What about the Peace Hanging?'

'It's at Gwen's. Don't worry about me.'

The moped wobbled down the lane and Fran came back inside. Babette had surprised her again. Choosing Gwen. And Gwen had surprised her too, bonding with Babette like that. Creative embroidery did not seem Gwen's sort of thing at all.

Fran decided not to brood on Babette's peculiar hostility. It was probably, quite simply, that their friendship had not survived her love affair with Jake. Babette must be jealous. Especially now that her own attempt to form a partnership with Rupert had faded, although Fran still didn't understand what had happened there. Twice Babette had started to explain and then said wearily 'Oh forget it.' And as Fran had never actually met the man who replaced her in both the school and the school-house, this had seemed perhaps best.

Fran changed quickly into shorts and crop top and jogged up the lane. The evening was still light and a warm breeze touched her midriff. *Don't worry about me* said Babette calmly in Fran's head, *Don't worry about me* she said reproachfully. *Don't worry about me* said Babette coldly. *Don't worry about me* said Babette bleakly, and forlornly, and inscrutably. *Don't worry about me* said Babette manipulatively.

The man in the palomino-pale coat was sitting on the bench near the factory again. Fran perspiring, wondered why he didn't take it off. He must be so hot, she thought.

'So Babette's charm school course finally paid off' said Jake on Friday when Fran had recounted her tale of the visit to Hill House, Gwen's unexpected cohort, and Leonora's capricious approbation. It was evening but the sun was still bright and the air exceptionally warm. They were in the garden, sitting among the daisies in the long grass. Portishead was on the CD player on the kitchen windowsill. *Nobody loves me like you*, Beth Gibbons promised smokily, *you got dm dm de dm*, Jake hummed, not remembering the words. 'Leonora was a bit old to be a flower child, wasn't she?'

'Age has never stopped her behaving badly.'

'Badly? Don't be such a prude, darling.'

'I'm not. Behaving badly is a contemporary compliment, didn't you know?'

Jake laughed. 'She's a marvellous woman. She produced you, so I can only admire and adore her.'

'Mm.'

It wasn't easy being on the edge of my mother's rapacious zest for life's experiences, Fran wanted to tell him. Behaving badly is only fun in the anecdotes, not when it's happening. But she knew Jake would blow away her complaints like so much thistledown, so she smiled and agreed. Jake went indoors for more wine, kissing her slowly as if reconciling himself to a long separation.

Within the cottage the phone was on answering machine, so Fran was surprised to hear Jake pick it up quickly when a woman's voice came on. She heard him say 'Yeah' and then there was a long pause while he seemed to be listening, and then he said 'OK' and hung up.

'Who was that?' said Fran when Jake came back out. She wished he hadn't left her to ask.

'Selene . My ex. She's going away for a few days and she wants to know if we'll have Cassie. Next week.'

Fran looked at Jake to see how she should feel but he gave no clue.

Fran decided, all on her own, that she felt pleased.

'I'm glad,' she said, 'It's really important for a little girl to know her father.' Jake took her in his arms again.

'You're a wonderful woman.'

'It's a bit short notice, though. Can you get the week off?'

'No problem. A few phone calls – I've got the lap-top here.'

'I wish I could be here too –'

'Take the week off,' Jake ordered – no, urged. Fran felt her pulse flicker but answered tenderly.

'Jake, I can't – I'm needed for holiday cover in Bindery, remember? The deadline's at the end of the week.'

'Oh well, I'll manage. Don't look at me like that, I promise you it will be OK – it will be great. After Babette, a little girl will be no problem.'

'Of course not,' murmured Fran. In the relief of Leonora's placement and Babette's departure, a little girl would be bliss.

'And your study's already set up for a bedroom.' For it was obvious to Jake that his study need not be involved.

Fran agreed.

'So you see some good did come from Babette's stay,' said Fran in the tender post-coital, pre-coital moments (for on Fridays they often merged).

Later when Fran tried to phone Leonora at the Home she found her line engaged. Relaxed and sleepy, Fran felt quite relieved not to get through. Conversations with her mother often left her worried. It was good that Leonora was busy with other people and not just lying there waiting for her call.

Fran would find out soon that she should not have felt relaxed at all. She should have been worried.

Gwen had been slightly worried about the militant aspects of Peace, but the serene white doves along the hanging's border consoled her. Babette was no longer planning to auction the finished collage; she announced that money donations were no solution to warring countries. In fact, they were part of the problem. Art-for-Peace had a touring exhibition going out to Bosnia soon, and Babette planned to contribute the Hanging, probably donating it to an orphanage somewhere on the route. Maybe she would go along, too. Gwen stroked the appliqué-pebbled coastline, feeling almost sorrowful. She had thrilled to the notion of the finished piece hanging resplendent while the Auctioneer told the raised faces of the bidders *It's for a very good cause...* 'It would look lovely in an orphanage hallway,' she conceded. In Gwen's world all institutions had hallways.

The Peace Hanging completely filled Gwen's spare room. There were bags of fabric on the floor and boxes of beads on the bed. Pinking shears and rickrack shared the dressing-table with pincushions and trays of coloured skeins. Gwen was pleasingly reminded of the sewing room at school. The needlework teacher, Miss Vincent, had been kind to her. Babette was kind too, praising Gwen's meticulous hemming just as Miss Vincent had done all those years ago. Though in slightly different vocabulary. 'Yeah, that's cool. Neat as a ladybird's arse.' *Babette is rather a rough diamond but means well.* Gwen confided to her diary, smug at her own broadmindedness. *I feel I am helping a worthy cause, and she is appreciative. It is nice to have someone to talk to who listens.* Indeed, as the hours scrawled past and the two women sat together stitching, Gwen found herself unburdening extensively to her new friend. Babette seemed to know what she meant even when she hadn't said it.

'So, you think your ma-in-law should stay in the Home

when the fortnight's up,' concluded Babette calmly. She teased out a scarlet strand from the embroidery skein and licked it for threading.

Gwen sighed. 'The bungalow is a death-trap, and so close to the canal. I feel on red alert the whole time I'm there,' she confided, and Babette made empathetic snorting sounds at the back of her nose which Gwen found immensely comforting. Neville never supplied such noises.

'Well don't let her badger you about coming out before she's given it a proper try. Old people can be very manipulative.'

Babette had put her finger on the nub, thought Gwen, but there was still Neville to convince. And Fran.

'Fran has been very tardy in her contact, I feel,' she confided.

Babette said 'Oh, Fran. We shared a house when she worked at the school; she's a sweetie but vapid. And I do get irritated by her constant air of muted Pre-Raphaelite euphoria.'

Gwen shimmered. She had not the faintest idea what Babette meant but it felt distinctly critical.

The following day Gwen decided to make the trip to Leonora's house to see how the repair men were progressing. Men need to be watched. This is in itself properly a man's job, but Neville had merely said 'Looks all right to me,' when Gwen showed him the quote.

'The heading says FLATROOFING, Neville' Gwen had pointed out. 'The bungalow roof is distinctly pointed.'

'Probably the same technique,' was Neville's only comment. Gwen started to say 'Not the point, Neville,' but suspecting he might snigger and make some punning comment she subsided into silence. *It will all fall on my shoulders again*, Gwen noted resignedly in her diary. *Though not literally. Of course.*

The repair men appeared to be busy repairing when Gwen arrived at the bungalow. She went inside, stepping over Leonora's post on the mat – a chunky brown envelope which looked like a brochure of some kind. It said PRIVATE on the front but Gwen felt it would be best to check the contents before taking it to the Home. She opened the envelope and withdrew a magazine subtitled QUALITY EROTIC ENTERTAINMENT FOR THE DISCERNING. This lettering partially concealed two caramel-coloured naked bodies entwined with such complexity that Gwen had to check the nail varnish in order to interpret who was clasping whom. She thrust the magazine back in the envelope and hurried to the swing-bin to trash it. Really, this junk mail was outrageous. It was scandalous that such a magazine might have fallen into the hands of an old lady. Gwen breathed deeply and washed her hands. She looked out of the window into the garden, where the repair men had taken thermoses and sandwiches to the edge of the canal for a lunch break. Cheery music fuzzed on their transistor and the men occasionally chucked crusts to the ducks. There was no sign of the gardener.

It occurred to Gwen that the men might possibly use the swing-bin for their discarded sandwich wrappers before leaving and would thus see the guilty contents. She retrieved the envelope and retired to Leonora's bedroom holding it cautiously. She looked again at the address and the account number on the envelope and realised with a dull feeling of deepening confusion that Leonora was no accidental target of a misplaced mail-shot. Leonora had her own reference number. Leonora was a customer.

Gwen sat on the bed and took the magazine out of the envelope again.

After a few moments scrutiny of the cover, she opened it and was rewarded by a full-page picture of a wickedly fat snake uncoiling nonchalantly from some kind of bush. Gwen's breath sharpened tensely and her eyes refocussed. The caption explained that she was contemplating penile enhancement, and Gwen's breath released in a gasp. Neville had never in his life released a creature like that at her. And his surrounding thicket was far less profligate in its profusion than this proffered groin.

Gwen turned the pages with fascinated revulsion. What could possibly motivate Leonora to look at such a magazine. All these young men with their tongues hanging out, lapping like cats wherever they could reach. An image of Leonora's gardener invaded her mind. She turned page after page and reached the personal advertisements. Not only men's listings, either. *Bored sexy housewife loves to show her panties. Voluptuous wife craves intimacy,* Gwen read. Like the other women illustrated, the voluptuous wife bared everything except her eyes, which were discreetly covered by a white rectangle as if driven by a fundamentalist religion decreeing ultimate opposition to the yashmak. To Gwen this seemed irrational. How could privacy be an issue for women who were prepared to pose splaying parts that Gwen would have touched only for essential applications of ointment?

Gwen turned the pages tremulously, apprehensive of uncovering a picture of Leonora in the buff brandishing her walking stick and offering favours. Fortunately, she found no such image. There was no-one Leonora's age advertising friendship and fun, though several of those illustrated were certainly old enough to know better. Gwen lingered for a while over one woman on a floral settee in a peephole bra and straggling suspenders. She's probably older than me, Gwen thought, almost respectfully. Fatter, too. *Affectionate female into O, toys, videos, and leather.* Something in that posture of hopeful yearning made Gwen feel quite sisterly, although she had not the faintest idea what O was.

On her journey home Gwen gazed at the fleshy neck of the taxi driver and speculated idly on possible poses. Plump ladies often proffer their bottoms, she noticed. Porky buttocks and shorty jackets. *50ish, no, late 40s attractive affectionate brunette, first-timer, seeks...* Various phrases, unwittingly memorised, floated through Gwen's mind but none seemed right. *Seeks initiation,* Gwen decided. Not that she ever would, of course.

Gwen confided none of this to her diary. The magazine was hidden deep within her shoulder bag and her imaginary advertisement did not survive the taxi journey home. At bedtime Gwen stroked her thighs and traced the pretty, silvery, lines of cellulite and wrote instead *I shall have my hair bobbed next week. I may plump for auburn lowlights too. 48 is no age, really. Magazines are full of women more mature than I. I might ask Neville to take some photographs. Purely for our own personal records, of course.*

'We're a good team' Babette pronounced next day. Gwen was helping her pin and tack the panels of the Peace hanging.

The variegated sections were coming together in an expressive landscape. As the women sewed, they talked. Babette had a lively curiosity which in some women Gwen would have considered nosy, but she found herself relishing this attention. This is what friends do, Gwen thought purringly. Womanly intimacy. She had seen it on the television.

'And what does Neville do?'

'He's in computers.'

'Well, obviously. But what sort of programs does his firm develop?'

Gwen didn't know how to answer. Computer programs, of course. She had never really wondered. Workwise there was a chasm between her and Neville; like the difference between the checkout at Tesco and the old ring-till at the Heart shop, she thought. Each to their own.

'I think they're doing something for the MOD at present,' she said vaguely.

Babette looked at Gwen as if she'd slapped her.

'Computer programs for warheads,' Babette said, sounding stricken.

Gwen drooped over the doves of peace, blushing and flustered. Babette lifted her arm and Gwen flinched, afraid. But Babette enfolded her in a soft maternal hug. 'Bloody men,' said Babette throatily, and Gwen's eyes moistened. She was not weeping from the shock of her sudden fear of Babette but for Gwen; for poor Gwen, for the meagreness and ignorance of being Gwen. *I wish I could be like Babette, understanding things in an instant, and knowing what to feel,* Gwen wrote in her diary that night. *I wish I could be pierced by something important and real.*

The men were driving off in their van when Gwen returned to the bungalow on Friday. One of them shouted and waved a clipboard in a businesslike way but Gwen had no idea what he meant. She felt hot and bothered, and frustrated by their cheerful disappearance, which seemed to underline the futility of her supervision. She checked the mat for post but it had been collected and placed on the sideboard. The sight of this slender pile reminded Gwen that the gardener was still in residence and she caught her breath at the thought that but for her intervention he would have discovered Leonora's sleazy secret. Then it occurred to her that perhaps this was no secret – perhaps the gardener sat beside her mother-in-law while they perused the raunchy images together. Gwen thought of that man's hands turning the pages she had turned and seeing the things she had seen, and she found that she was quivering.

She stepped into the garden. As Gwen hesitated and shaded her eyes, she thought she saw the outline of a man in the greenhouse. She strode down the gravel path towards it.

Gwen stood in the doorway of the greenhouse in her blue button-through dress, watching the gardener. He was watering a row of tiny pots and the beads on his pigtails clicked quietly as his head moved slightly, rhythmically, up and down.

'I want some basil,' she said, eventually.

'By the back door,' he said, without looking up.

Gwen lingered. There was a curious buzzing in her ears, a pulsing sensation, and the air seemed tremulous with a faint shimmering sound. Dazzling sunlight etched the greenhouse windows and Gwen felt giddy. She stepped through the doorway and steadied herself against the post.

The gardener looked across quizzically. He pulled the black thread that crossed his chest and as his slim headband slid away Gwen realised the waspish buzzing noise was sound-leak from the personal CD clipped to his hip. He disconnected the wires and trance-like music sounded loudly between them.

'Ambient Amazon,' said the gardener inscrutably. He pressed somewhere close to his groin and the sound ceased.

Gwen closed her eyes. She could feel a mist of perspiration clinging between her bra cups. She wanted to look down to check there was no telltale dark stain showing but she dared not peer at her breasts for fear of drawing the dragon boy's eyes nipplewards. She fiddled with her shoulder strap, surreptitiously feeling for telltale damp.

'Tension,' observed the dragon boy. He was watching her coolly without moving a sculpted muscle.

Gwen gave her little gasp and coughed. She found she was nodding, as if in agreement. He moved behind her and Gwen felt his powerful hands descend on her shoulders, his knuckles slowly kneading into them, his thumbs pressing into points of delicious pain. Gwen closed her eyes.

'Stress gets mostly trapped in here.' The dragon boy's laconic voice was very close. The delicately spiralling pressure he applied was like a gimlet of silver pleasure. Gwen could feel tiny molecules silently popping like champagne bubbles and flowing away. The tension released. The sensation of ecstasy continued.

'You want to get that done more often.' The dragon boy eased his pressure and moved back to his potting activities.

Gwen remained.

'There's all the oils in the house. Do you properly, if you like.'

'No,' said Gwen.

'Look lady,' said the dragon boy, 'I'm not the gamekeeper. If you want something else, you'll have to ask.'

Gwen had not read the novel about the gamekeeper and the lady but she understood his reference and waited for her body to tense, insulted. It did not. The dragon boy looked up with those wonderful aqua eyes. She stayed where she was in the doorway while he wiped his fingers on his frayed jeans and stepped towards her. He cupped her face in his hands, pressing her hair sleekly to the side of her face.

'You should grow your hair long,' the dragon boy instructed softly. He lifted her face and kissed gently the soft skin underneath her chin and on her throat, sucking softly with his teeth and tongue. Gwen breathed quietly. She felt very beautiful.

The dragon boy unbuttoned her dress to just below the waist so that when he drew it gently from her shoulders it slipped to her hips and remained there clinging like a mermaid skin. He unhooked her bra without fumbling and removed it smoothly.

Gwen looked down as her breasts, pale and surprised, rolled quietly towards her midriff. The dragon boy scooped them up, a hand under each so her nipples perked up like button mushrooms. Gwen regarded them in this new position, plump and full and rounded. They looked rather nice. She was pleased to see that the dragon boy was no longer impassive. His breathing had deepened and quickened and he moved his legs very slightly further apart. His face was slightly flushed and his lovely azure eyes were heavy. I am exquisite, thought Gwen. She raised her gaze to the apple tree beyond the greenhouse. My heart is singing, she thought.

'Shall we go into the house now?' whispered the dragon boy.

'No,' said Gwen calmly.

She knew that there was no way this interlude would transfer outside the greenhouse across the lawn, even if she closed her dress and closed her eyes as she sped.

The resourceful dragon boy, undeterred, lifted her onto the shelf next to the Growbags. Tomato plants rolled around her and a flowering pepper plant leant across her shoulder. She sat docile while the dragon boy with great dexterity and economy of movement manipulated a bedding tray with his feet and stepped onto it while sheathing himself with his hands. She was pleased at this precaution, though conscious of a fine spray of Levingtons Multipurpose.

Gwen sat clinging to the edge of the shelf with her knees very wide as the dragon boy pressed suddenly and closely into her. His hands scooped under her buttocks and he gasped into her hair as he struggled fiercely between her thighs. Gwen gripped the slats behind her so that she could push forward further and wider and the dragon boy sang dolphin songs into her neck and breasts. There was a tumbling scuffling sound as shaken plants cascaded around them and the sweet scent of fresh young tomatoes suffused the air.

Afterwards they buttoned themselves away and Gwen said shyly, 'I should know your name.'

'They call me Polo,' said the dragon boy.

'What a funny name. Why do people call you that?'

'Because I nick 'em.'

'What, the sweets?'

'The cars.' Then he laughed and said kindly, 'Not really.'

Polo tidied the greenhouse shelf and Gwen tidied her hair. They smiled at each other.

'Do you do that with Leonora?' Gwen asked just before she

left the greenhouse.

'Nope.' said Polo, without any particular emphasis.

Gwen went back up the path and found the basil, just outside the back door. She picked several sprigs.

On her way home in the taxi Gwen wondered if perhaps, since she had finally become involved in something that WAS against the Commandments, she ought to pray. She closed her eyes. Gwen imagined God as she had since childhood: rather like a garden gnome without the hat and fishing rod, with a benign expression and milky eyes glazed with worry at the troubles of the world. She did not of course still believe in the God she imagined, but sometimes she wished that she did. The God Gwen now believed in was unimaginable; an incomprehensible distillation of recrimination and rebuke. This was the God that Gwen expected would twist her in His knotty unimaginable fist as the taxi crawled across the toll bridge, sending fire and brimstone or at very least a migraine. But Gwen arrived home uncharred and lightheaded, with a tremulous undefined sense of Isis rising.

Evening lounged over the rooftops of Bath. Gwen was sipping a gin and tonic. At her feet, white felt birds fluttered; on her lap lay her diary. Gwen doodled in the margin trying to decide what to write about today.

She had already mentioned the roses at the bungalow, which were exceptionally sweetly scented. There was more she would like to transcribe but Gwen was not sure how. She had no way of thinking about the events of the day; they simply did not fit anywhere in her sentient landscape. Leonora had once referred to Fran's father as a fling. *Simply a fling*, she had said gaily. Like a bright frisbee casually slung across a sunny beach. A strange word for an encounter with so enduring an outcome as a daughter. Encounter – now that was a better term. There was something adventurous and significant about an Encounter. Accidental, possibly, but not trivial or ignominious.

Today I had an encounter, (inserted) *important, encounter which has made me feel more positive about myself and hopeful about*

about

Gwen rose and stepped over to the latticed window. She tweaked the curtain and looked into the dusky world outside. The herbaceous border was a blur through the myriad diamond panels. On the television there was news of further lorry loads of relief for Bosnia. She thought of Babette's Hanging for Peace, and said to Neville, 'Do you think the peace will last?'

Neville replied without shifting his eyes from the screen. 'Historically, the Balkans have always been a trouble spot. Both sides are as bad, it's in their blood. They cut each other's throats sooner than shake hands. There's nothing we can do about that.'

Her husband had been watching the screen so placidly that Gwen had no idea his opinion would be so vehement and so fatalistic. She sat down again and looked at her diary and read *hopeful about...* Why don't I know about things too? Gwen thought. I must have learned history at school. Why can't I say knowing things about the world? Suddenly the futility of being Gwen welled up enormously within her, swelling like a deluge of grief until nothing was left but ignorance and absurdity. On the TV screen coaches were rolling, bringing relief. Succour for orphans. Motherless Gwen watched wet-eyed.

'What's the matter, dear?'

Neville had noticed. Another wonderful thing happening today. Had the unthinkable encounter with Polo made her suddenly no longer invisible?

'It seems so sad for those poor people,' she said eventually in a watery voice. 'I should so like to help.' She rescued a crumpled dove of peace from the carpet.

'You don't drive,' Neville pointed out equably. 'You'd be a liability.'

Neville had put his finger on it again. *Neville thinks I am a liability*, wrote Gwen neatly in her diary. Then after her usual pause for contemplation she crossed out *Neville thinks*.

She doodled a small circle with two dots and two lines to represent features the way Clive signed the occasional instructions left in his bedroom, curling the mouth line slightly down instead of upwards. This seemed a surprisingly satisfying and simple way of expressing her emotions. She fiddled with the mouth line and added some lines of hair.

You should grow your hair long, whispered the dragon boy in her head. Gwen's body shivered with a tiny tingle of unfamiliar sensation. Perhaps it was hope. She crossed out the rest of her last sentence and continued from *hopeful about:*

possibilities for change. After all the Heart Shop takes up very little time and I feel I have more to offer. The Hanging is merely a start.

Gwen was about to write more when she noticed something. She examined the binding of her diary closely. She pressed the something and drew her finger down the page which now had a very fine smear of what was definitely cigarette ash.

Gwen waited for her shoulders to tense in annoyance but they did not. Neville was actually listening to her.

15   Calm Seas

Fran and Jake were drinking coffee on the Bristol Quay. They had been to the Arnolfini Gallery – or Arnie-phoney, as Jake called it – mainly because Fran wanted the loo and Jake enjoyed making loudly patronising remarks about the current exhibition while he waited for her. They left through the cafe, which reminded Fran she could do with a coffee and prompted the purchase, and then took their cups to the tables outside.

'Who's the bloke looking like he's missed the last bus?' Jake wanted to know, wafting his cup towards the seated statue of John Cabot staring across the estuary from the quayside.

Fran knew that one and told him, adding '15th century explorer – he sailed from here to Newfoundland, and claimed it for the king. Henry VII that would be.'

'Ah yeah. He thought it was Asia, as I remember. Like Columbus arrived in a land full of thriving indigenous peoples and claimed he'd 'discovered' America. And then proceeded to enslave and kill the existing populations, by disease even if not outright slaughter.'

'"Man's inhumanity to man makes countless thousands mourn", Fran murmured, eating the froth off her cappuccino, 'That's Burns. We did him at school. I wanted to do the Liverpool poets, but they didn't count for exams, apparently.'

She watched the sea-gulls swirling above the dock and lifted her face to the sun. Jake was still staring at Cabot's back. 'I'm surprised they haven't got a statue of Colston gazing out with satisfaction over these docks,' he said, 'This harbour must be thick with the bones of the slaves he dumped because they were too sick to sell. Men women and kids, thrown overboard for the insurance money. It's beyond disgusting. They don't tell you about these things, though, do they – it's all hidden history.'

'There is a statue of Colston,' Fran said, digging out her tiny fold-out map of Bristol city centre, '– it's just up the road, there. And of course, there's Colston Hall. There's been fuss about it for ages, people campaigning to change the name – Massive Attack say they won't play there till the venue's renamed.'

'Well that's not going to happen, is it,' said Jake amiably. 'The English are totally complacent about their colonial past.'

'I'm pretty sure there are some campaigns...' Fran said uncertainly. She wasn't sure actually – she made a mental note to ask Leonora. Leonora would know. But that was the trouble, wasn't it? Initiatives like this were always the domain of fringe elements – wild old women and so-called 'tree-huggers' with no social status to make any impact.

'What we need,' she told Jake reflectively, as the seagulls on the quay squawked loudly around them, 'is some kind of unifying figure to lead a national movement for more enlightened views. In fact, not just national, international. It could happen, Jake – being in the EU means we can maximise our impact, and it could spread across the world once it got started.'

'Don't be silly,' said Jake, fondling her hair under the pretence of smoothing it from the wind, 'The EU is a trade treaty. It's about profit not idealism. It could just as easily break up, if a few individuals decided they could make more profit outside of it.'

Fran did not argue but she knew Jake was wrong. The links slowly being forged across the world were heralding better times, and an end to prejudice and cynicism. It had to come. This was a new millennium, and the selfish values of the old regimes would recede into history, just as the slave-owning regime had done. She said no more, and let Jake kiss her as the seagulls swooped around the quayside.

Back in the cottage, Jake remembered it was time for his next column. It was annoying, lugging the fax back and forth from London but for situations like this, he reflected, it was vital. The placid scene at the docks had put *The Fall of Icarus* in his mind. Without more reflection, Jake wrote:

"Everything you need to know about Bruegel's uncannily serene seascape, painted in 1560, has been written by Auden in his

stupendous poem Musee des Beaux Arts. The triviality of tragedy is here celebrated in grand style. The peasant behind his plough does not care which leader falls – he doesn't even care if the ship reaches harbour, unless it deals in wares that he can buy or provide. Death here is not important, it is merely a consequence of mortality, which is one of the attributes of life itself. Everything is finite: the ploughman knows the seeds he will sow in these furrows will first ripen then die.

But we should not read this painting as merely a calm celebration of status quo: pandemics were rife across Europe, as Bruegel knew well and had depicted already in his grim painting Triumph of Death. In addition, Bruegel's Flanders was at the epicentre of the 16th Century Beeldenstorm – 'statue storm' – which saw mass destruction of religious images as protestant mobs attacked artefacts in churches and public places – another phenomenon which, like plague, we are unlikely to see again in more tolerant, or perhaps indifferent times.

So the context of this pragmatic portrait of real life is in fact not a Greek legend, but a maelstrom of public reappraisal of iconography, asking the question that we no longer hear in our own complacent community: Why should I honour this image that I no longer value? Perhaps the artist is, in his own way, making that protest. This is a deity from an old order – does his fall matter one jot to him?"

Then he added 'Pieter' and 'the Elder' to 'Bruegel' and 'WH' before Auden, and faxed it off. He knew he should have said more about the technique, and the general body of work from the Breugel studio, but that was exasperatingly accessible now on Wikipedia, which was beginning to seem a pretty good reason for the end of information-based schooling, Jake thought. No need ever to 'teach' facts, the age of reason and debate could finally truly be heralded now for a generation with facts literally at their fingertips – the next century would surely see the end of schools as buildings and examination testing.

Jake was glad. He hated to think of his wise, loving, little Cassie caged in a fetid institution run by the unimaginative and the disillusioned. Self-motivated learning on a chosen interest should be the way, as in the days before 'schools' were designed to mould the mob to a life of adult obedience. Thanks to technology, no-one needs a teacher to tell them what to think or learn. With factual data at everyone's fingertips, education could become worthwhile again. Times were, finally and not a moment too soon, a'changing.

16   Leonora's Forte

Meanwhile, at Hill House the telephone was ringing. Leonora could hear its muted trilling echoing through the pallid corridors, and she twitched yearningly. Leonora thought she would enjoy a conversation, even on a phone. She had not enjoyed anything much so far today.

She had spent her morning in the reception room with her crochet. Pansy sat beside her sucking a hanky. The television was on with the sound down but Pansy's gaze remained glued to a Degas print hanging on the pale wall. After a while Leonora spoke.

'I was a dancer before the war,' she told Pansy, 'the second war, that is. Perhaps you remember it.' Pansy began to cry, dribbling down her fists, and a carer with blonde hair came in and turned the sound up on the television. Leonora hobbled to the French windows. 'Not yet, my lovely' said the blonde carer.

Leonora paused in mid hobble.

'Mrs Milsom don't let us open up the garden till the afternoon, when the extra staff comes on. Can't have you tumbling, can we?'

Leonora allowed the blonde carer to reseat her. 'I married a Lance-Corporal after the war,' she confided hopefully.

'Men in uniforms look so nice. My Mark is a traffic warden.' The blonde carer smiled as she slid an expert hand to check the incontinence cushion.

'He was shellshocked and in civvies when I met him. We had what was termed in those days a shot-gun wedding. Ironic, don't you think?'

'Lovely, my lovely,' said the blonde carer and hurried away.

"Nothing came of either enterprise, however,' Leonora informed no-one in particular, as no-one in particular was paying any attention.

When lunch was over and the garden no longer out of bounds,

Leonora was escorted to a chair on the lawn where she sat facing the astounding view, right across the city.

'I lived in a teepee for two years in the seventies. I organised the settlement school. I still have some of the children's drawings' said Leonora to the distant roofs glowing mellow in the sun.

Afternoon tea was served by a volunteer helper. Leonora gripped the girl's arm so tightly that tea sloshed over the rim of the cup as she told her, 'During the 'eighties I spent six months at Greenham Common. I was photographed for the Sunday papers – I still have the cuttings.' The helper had never heard of Greenham Common. She shook the slops onto the grass and said forgivingly, 'There you are, Gram-ma.'

And now the day was ending. Leonora, back indoors, waited for suppertime and listened as the office telephone continued to ring. Through her bedroom window she could see Samantha, the receptionist, plodding across the garden with Mrs Milsom. The matron was gesturing at patches of weed in the lawn and Samantha was nodding. Shortly the unmanned switchboard would inform the caller that there was no-one in the office at present and play an irritating jingle. Impulsively Leonora picked up the phone in her room and keyed in the number to receive an outside call.

A husky voice enquired, 'What colour are your knickers?'

Leonora sighed. Underwear was a contentious topic for her, since Gwen had confiscated much of hers as unsuitable to be revealed to the Home staff and replaced them with some of her own stock of Damart: a five-pack in black, white, and neutral. She contemplated her response. 'Putty,' while truthful, lacked allure.

'Your knickers? What are they like?' urged the lascivious voice impatiently, and Leonora yearned for the days when her underclothes were not neutral tones in serviceable thermolactyl cotton.

'Silk,' said Leonora firmly, 'apricot silk, with deep matching lace and narrow ribbons.'

'Cutaways?' hazarded the voice, but Leonora was deep in her own fantasy. 'French knickers. They are scented faintly with jardiniere, mingling with my own, essentially feminine, aromas. The ribbons are satin and a darker peach in tone,' she said 'threaded across my thighs. Look, I'll show you.'

The voice at the other end gasped and gurgled. 'Higher,' it begged, 'lift a little higher?'

Leonora made a breathy little panting noise like a puppy excited by a toy. She was finding the exchange immensely diverting, and would have been content to continue on this coquettish theme but the voice on the phone, now sounding deeper and more treacly, changed the subject.

'Do you gobble?'

Leonora replied severely, 'I do not, young man. That is a very naughty notion. I think you should be severely spanked.'

A purring sigh came from the other end. 'With a wet hand,' added Leonora. The phrase dislodged unwanted memories of childhood. Leonora scratched her stiff ankle, peering at the blue and yellow bruising, and decided to eschew sado-eroticism. 'I will describe my preparations on retiring,' she offered instead, and to enliven her account she assumed a desultory Piaf-style French accent.

'Eet eez a sumptuous nightgown in sateen, sleet up ze sides and weez cuts at zee bozoms. Zo! You see where my feengers are circling? Zees way my neeples stand out like polished nuts, shiny weez ze oils I apply, big and full and teengleeng weez excitement.'

Her caller was now making puppy-like short gasps and Leonora gave further detail. She lingered further over the application of lotions and then decreed, 'That's enough for now.'

'Can I call back?' begged the voice humbly.

'You may,' Leonora conceded, 'but if you wish to speak to me again you will have to use my private line. It was a mere quirk of fate that it was I who lifted the receiver. You might have got Mrs. Milsom, and her knickers are of sterner stuff.' She repeated the number, twice, before replacing the receiver.

Leonora enjoyed the call so much she contemplated ringing up men at random in order to describe lingerie to them, but decided the increased phone bill would be noticed by Mrs. Milsom. Incoming phone calls were a different matter. No-one could object to that, could they? It would certainly add spice to the long hours of crocheting. Perhaps I have found my forte, Leonora thought.

Her new hobby was discovered within hours, when the carer on sleep-in heard the phone ringing in Leonora's room later that night. The carer, waiting at the door in case of bad news, heard only Leonora's side of the call, but that was enough.

'Hot! You want to know if I am HOT?' The setting of the Home heating was a particular bête noire to Leonora. She had several times been scolded for struggling to open a window in her airless room. 'I am positively perspiring....Yes, I am most certainly sweating there.... In this heat,' confirmed Leonora sententiously, 'my breasts are like partially poached peaches, sticky with syrup. My legs are rivulets of warm champagne. My crutch is a limpid pool...' The carer tiptoed away.

This was something else for the staff to talk about, and certainly more interesting than Pansy's hankies and Madge's incontinence.

'You have to admire her,' said Denzil, who was head of the care staff, 'she's a game old bird.'

Mrs Milsom said she was not running a poultry farm.

'I wonder where she gets all her ideas from,' said the blond carer, and the kind carer said, 'She wrote a play that was on the radio one time, she told me, about an old pro who stayed on the game even though she had sciatica!'

'Not, I am sure, for the BBC,' said Mrs. Milsom.

'Oh, probably for local but, you know, the research could have given her ideas. I asked her how she went about it and she said, 'You can get anything through the letter box these days – I'm still on the mailing lists!' The kind carer giggled but Mrs. Milsom said she was not running a playwriting course.

'Still, she is a trooper' Denzil said, but Mrs. Milsom was picky about battle metaphors too. 'She is bringing the Home into disrepute,' said the matron sharply, and Denzil knew this was serious.

Mrs Milsom summoned Neville and explained the situation.

'I haven't confronted your mother myself because I don't want any unpleasantness. But I would appreciate it if you could tackle her,' she concluded.

Neville nodded and made his way to his mother's room. Mrs. Milsom followed. Her chosen verb had made Neville a little uncomfortable but he spoke coaxingly to his mother.

'Leonora, you'll get no income from this man's calls. You haven't negotiated with the telephone people. That is the prerequisite of a dirty.. er, a telephone answering service of any specialist kind.'

Leonora smiled stubbornly. 'I see this as a charitable social service,' she said crisply. Neville and Mrs. Milsom exchanged severe and piquant glances. 'If a man is confiding his lustful secrets down the telephone to me, he is not out prowling the streets and molesting other women.'

'But suppose when he puts the phone down he is excited to such a pitch that this is exactly what he does? Not a nice thought to have on your conscience, Leonora.'

'That is where my especial flair comes in,' Leonora said smugly. 'I ensure that he feels no such need. He is replete.'

Mrs. Milsom winced. Neville patted his mother and left, shrugging, followed by Mrs. Milsom. 'What would you like us to do?' he said. 'She may be one radish short of a mixed salad, but she's booked for another week. Can it wait till then?'

Mrs. Milsom folded her arms dissatisfied as Neville drove away, and decided to tackle Leonora herself.

'I want you to promise that this silly game will stop right now,' she said grimly.

'I see nothing wrong with discussing underpinnings,' Leonora said, quietly but firmly, 'We all need support.' She looked shrewdly at Mrs. Milsom's bosoms, which were quivering with irritation.

'It's not just the prattle about lingerie, Mrs Forth. You know perfectly well that you lead these men on.' She spoke the last four words sotto voce, looking anxiously at Madge as though such excitement might be disastrous for her bladder.

'My monologues are carefully crafted,' Leonora insisted, 'They are sensual and erotic.'

'Mrs. Forth, they are vulgar and raunchy.'

'Now you are simply splitting hairs,' Leonora objected, and turned again to her crochet. Her telephone project had enlivened the week immensely. Even the staff were talking to her now, though support was divided. Denzil clearly adored her, but some of the carers were siding with Mrs. Milsom.

'Talking about your underwear on the telephone to strange men!' scolded the carer with the dyed black hair as she whisked the curtains closed that night.

'My dear – thing, there's nothing novel about the pairing of unfamiliarity with undress,' Leonora asserted. 'Men are faced with strangers' underwear on a daily basis. They can't open a paper without being proffered some woman's cleavage or crutch. They can't pay for car repairs or even petrol at a garage without a naked woman dangling above the till on a calendar.'

'Yes, but they're young!' said the carer. 'It's not very suitable, at your age, is it? Not being horrible or anything, but it's downright disgusting.'

But I am still me, Leonora wanted to say. To you I'm an old woman on the way out, but there is still an essential 'me' within this body. Larger than my frailties are my feelings: I still have needs and even hopes. My age isn't a number of years, it is all the moments of my life, turning like a kaleidoscope of tumbling colours.

But the black-haired carer hadn't shown any previous interest in existential philosophy so Leonora did not say this. Instead she pursed her lips and looked stubborn.

'I see this as voluntary work,' insisted Leonora, 'challenging, but stimulating.'

The black-haired carer made her report to Mrs. Milsom. Denzil listened to the new instructions about medication and looked troubled.

'We can't stop our people from having calls, even if they are a bit quirky,' he said. Mrs. Milsom dismissed his protest, waving her fingers in the air as if flicking treacle at passing flies.

'I have her son's agreement that she has become mentally unstable,' she said. That's that daft quip about the radish, Denzil thought gloomily, but he obeyed the instruction to increase sedation.

Neville had decided, on the whole, not to tell Gwen about his mother's little difficulties in adjusting to Home life. He had mentioned his visit obliquely and suggested another trip might be in order at the weekend. His wife had surprised him by smiling agreement, and they arrived just as tea was being served in the garden. The ladies were seated in a semi-circle of stacking chairs on the long lawn. Leonora looked up as they greeted her but her expression was opaque.

'Don't bite your hanky,' said the ruby-haired carer to Pansy. 'Put it in your pocket. That's better.'

Leonora was mumbling. Tea sloshed unsteadily into her saucer as she took a trembling sip. 'I wonder what it's like to be...' Leonora murmured to the air.

'What, dear? A bird?'

Recalcitrant Pansy was chewing her hanky again. Leonora's clouded eyes drooped. She whispered, almost inaudibly, 'I wonder what it's like...'

'What is it this time, dear?'

'...to be Pansy.'

Gwen's eyes met Neville's.

Gwen rose and walked – no, strode – up the lawn into the house. Within half an hour she had packed her mother-in-law's suitcase and acquired the necessary paperwork from the office for Neville to sign, and Leonora was settled in the car.

As they drove away, Gwen's mind was racing. She had never acted so decisively in her life, and it felt good. There would be some re-planning required, but not much: she had a rubber sheet that could be popped on the spare bed just in case, and there were sweet peas in the back garden she could put in a vase as a thoughtful welcome gesture. Of course, the spare room was rather full already with the Hanging, but Gwen continued feeling euphoric. *'Hey sista, go sista, soul sista, go sista'* sang Lady

Marmalade on the car radio, *'Voulez-vous coucher avec moi, ce soir?'* Neville's hand moved nervously to the radio knob but Gwen said 'Leave it on, dear. I like this one,' and she nodded along as they made their way back to Bath.

17 Babette's Bee

Babette's Sewing Bee had been buzzing all week. Gwen, sitting beside the patio fountain with her diary on Friday night, hardly knew where to begin. She curved her hand protectively around the open page although all she had written so far was *The heat wave continues*. Gwen was taking authorial responsibility more seriously these days. She was writing for two now.

It has been a pleasant week though busy, with Leonora to care for and the border of peace doves to appliqué. Gwen reported virtuously. With two house guests and a Hanging on the go, Gwen's week had been so busy she hardly had any spare moment for reverie about her *amour*. Yet she imagined the flushed face of Polo constantly in her peripheral vision, his hot sensuality and palpable presence always somehow at the subtle edges of her physicality. He loomed in her dreams like a prince, he sighed in her daydreams like a dragon's breathing. Hidden in dreams was, Gwen felt, the best place for such recollections. She did not want that extraordinary episode to stumble clumsily into her real life. The memory would collapse inevitably from magical to bizarre, and then to something worse. Gwen intended her *amour* to remain on the misty outskirts of conscious thought, like Mr Darcy dripping from the river on the video.

Babette is delighted with our progress on the Hanging, Gwen wrote. *She is quite a zany character, very eye-catching in her attire.* Babette had arrived in a tie-dye top in varied tones of marigold and swarming with astral symbols in shimmering bronze, with black Lycra leggings which stretched exhaustedly across her sturdy knees and clung as if terrified to her calves and thighs. Gwen surveyed her admiringly. This was a woman who did not agonise over figure-fining styles or reducing shades and vertical lines. *Babette sees little point in dieting. It is a malaise of our culture to admire skinny women. Eating is a natural occupation and refreshments give a message of welcome too.* However, Gwen was unsure what refreshments were suitable to proffer at a Bee so she put out a tray with a few dips and crudités and a bottle of Campari. She couldn't find a fresh lemon so she added a splash of Jif.

'Isn't this nice?' she announced as they settled down with Babette's collage and the bags of attendant implements: 'Three women together. We can have cosy chats as we work.'

Leonora had already started.

'My dear woman, this must have taken weeks. Why ever did you begin it?'

Babette, who had started smiling proudly before Leonora's imperious demand, sighed. 'Fran asked me that, too, and honestly, I dunno. I've never sewed before, not so much as a bib. It is sponsored – well, sort of. I heard about this Art for Peace project, and I thought, well that sounds more use than pictures. I contacted them, and they said if it's good enough they'd use it. It was to do with stuff happening in my life at the time, too. I was about to leave Rupert because that hadn't worked out and I just wanted something I do to be, well, good enough.'

Leonora seemed satisfied. She shifted without further ado to her next cosy chat topic.

'And why did you leave Rupert?'

For the second time in as many minutes Gwen found herself freeze-framed in uncertainty over the social acceptability of her mother-in-law's chit chat. But Babette appeared to relish the question.

'It's more like, how did we ever get together,' she said, uncannily echoing Jake. 'We disagreed about everything, from my cigarettes to the state of the world. Simultaneously, often. He used to come in the room and do this ostentatious little cough and wave a magic spell around him in the name of passive smokers everywhere. He boasted of his weak chest. 'My father was a heavy smoker,' he told me, 'I suspect that's the cause.' I said 'So sue him. That's the thing to do these days, isn't it? If you're not happy, find someone to blame and sue them.' And you know how one thing leads to another: he said cynical sneers didn't suit me and I said his foreplay was pathetic. Well, it was. A quick pinch and "Time for a quicky?" A girl needs more cosseting.'

Leonora nodded. Gwen murmured in noncommittal appreciation.

'We were totally incompatible. Mind you, incompatibility can go on for years – it gets to be a habit.' Again her audience assented with nods and murmurs. 'The reason I actually left was because he couldn't understand how I felt about losing my baby.'

Babette confided her difficulties with Rupert. Gwen wrote. *It is a tragic tale. She lost a baby at five months old, through cot death I think, and Rupert simply could not appreciate the depths of her emotion. When I hear what other women go through I know I am truly lucky. Clive is admittedly sometimes irksome, yet it would break my heart to lose a child like that. I felt in view of all she has been through it would be a kind gesture to invite her to stay while we complete our work.*

In fact, even after two glasses of Campari, Gwen's principal intention had been a kind gesture rather than a second lodger.

'I wish I could invite you to stay,' she had said, 'but unfortunately our spare room is...' is full of Leonora, was what Gwen meant, and she quavered into uncertain silence. Clive materialised at that moment with a bowl of cornflakes.

'She can have my bed,' Clive said indifferently. 'I'll stay with nudge.' At least it sounded to his mother like nudge. It might have been Nadge.

'Are you sure it will be convenient for your friend...' Gwen began, but Clive interrupted with a clicking noise as his tongue kissed his teeth sharply. Her words faded again. She knew the sound, and the irritation it flicked her way.

'That's very good of you, dear,' said Gwen faintly.

'I'm off, then,' said Clive, and he went.

'And since she is now staying , we have continued with the work all week and it is nearing completion.

All that was left was to tack and oversew the last pieces together and back the hanging. 'Won't take long now,' said Babette. She sounded almost sad. Gwen noticed she continued to embellish pieces already included, adding little flourishes of personal mythology in embroidery or buttons and beads. Privately Gwen thought Babette should let well alone. The initial concept, a graphic map of war zones across the world, was simple and impressive. The central section represented the southwest of England, from where the inspiration had emanated. Some parts of this section now were overlaid with wider aspects of protest, and Gwen felt Babette's iconography was sometimes slightly *de trop*: the blood-red sequins on fox-hunt lands, CND mojos by Hinkley Point and a toy mole representing the A30 protest near Exeter, for example. However Gwen had enjoyed plying her needle and coloured threads far too much to challenge the busy scene of rural protest. She enjoyed too the feeling of making valuable contributions, the sort of thing people talked about on thoughtful afternoon programmes on the radio. And as the separate pieces joined together, each acquiring a different sense of scale and proportion when combined with the others, Gwen abandoned her aesthetic reservations. She began to feel excited by the vitality and energy of it. *As I tacked the Glastonbury tor piece in place and thought of all the times I have seen that silhouette in the skyline, my hands almost fluttered. We are living the collage, I thought.*

Leonora had found memories there, too.

'Solsbury hill,' she said sentimentally, stroking the green felt mound overlaid by Babette with indignant zigzag rickrack to represent the invasion of the new road. 'I remember it well. That was my last active protest. With my last serious partner, too. If partners can ever be considered serious.'

'Oh... I'm so sorry.' Gwen wasn't quite sure why she was apologising. She felt mystified. Babette had reached into the past as if it were almost tangible. Leonora's manner of reminiscence was altogether different. Casual, was that the word? No, Gwen decided; it was indifferent.

'Bloody good thing,' decreed Babette. 'Men. Why do we put up with them?'

Leonora, who might or might not have been about to elaborate her tale, chuckled. 'That P word, probably' she said.

'Pity,' said Babette tersely. 'Patience?' suggested Gwen.

Leonora shook her head silently. She lifted her crochet work so that a tail of wool unravelled slowly and then resettled herself. 'Patience is a virtue. I have very little interest in virtues,' she said. 'Vastly over-rated, in my opinion.'

'Most of them are,' Babette agreed. 'Just social mores. Or else concepts so vague as to be useless. Truth, for instance, is pretty slippery stuff. Whenever you decide to be totally honest, even while the words are coming out of your mouth you think, this is bullshit. Well, I do.'

Babette sloshed Campari round the glasses again, and Gwen's eyes flickered only briefly to the unused coaster.

'A little honesty goes a long way,' Leonora mused. 'Truth like chilli pepper should not be overused. Forgiveness – that's a poisoned chalice of a concept. It presupposes culpability and presumes remorse.'

'Never regret,' advised Babette.

'Rien de rien,' Gwen added with shining eyes, feeling almost sophisticated. Exhilarated by the philosophical turn of the conversation she shared round the Campari and asked, 'What is the most important thing a wife should bring to a relationship?'

'Faking orgasm,' Leonora decided promptly. 'A skill sadly undervalued these days. It seems to me that modern women prefer to mortify their menfolk rather than do a little shuddering and moaning at a critical moment. Or an uncritical moment.' she added after pedantic reflection.

'Squeamish?' wondered Babette.

'It's the modern attitude. They don't mind masturbating but they don't like faking orgasm.'

'I wish I knew how to do that,' admitted Gwen shyly.

'Haven't you seen that clip from *When Harry Met Sally?* demanded Babette, and Gwen fearing demonstration clarified quickly, 'I meant the other thing you said.' Leonora looked for a moment as though she might fumble with shaking fingers through the voluminous folds of her crocheting to demonstrate but she merely gave a quiet snort of laughter and unrolled more wool from the lemony ball.

'Sin joyfully,' Babette advised. 'I was in therapy for years.

My therapist was very keen on seeking causes. She talked about repressed memories of abuse in a way that got me quite wistful. We pored over my dreams for significant symbols, like looking for a lost pearl in a bag of toffees. I began to feel I was letting her down. I think she felt that, too. I got very envious of other clients who all came up with interfering relatives and babysitters during hypnosis. I hinted a bit about my father in order to hang in there, but then I lost my nerve and withdrew. I was isolated all over again.'

Gwen found it difficult to tell from Babette's tone how serious she was. This might be one of those times when cynical comments were actually jokes. Gwen had an uncomfortable memory of a smirking dinner party conversation when someone had accused her of irony deficiency. She looked across at Leonora for guidance but from her pose of impassive serenity Leonora appeared to be taking one of her intermittent naps.

'Not your father...' she ventured. 'You couldn't want... that, surely?'

Babette shrugged with a mouthful of pins sprayed out like fangs. She removed them and said 'How do I know? No-one knows if there are people who enjoyed this kind of initiation. There's no studies. We know it happened a lot in remote areas, historically, but the only records we've got nowadays are the people who got hurt.'

'Are you saying– you're not saying...'

'I'm not saying anything. I've seen enough damaged kids, at the school. I believe in their hurt. I just don't believe everyone gets hurt.' Babette scooped the last of the taramasalata, meringue-pink and sloppy, onto her finger and sucked it appreciatively. 'It's like getting fat,' she explained. 'For me, it was better to acknowledge I was greedy than to choose something else to blame.'

Gwen, already disturbed by the zigzag tacking of their conversation, felt even more uncomfortable. 'Fat' and 'greedy' were words that landed in her ears as awkward lumps, refusing to be reclaimed as positive. Echoes jeered from the playground. Greedypig, greedyfatpig.

'Just look at black women,' Babette said. 'They know how to

carry their bigness. Have you ever been to Trinidad? That would open your eyes. Fat sassy women strolling indolently with self-accepting grace. Big and at ease with bigness. Cheers.'

'I have never felt comfortable with my body,' Gwen confided. 'There was a quiz in my magazine last month which said that all women dislike at least one part of their body. It gave you options like tummy and thighs, and other parts. I had to tick them all.'

'Neville likes you the way you are.' This didn't sound like a question, but could hardly have been a statement, for how would Babette know that. Even Gwen didn't know. She hesitated.

'I sometimes think that he might like me better if I were less rotund.'

Babette made that noncommittal noise in the back of her throat which Gwen found encouraging. Gwen sipped again, and looked across to check that Leonora was still dozing. She leaned forward and lowered her voice.

'After we got Clive, Neville wrote me a letter. A very sweet letter. He said that he found it difficult to talk but he wanted me to know that he didn't really want to try any more.'

'To try?'

'To, you know, try physically.' Gwen blushed, not at her euphemism, but at the painful sense of shame she had carried silently for so long. Unable to inspire her husband to conjugal congress. 'But he did say some very sweet things,' she added quickly, 'about being understanding. If I ever felt the need.'

'What did you say?'

'I didn't say anything. I would have written back but I didn't know what to put.' Gwen realised now that the hurt of Neville's clumsy permission had stayed there silently all these years. Neville was content with celibacy but recognised she might not be. She was the greedy one. The greedyfatpig. The unspoken imbalance had become an unspeakable pain in their relationship. Gwen had become ashamed of her need for contact, and told it to creep away. And it had. Hadn't it? Gwen felt her eyelids swell and become sodden with seeping tears.

'Why couldn't he speak to me? If he had talked to me, to explain how he felt, I would never have wanted to.. do... anything he didn't want.'

'Do you want to?' said Babette, stealthy like a hawk on a stoat.

'No. I thought I did. Or rather, I thought I didn't. But that made me afraid that I did. But, no.'

Leonora snored snortingly.

'So, after you 'got' Clive, you never...'

'No.' Gwen got up and fetched her set of coasters with the hunting scenes and placed one of them close to Babette's glass in its circle of messy rim-marks.

Leonora was stirring.

'Rather an old-fashioned term, 'got'?' said Babette quietly.

Gwen bent over her threads to tidy a piece of erratic feather stitching but did not reply.

'Secrets are better out in the open, in my opinion,' said Babette.

'Did you tell Fran about your baby?'

Babette shook her head. 'She wouldn't understand.'

Gwen felt obscurely pleased. 'Perhaps it would be difficult for her, since she's never had a child,' she offered but Babette said, 'Fran's always seen herself as an abandoned child. She wouldn't sympathise with a mother.'

Gwen had never thought of Fran like that. She remembered the quiet composed young girl, turning heads wherever she went. Capturing the gaze of everyone. Perhaps, though, not her mother's gaze. Leonora's heavy-lidded eyes were still judiciously closed. Gwen thought about the emotional narrative oversewing the rich collage of Babette's life and had a strong and yearning impulse to share her own recent adventure, but her mother-in-law's quiet attentiveness deterred her.

'He came back to me, you know.' Gwen jumped. Leonora had rejoined them, apparently still mentally on Glastonbury Tor. 'He was seriously ill. I nursed him in his last days, in fact.'

'What was it?' Babette asked.

'Oh, terminal,' Leonora said vaguely.

'Cancer? Leukemia? Meningitis? Diphtheria?'

'How annoying. I've forgotten,' said Leonora. She opened her eyes fully and looked directly, cryptically, at Babette. 'That thing that begins with P,' she said.

'Pox?' Gwen hazarded, then wished she hadn't.

'Plague?' said Babette.

'Not in these days of penicillin, surely,' Gwen said, as Leonora seemed still uncertain.

Babette pulled out the last of her pins and snorted. 'Haven't you read Camus? *"The plague bacillus never dies or disappears for good, it can lie dormant for years and then it comes back for another killing."* Or something like that. We did it at school. Actually he's talking about fascism, but it's a correct analogy, medically speaking.'

Gwen held her ground. She hadn't read Camus herself, as existentialist literature was not on the curriculum at her school, but she was pretty sure all this was incorrect, medically if not politically. Politics was a different field entirely, discussed in sections of the Sundays which Gwen never waded through, but she was pretty sure of the medical side. Penicillin had changed the world. And antibiotics, and jabs. Flu jabs and vaccinations every year to keep everyone safe. Never again would whole towns and cities be closed down because people were dying in hundreds, daily. Especially in a civilised country like England, a world leader with its wonderful NHS. Babette could be quite naive sometimes.

Gwen was still formulating an appropriate riposte when Leonora joined the debate.

'Pneumonia,' she finally announced. 'Is that it? have we done it now?'

The three women stood up, each holding a section in rotation so that Babette could scrutinise the complete work.

At length Babette said laconically, 'Yup' and Gwen wondered if she should get another bottle of Campari to celebrate. Then she had a better plan.

'We should take a trip to some of the places on the Hanging!' she said. 'After all, we've made quite a feature of our own dear West Country landmarks!'

'A pilgrimage,' Babette declared, and Gwen solicited Neville's permission as soon as he arrived home. Neville queried the venture, quoting Leonora's oft-flourished anxiety about finite fossil fuels, but his mother had clearly hurled her global values aside today and the three pilgrims set off with sandwiches and a flask.

Babette drove with zest and Leonora in the back seat sang out, 'Clear left!' at every turn, either to assist her or as an injunction to unwary pedestrians.

At Glastonbury we watched birds whirling round the softly tiered splendour of the hill. Hazy distant fields dotted with buttercups and dandelions. There is an odd cavern-like place under the rock beside the road where one can purchase tea and crystals. A woman with Bambi eyes and a gem on her nose like magic snot told them about the rejuvenating qualities of tiger-eyes. Gwen fingered them all and chose a darkly striped glossy pebble with an underbelly fire of sheer gold.

And then we walked to the top. Three women slowly climbing the steep womb of earth with its strident phallus. *Leonora was determined to achieve the summit although she has not yet had medical clearance. She relies on the benign power of the universe, she says, plus aromatherapy, Indian Head massage, and a little alcohol. The tor also is itself a place of spiritual healing. Apparently, the whole place is crisscrossed with ley lines – a positive cats cradle.* Gwen thought of the huge dark cradling earth cat. I would like to be kiss-cossetted and laid on every line, sang Gwen, but silently.

On our return we had an unfortunate accident in the garage. Gwen had in fact accidentally nearly broken Babette's shoulder but could find no nonchalant words to minimise her embarrassment. Another notable omission, thought Gwen, and she wondered why she was writing a chronicle at all. It must be something to do with finding herself, or perhaps inventing herself. She looked dreamily into the garden and thought of the husky musky smell of the dragon boy's firm arms.

It was particularly unfortunate for Babette. Particularly ironic too because Babette had spent the return journey expounding her theory of mind-body symbiosis. Physical ailment, according to Babette, is mentally invited. 'Your ankle, you see,' she told

Leonora 'was a metaphor for your feeling of immobility at the time. Look at you now, you're spry as a fly.'

Gwen's own view was that respite care was what had set Leonora on the mend, but the concept of complicit victim was helpful now to reduce her responsibility over the affair of the garage door. It was good of Neville to come to the hospital and wait. Leonora had simply gone to bed. There are different rules for old people.

As so often these days, Gwen began to wonder what it was like to be old for someone like Leonora. Old women are expected to simmer down. Like stock when the meat has gone from it. Elderly women are not allowed lust and rage. Those are the permitted hobbies of old men. Old women have – what? Grandchildren and crochet. Even the outrageous Leonora had started to crochet. I wonder, thought Gwen, when being old will overtake my whole identity. Is it all of a sudden, one birthday, blowing out the eightieth candle and suddenly finding the spark within has gone? Or does one's vigour drip away, tear by disappointed tear, seeping out through greying hair, slipping down the folds of a crepey neck, trapped in stiff joints, sore teeth, until the day the sad woman in the mirror will be no longer a stranger but the only *me* I know.

Gwen's thoughts were making her mournful. She concluded her resumé briskly.

Babette fortunately is undiminished. She certainly has verve, and this week has been most fulfilling for all our little team. Gwen considered adding some pungent aphorism about Art and Life but couldn't think of one so she drew a squiggly line beneath her last entry instead. Before closing the journal she examined the binding carefully, and sniffed the recent pages for any tell-tale smell of cigarette smoke.

There was no ash in the border of Gwen's journal tonight, merely the faintest hint of digestive biscuit crumbs. Gwen thumbed back, half-hopefully, and was wholly rewarded. Beside her recent entry about France was a tiny black-penned scribble written sideways in the margin.

song and Provençal mirth

with beaded bubbles winking at the brim.

Gwen sat enraptured. Of course, Keats's ode was more about feeling like death than wine-tasting, but Neville couldn't be expected to remember that. She fetched the limp-bound Works and it fell open at her favourite page, the one that read *To Mummy with love from Clive* in newly-joined-up writing. 'Daddy got it really,' the little boy had confided from the recesses of his mother's hug. Gwen, remembering, breathed in deeply, and released her breath in a long ecstatic sigh.

Returning to today's journal page she wrote *Perhaps it requires some wild and unexpected event – like the occurrence in the garage I mean of course – to truly value the richness that one has. Perhaps it is good to travel to fully recognise this. Further afield than Europe, closer to the sun.*

Gwen paused for a moment, imagining sun-white sands seared with shadows of palm leaves. She pictured her own shadow dancing there, big and sassy and bold. She arched her back catlike as she sat, the way her yoga teacher had shown, and shifted from side to side slowly, rhythmically. Supple energy, her yoga teacher called it. Or maybe it was subtle energy? I wonder how many yoga positions it is possible to make love in, Gwen thought. Most of them, I expect.

Gwen closed her journal and went quietly down the stairs. Her house guests had retired and Neville was alone in the living-room dozing to the Discovery channel. He opened his eyes and shifted accommodatingly so that Gwen had room to perch on the end of the settee. Gwen consented to descend, but her misty eyes were not on the screen. Gwen was wondering whether to say *Neville, we must talk.*

'What's up, pudding?' Neville asked, sensing something unusual. Gwen did not usually stroke his socked toes, for one thing. Gwen roused from reverie.

'I may repaint the living-room. It could do with some warmer tones. Buttercup, perhaps, with mango in the alcoves.'

'Will you get a man in?' asked Neville.

'No' said Gwen. 'It's only anaglypta. I shall do it myself.'

18   Daddy's Girl

Jake knew that little girls cried, of course he did. You could see them on the advertisements, crying for some consoling product. You heard them in shops, crying at the checkout. Mums gave them things. Sweets, slaps. When Cassie was a tiny baby she used to cry, and he had rocked her until she quietened. He had no reason to fear the phenomena of crying.

But this was different. Cassie was looking at him with enraged black eyes which refused to spurt tears no matter how viciously she forced her face into a gargoyle of grief. She was pink and ugly with malice and distress. Under there, under this alien mask which was frightening them both so much, Jake knew his little girl Cassie was hidden. Perhaps she's hidden in a tear, that's why they won't come out, Jake thought absurdly. He had dropped onto his haunches to try, bravely in his opinion, to hold his child in eye contact at least. Cassie pushed out a fist to hit him, then screamed as though she had been hit herself.

She's been utterly spoilt, thought Jake, straightening up quickly. He poured himself a drink. Behind him he could hear the wails fade into petulance, hesitate then redouble in volume again.

'Fuck it!' shouted Jake helplessly, at her, at himself, at his ex-wife, at the long awful week stretching ahead. Cassie stopped crying.

There was a moment of intense silence, as if both were so fearful of the sounds they had created they were too cautious to attempt any further noises. Then Cassie said in the voice of a very young child, 'I'm thirsty.' A moment later as he was pouring juice Jake heard Fran's key in the door.

'Hello,' said Fran shyly.

'I'm Cassie,' said her young visitor. 'And this is my Daddy.'

She hugged his knees proprietorially. Jake winked, a slow

luscious wink, and both rivals forgave him instantly for the pain of his infidelity.

Fran had arranged flexitime for Cassie's week so she could be home earlier.

'And thank god you did,' said Jake with his feet up and spaghetti hoops with Jacobs Creek wine the best he could muster up for supper. 'She likes you. I can tell.'

Fran wanted Cassie to like her. Since Selene's call she had gone to a lot of trouble to choose various toys and activities. The trouble was caused by the unforeseen difficulty that all toys seemed to have global implications. Fran had originally intended to buy ethnic items of interesting origins in the heavily scented Central American shop in Bath, but although she found the experience enriching (and did get herself a rather lovely mirrored bolero) the toys, beautifully carved and painted as they were, didn't seem designed for children. She had next contemplated software for the Macintosh but Jake had been horrified at the notion.

'Four is too young,' he'd protested, even though Fran said it was computer games she was suggesting not computer dating.

So she had left Jake rearranging his schedule for the following week and gone into town to look for toys. 'What are you looking for?' he asked as, prevented from rising by his laptop, he kissed her knees goodbye.

'Something in wood maybe, though not tropical wood, obviously. Non-toxic paint. Educational.' In the toy shop in the town lots of things had Educational written on the box but the contents were mostly lurid coloured plastic. Who would buy a teapot with a smile like the Happy Eater on acid, Fran wondered. She followed a small girl with black braided hair and a dusky face, hoping for at least a multi-cultural solution, since most of the dolls appeared blatantly untroubled by the feminist revolution. The child went straight to a shelf of flaccid gargoyles with hair like a primeval scream made manifest in violet bri-nylon.

'Not another troll, Jasmine,' came a weary maternal voice, "I'm fed up finding them in the washing-up.'

Fran turned and found the mother's face faintly familiar. The woman smiled and said, 'Hi.' She had short, nondescript hair and a pale freckled face. Fran tried to place that slight recognition.

'I seen you out running.'

'Oh, that's it,' said Fran. 'You run, too?' The woman nodded.

'I wouldn't do it on my own, like you. Too dangerous. I go with my girlfriend, and we carry a whistle. There's funny sorts round here, you know. No, not that either.' This last to Jasmine, who had sidled up with a hopeful expression and a boxed Gymkhana. 'You had one at Christmas, remember, and the dog got the jumps.'

Jasmine made another sortie and her mother spoke further to Fran of the danger of marauders and the price of toys and, hearing her mission, advised Fran to go up the hill if what she wanted was, like, rainy day activities; these were more birthday prices really. 'Colouring books, crayons, all sorts, you get there.'

Fran felt pleased and instantly more purposeful. 'I'm so glad we've spoken. I thought I knew you from somewhere.'

'The factory,' said the woman and, as Fran flushed, still uncomprehending, 'I'm Polly.'

'And the reason I didn't remember her,' said Fran to Jake as she unloaded the tale and unpacked the carrier bag of goodies 'is she seemed so different. I mean her whole manner was different. You know? She was talking about running. She's not friendly like that at work.'

'Of course not' said Jake.

'Well, she sees me every day. I'm only another woman.'

'Don't be silly," said Jake, 'You're Management. Your brother rang, by the way. They seem to have acquired Leonora.'

'Why? What went wrong with the Home? She's supposed to be there till the repairs are done.'

'Dunno. Perhaps she got expelled. It seemed to be Gwen's idea. Typical of these neurotic women – they insist on making everyone do things their way and then change their minds. Oh look, magic painting! I used to have one of these. Same artist did the elephants. We'll have a great time.'

And once the trauma of her arrival was behind them, they

did. Cassie coloured in her colouring books. Jake helped. He made her a kite. Cassie helped (but not much) and they flew it from the top of the hill with the white horse. They visited the birds in the Bird Garden and the pets in the Pets Corner. Every evening Cassie recited the exploits of her day and Fran wrote them in her Holiday Book, supplied by Selene and helped her Pritt in her picture postcards. Then Cassie added some Cs and Ss with the occasional A. Selene was teaching her to spell her name, an exercise not encouraged by Fran, who disapproved, or by Jake, who forgot.

Then Cassie, pink and fragrant, with her wet hair fiercely parted (Cassie loved her comb) sat in her pyjamas with the squeaking bunnies (*Aren't they sweet*, Fran said on the first night, receiving the sage reply *Mummy says they're tacky*) and listened to her story tapes on Jake's stereo system until she became sleepy enough to agree to Fran leading her up to bed.

After this Jake talked until late. He said he needed cerebral stimulus. Little girls were fine in their way but spending more than five hours with one seemed to have an enervating effect on the brain. Cells became dislodged, he thought. Perhaps it was something to do with bending down and the magnetic north. Fran thought it was more to do with being unused to listening.

'It has to do with you being a naturally very dynamic man and now you're being so very patient and attentive,' she explained.

Cassie was opening a new world of experience for Fran, too. Her clothes, for one thing. Cassie dressed in the sort of flounced frocks with collars and puffed sleeves that Fran thought extinct. Cassie had her own cherry-red velvet-covered jewellery box and her own make-up kit. Cassie's dolls had their own jewellery boxes and make-up kits, too.

'I used to have to wear things like this,' Fran told Jake as she hung up Cassie's little-princess dresses.

'Quite right too.'

'The Laura Ashley look. Mum wore Biba.'

'You must have looked an incredibly alluring pair.'

'I always thought we looked ridiculous. She was ages older than my friends' mothers.'

Jake did not understand why a kind of bleak lassitude came over Fran when she contemplated her childhood. Fran was perfect, ergo Leonora had been a wonderful mother. Fran could not explain the cloying isolation and self-conscious sense of frozen sadness that was the memory of being Fran as a little girl. 'She called me Francilla, in a particular sort of way.'

'It's a lovely name.'

'She told the other girls off for shortening it to Cilla. In the end they didn't call me anything much.'

'You did pretty well at school, though?'

Fran shrugged. At school she had developed a gleaming team persona, the kind of girl forever applauded but rarely sought: she was aware that even now she socialised through contiguity and not intimacy. She would have liked to asked Polly to bring little Jasmine round to play with Cassie, but since that chance conversation their encounters at work had been noncommittal and routinely formal. I don't really know how to make friends, Fran thought. Even Babette walked out on me. Even Babette! Jake is the only person in the whole world who loves me. Meeting Jake made the whole of her previous life seem a vague haze merely waiting for the intensity of this passionate commitment, as if her yesterdays had simply dissolved, like water drips on hot rock, since the night they met, when Jake had whispered *Don't tell me anything about yourself – people are all essentially unknowable*, and she had obeyed.

Jake didn't talk about the past either. He had told her nothing about Selene. Did that mean he had no feelings about her? Fran tried to have none, too. Not as her lover's ex-wife, anyway. But as Cassie's mother it was hard to avoid a peripheral awareness of Selene this week. She lingered, perceptible as a flower fragrance, just out of sight. Fran couldn't help thinking about her – couldn't help wondering what it was like to have a child in your life, another being in your home and your thoughts, all the time, day and night. A small determined person with its own feelings and opinions, observing you, carrying around a growing impression of you, building a memory of you. As if your shadow and your mirror were both watching you. But this constant witness has a separate identity too – makes its own choices, has its own voice. It must be very strange to be a mother. The responsibility of shaping someone else's experience, bound up together with the frustration of knowing you will never, ever see the world through the eyes you have made.

And Jake had been part of this, too. The Cassie who grows into a woman will be different because of Jake, because he heaved himself into Selene six years ago, because of times he spent with her and because he went away. Everything Jake had done or not done is a thumb-print somewhere on Cassie's life. Is this how it was for Leonora? Feeling responsible for something tiny and precious, like a jug you don't want to chip. Maybe that was why Leonora didn't touch me much, Fran thought. In case she smashed me. *Your children are not your children*, Leonora's voice reminded Fran from the recesses of her mind: *they are the sons and daughters of Life's longing for itself*. But I wanted to be somebody's child, she whimpered silently. Life, like Death, longs for everyone.

Fran shook her morbid thoughts away. She did not want to be morbid, not ever, and especially not around Cassie when formative experiences are so important. Fran wanted to be Jake's golden girl, not drab from feelings of vague dismay at memories of childhood. Fran didn't do childhood stuff. Why now, this perfect summer, did it all keep coming back? It was almost as though there was something she needed to understand.

Fran watched Cassie at play and noted her contented self-confidence. Selene must be doing something right. The little girl was clearly used to being hugged. She adored rough and tumble, loved snuggling up, taking Fran's face and pushing her cheeks forward to make her lips pout moistly for kissing. She soaked up every kind of tactile contact like a tiny sponge in coral waters.

Fran watched Cassie indulgently, with her gender-watch hat drooping considerably; it was easier actually to take it off entirely and let Cassie wear the hats, offering her own rarely-worn adornments for dressing-up games. Cassie loved anything feathery or beaded, and tended to regard them as trove. Fran found several items squirrelled away in Cassie's room, and her peacock earrings and Venetian fan she never recovered at all. Jake was a surprisingly good audience. He didn't hail her as Daddy's little princess or pretend non-recognition. He listened seriously to her exposition of each persona and trekked respectfully through the realms of her imagination. Fran was impressed. 'I'm finding out a lot about you this week, and it's all nice,' she whispered after Cassie's bedtime.

'Nice' he sighed. 'Oh, not too nice, I hope. I'll have to do something about that. Is the door shut?'

The phone rang later while Fran was in the bath. As the answerphone was on Jake ignored it. Gwen's voice became audible, moaning as if in pain.

Fran sploshed hurriedly from the spritzy tub, trailing a towel which she assembled around her as she lifted the receiver.

Jake heard her say 'Oh dear,' and then, 'Oh dear, how dreadful.'

In the study Cassie whimpered quietly in her sleep. Fran closed her door gently as she passed and came into the bedroom looking shocked.

'Darling, that was Gwen. It's Babette. They all went for a drive to Glastonbury in the Volvo. When they got back Babette drove it into the garage. And because the door's been broken for ages, someone has to hold it up with a prop. But they were talking, or something. Anyway, it slipped. The door slipped and fell.' Fran stopped speaking and looked awed.

'And?'

Fran gave a tiny grimace and slapped across her heart so that her hand rested on her left shoulder.

'Shit" said Jake, slowly, reverentially, then 'What broke? Clavicle?' Fran nodded.

'So poor old Neville's in a sling?'

'Not Neville. Babette.'

'Babette?'

'I said Babette. Jake, you weren't listening.'

'I was listening. I thought you meant she dropped it on Neville.'

'Gwen dropped it on Babette. Gwen was holding up the door, but she let it drop too soon. Apparently her and Neville are synchronised. Babette wasn't ready. Gwen is feeling terribly guilty. Well you would, wouldn't you.'

Jake nodded. In his mind a dark witch was flapping bat-like slowly away, receding into the grim and grimy distance. Babette stricken. A sad woman wounded. Jake could almost feel sorry for Babette.

'And she had to wait ages in Out-patients. It's strapped up now, she won't be able to shower or anything, for ages.'

Jake held his troubled woman and kissed her bath-scented hair. He breathed mantras of jubilation but he did so silently. It was important to show compassion.

'Babette's still there. Should we offer to have her here, Jake, when Cassie's gone?'

'Shit, no,' said Jake, reaching the limit of his compassion swiftly. Fran seemed to somehow find this reassuring so he hugged her again. 'Do you want to share my bath while it's warm?' whispered Fran, after a while.

Jake smelled her neck, tasting strawberry shower gel. 'We could start there,' he conceded.

Jake took Cassie into Bath for souvenirs at the end of the week and saw Mandy in the off-licence. In the cavalier manner of one who rarely recalls faces outside their appropriate environment, Jake did not at first remember her as Leonora's social worker. He noticed her shy lingering look and tentative smile and thought perhaps she was a woman he had met and laid in London. She remembered him instantly, if not sooner. Women usually did.

Mandy noticed Jake's delightful, all-purpose, smile and said helpfully, 'We met at your mum-in-laws.'

Jake's smile intensified with his amnesia. Selene's mother lived in Putney.

'So sorry the Home didn't work out,' said Mandy, 'but family care is usually best. Especially when there are daughters.'

Now Jake placed her. 'She'll be back in her own home soon,' he said confidently. Mandy stretched her mouth sideways like a letter box and spoke of trips and tumbles and how old bones take a long time to heal, which the family might need to take on board. Jake smiled and spoke of the importance of independence and dignity.

'Oh yes. Such a dignified old lady.' Mandy enthused. 'Such a sense of humour. I said, *now what do you want to wash down your antibiotics?* and she said, *anything alcoholic!*'

'She would have been serious,' said Jake, who had been in a similar situation himself.

Mandy laughed again as at some further witticism and said, 'I wish more of my People were cheerful like that.'

My people, thought Jake. How patronising. The constraints of correctness are making her sound like some Sultan or Tsar. Mandy, ignoring Jake's sceptical expression, carried on. 'I wish all my People with needs were such a pleasure to visit.' She turned her mouth down and drooped her shoulders and Jake thought, now she looks like a small unhappy Tsar or Sultan who hears rumours of trouble in the land; he felt instantly sorry for her and wanted to put his arms round her to comfort her. Instead, he took Cassie's hand, smiled his farewells, and hurried away.

'She's an old-fashioned little thing isn't she?' Jake said fondly as the weekend inched closer and Cassie squatted in the garden making nests for ladybirds.

'I did tell her ladybirds don't need nests and they'll just fly off. She didn't even look up, just said, "They need them to fly off from, daddy", and carried on tucking leaves in into her little tangle of grass and wildflower stems. I thought she'd want videos every day, and have lots of whatever's being hyped this summer. Street-fighting turtles or dirty-dancing dinosaurs or whatever.'

'Perhaps that will come next year, with school,' suggested Fran.

'Probably. Pity. I like her cottage-garden simplicity.'

'That's sentimental, Jake. She can't stay a Kate Greenaway child forever.'

But Fran too wished Cassie could. There was something idyllic and untouchably pure about these evenings, with Jake on the floor being a bear and the solemn little girl thrilling with laughter, hugging his neck and fiercely kissing him.

'You're quite gentle, for a boy who only had brothers,' she told him.

'I had a sister,' Jake said.

Fran sat up, shocked. 'Seriously? You never said. You said you had two brothers.'

'Well, I do. My sister died.'

'Oh Jake! That's terrible... tragic. What happened?'

'We were playing and she got run over, that's all.'

That's all! Fran felt a cold touch dance slightly up her back, her neck, into her hair. Why was Jake's voice so bland and unperturbed as he rolled this horrible burden like a marble across the floor. Why hadn't he told her about that before?

'Did you blame yourself, Jake?'

'Of course I didn't. I was five, for fuck's sake. Don't start Babetting me. It was a long time ago, darling, I don't need psycho-mumbo-jumbo now.'

Fran decided it was important to respect Jake's privacy. She kissed him and asked no more.

The phone rang and Fran answered. Neville was wondering if she knew when Babette's term would be restarting. 'She's been staying with us since the accident,' he said, sounding slightly gloomy.

'Not till sometime in September – but I'm sure she and Rupert will sort something out before then,' Fran said encouragingly. It seemed best not to mention Babette's quest for a career change. 'At least Mum can go home this weekend, can't she? If the repairs are finished on time.'

Neville confirmed that the repairs were finished, and Leonora's social worker was taking the occupational therapist over to check the bungalow tomorrow.

'That's great, then. How's Clive?'

Neville said Clive was fine and rang off.

'Poor old Neville. Three women on the rampage...' Jake shuddered ostentatiously as Fran relayed the conversation. Fran felt obscurely culpable.

'What's a rampage?' enquired Cassie.

Jake scooped her into a demonstration chase around the room which concluded when she hiccupped herself into chortling collapse and he upended her and showered kisses on her belly, still crinkled by the agony of giggles. 'Tickles!' screamed Cassie in protest and then as he desisted she ordered again 'Tickles! Tickles!'

'All women are predators,' said Jake, sliding Cassie gently to the floor.

'Even my mother?' said Fran sweetly. She meant, of course, *even me?* Jake was aware of this.

'You are not a woman,' he explained, 'You are a unicorn girl. An essential virgin, untouched by the muddy waters of living.'

'How's that, then? I simply prance above them?'

'I have no idea. It's part of your magical charm that no-one knows.' He stroked her sleek reproachful mane. Fran trembled.

At the end of the week Fran and Jake treated Cassie to a pub supper at her request. The pub they chose specialised in baked potatoes with amazing fillings and had a big garden full of families with children of all ages playing on wooden adventure toys. The evening was warm and the amethyst sky darkened slowly into grey. It was late when they got back and Fran bustled Cassie gently into bed.

'I think we're home and dry,' said Jake lazily to Fran, though he was actually half-dozing in the bath.

Cassie giggled in the doorway.

'What's she doing?' Jake wanted to know.

'I'm doing my teeth,' said Cassie, in her busy voice, bustling in. 'Fran forgot.'

'Go away, Cass.'

'What's that?'

'Take her away, Fran,' said Jake, looking round for a flannel to conceal the object of her scrutiny.

'Don't be grumpy, Jake,' Fran said, dropping a sponge splashily.

'It's nothing to smirk about, Fran. That's called exposure.'

'She's your daughter, darling.'

'Exactly. I don't want anyone's daughter exposed to, and I certainly don't want anyone exposing themselves to my daughter.'

On Sunday, while Fran was packing Cassie's case and Cassie was filling her fluffy Eeyore back-pack with pictures and picnic bits ready for the journey home, the phone rang. Neville was sounding rather more cheerful. The O.T. had approved the bungalow, provided Leonora were not left on her own. Gwen had withdrawn her previous opposition to Polo, and Neville was to take Leonora over after Sunday lunch. Would Fran come over to settle her in?

'It's a bit difficult. Selene's collecting Cassie in the afternoon, I'd really rather be here to say goodbye. Can't Gwen go?'

Neville said that Gwen wasn't keen.

'Not keen? She used to go to the bungalow every week – she was the one keeping an eye on the repairs. Why not go now?'

No reason was forthcoming but after some background altercation Neville's voice came back on the phone to say that Gwen and Babette would both accompany him on his mission.

At around two Neville phoned again in panic. The gardener had disappeared. True to his word, Polo had stayed to the end of the month and then left. The bungalow was empty.

'I'll come over,' said Fran resignedly.

'What can you do?' Jake objected.

'Shit knows. But I don't want a family row. I haven't really done anything to help all week.'

Fran drove to the bungalow illegally fast hoping to be back before Cassie had left but she was not back when Selene arrived.

'You've missed Fran by inches' said Jake. 'Would you like to stay and meet her?'

'Stay, stay!' said Cassie, and burst into tears. 'Stay with Daddy. Stay with Fran. Fran, Fran, I want my Fran.'

Selene smiled bleakly and said that she thought she would rather be off, thanks.

'Don't worry about the tears,' said Jake smugly. 'She was like that with me at first,' and Selene said she was aware of Cassie's foibles, thanks. Thanks, anyway.

'It's unbelievable' Fran told Jake when she arrived home. For by the time Fran reached the bungalow there was no need to do anything except say, 'Oh, good'. Matters had been resolved. Babette was to remain at the bungalow as Leonora's companion.

Neville was placid as he informed his sister of this outcome. Gwen was still agitated about what she termed Babette's Plight. 'Who will look after Babette while her arm heals?'

'For goodness sake,' said Leonora, 'I will look after Babette. She will look after me. All aid is reciprocal, that is the basis of community.'

'Predator and prey,' said Neville enigmatically.

'D'you think they'll be alright?' Fran had asked as she waved her farewells, irritated by the unnecessariness of her call-out.

'Oh, I expect so,' said Neville easily. 'If not, she said she'll fax me.'

'Mum doesn't have a fax,' said Fran.

Neville mused. 'Possibly a joke.' he conceded.

'I met Leonora's social worker in town on Friday' Jake remembered lazily that evening. 'She was talking about her People. People – with needs, people – with disabilities. It's this PC thing, isn't it? Why is it suddenly a hanging offence to say mongols?'

'Because they're not. Mongols come from Mongolia. You're being boring, Jakey.'

She poured another glass of wine. They were sitting at the rustic garden table where only yesterday Cassie had assiduously crayoned in her Sleeping Beauty colouring book. Beyond the flower beds and roses, sunset seeped through the woodland. Portishead was on the CD. *Nobody loves me like you*, Jake hummed. His azure eyes disrobed Fran slowly.

Fran was edgy at the mention of Mandy. Fran did not have Jake's instinctive disdain for networks of care. Her mother was not yet quite eighty, she could go on for another dozen years. More, even, Fran thought, making allowance for

Leonora's capricious nature. She pictured her mother receiving congratulations on her longevity from Buckingham Palace, signed by whichever King then reigned, mumbling querulously about the absurdity of monarchy as her arthritic fingers fumbled to open the envelope. Or perhaps there would be no king. Leonora would live to see the monarchy dethroned, England a republic. 'She'll outlive us all' Jake had said once, joking. Now Fran was beginning to wonder. Would she spend her sixtieth birthday spooning baby-food into Leonora's toothless mouth while Gwen, now iron grey, pursed her lips and said, *'I told you so. The Home won't take her now, she's beyond it. She needs twenty-four hour care. You should have listened to me.'* Fran knew how much they all needed Mandy to care for her People. Long live the unpraised servants in the palace of Decrepitude, thought Fran fervently.

'We're going to have to take Leonora seriously, you know,' Fran said to Jake, long after he had relaxed into other notions entirely.

'Of course we are.'

'We can't just leave her, like we have been doing.'

'We'll visit,' Jake promised.

'Even with Babette there?'

'We don't want to break off relations,' Jake murmured gently, though he did add, 'breaking off shoulder blades will do, in her case, for a start.'

Fran laughed.

Fran laughed, but she was not really amused. She felt marginalised and bewildered. Her mother and her friend, both seeking refuge, had both found it with Gwen. Gwen! Fran's sense of her own failure was somehow compounded by the fact that Gwen had been their hostess and provider. There had been Cassie to consider, of course, but had Cassie really made any difference? Babette was already alienated, dismissed with minimal subtlety, and Fran suspected that to please Jake she would have found reasons to reject her mother too. *The isolation – the steep stairs.* Fran felt meagre-spirited and abashed. It occurred to her that this feeling was partly Jake's fault.

Jake was insensitive about some things. Like mothers, and friends. Women in general. *My sister died*, he said. He had never explained.

So Fran laughed when Jake joked about breaking off shoulder blades, but only limply.

19   Grass

Gwen had begun her redecorating that Sunday, as soon as they returned from installing Leonora and Babette at the bungalow.

Neville was sitting with his feet up on the beige leather settee, which was now smothered entirely with a white sheet. He was in the position he adopted for viewing television although Gwen had unplugged it while the skirting dried.

Neville had not yet adjusted to the absence of screen image and was having a cigarette while he decided what to do instead. Vaguely his focus shifted aloft. Gwen was patiently working into the corner of the alcove with orange paint. Was it orange? It looked orangey. A dusky pinky kind of orange. Rather nice. Gwen was humming something faintly familiar. Gwen looked rather nice, too.

Neville caught the falling end of his cigarette, mostly, and held it cupped carefully like the ashes of his forefathers. He wondered whether to indicate to Gwen that there was need for a suitable receptacle since she usually provided one at this point in the manoeuvre, but decided against it. He looked round cautiously but the ashtrays were all in the kitchen, washed up and put away. Neville let his hand drop to the carpet and coaxed the particles of ash beneath the settee. They bounced slightly on the high pile but eventually dispersed. He looked at Gwen, whose third eye was usually alert to such movements. She was still painting.

'You're making rather a nice job of that,' said Neville.

Gwen turned with a smile that made him think of scones and honey. Now Neville recognised the tune she was humming. It wafted from carefree fields of long ago, smelling of long grass and cream soda. Happiest days of my life, Neville thought, and he joined in quietly with the words of the old scouting song. *Ging gang goolie goolie goolie goolie watcha, ging gang goo, ging gang goo.*

'Clive out?' he suggested, and Gwen nodded. 'He is taking

those tablets your mother left behind to the bungalow. She said she didn't need them but I thought it best to send them on. Clive didn't mind; he said he meets his friends at that pub by the canal sometimes on Sundays.'

'How does he get there?' Neville wondered. Despite the substantial boots, he did not associate his son with country walks.

'One of his friends gives him a lift, I suppose. You know Clive, he never tells me anything.'

Gwen supposed correctly. Babette, browsing in her new quarters, heard the throaty snarl of a big bike on the canal path and then voices in Leonora's kitchen. She quietly slid closed the mahogany drawer of the bureau and went to join them.

'Just checking you're not dead, aged one,' said Clive, kissing his grandmother on the top of the head. He noticed Babette watching and became sulky.

'As you see, I am well provided for.' Leonora spoke serenely, leaving her spidery hand on her grandson's arm briefly. Babette remained in the kitchen doorway. The motorcycle outside continued to thrum.

'Who brought you?' she asked.

'A friend.'

'Someone with better wheels than mine.'

'Yes. Got to go, now.'

Babette followed Clive outside. 'You must be happy now you've got your room at home back?' she said.

Irritation flickered Clive's bland gaze. 'I'm not fussed,' he said.

'I know what's troubling you,' said Babette quietly.

Clive continued to regard her with vague expressionless distaste.

'It's what they haven't told you, Clive, isn't it?'

Clive stared with awful fascination. His face became opaque and childlike.

'What?' he said at last, as if the word was dredged from him.

'My poor boy. Secrets are better in the open. You should talk to Gwen.'

'What?'

'Tell her you want to know who your real parents are. Clive, surely you must have realised? You were adopted.'

Babette's lunging bear-hug enclosed him. Sequins scratched his bare arms and folds of fabric shrouded him. Clive swayed, speechless, but did not resist.

20   Bad Manners

Fran had taken the week after Cassie's visit off work. She and Jake talked vaguely about getting a last-minute holiday deal – taking a midweek break, in Amsterdam, or Barcelona – but the sumptuous sun deterred them, confirming that their own idyllic home was the best place to spend summer. 'People are paying vast sums for cottages like this,' Jake reminded Fran as they picnic-breakfasted late, listening dreamily to the trickling stream and the sensuous singing of the birds – 'for cottages not half as good, in locations not nearly as nice. Or touring in search of fabulous settings like this, having to camp or put up at bed-and-breakfasts.' Jake assumed the persona of a strident landlady with specific instructions for bathroom management, waiting for Fran's quiet, slightly childlike, laughter and then kissing her throat and her warm soft arms.

Perhaps Fran should visit her mother. This was one of the reasons she had given Don Glossop when requesting her holiday time at short notice. But Leonora was back home now, settling in with Babette. Probably best to let them do this without interference. And days with Jake now were so languorous and so lovely.

'I bet you can't guess who I met while I was in Bath,' said Jake, untwisting the slender wire from the neck of the champagne he had bought in celebration of a further commission which had arrived with this morning's cheque.

Mandy, thought Fran.

'Probably not,' she agreed. She was gazing at the amber pendant, his gift, his reason – practically – for going into town in the first place. The amber stone was huge and luscious, stunning sunlight encapsulated in a huge and honeyed drip of gilded buttermilk. 'It's for you – it is you,' Jake had said, with grand simplicity. In the hall mirror Fran had regarded her sun-touched flesh and sun-kissed hair, her smooth-lidded golden-treacle eyes and impassive expression, then smiled a slow and sensuous smile, the one Jake loved. She had looped the silver thread around her neck and watched the amber nestle low on her throat on the smooth flesh, in the slight recess at the top of her sternum. 'I love it, it's delicious,' Fran had murmured, so she could not now really mention that she would have liked to have gone into town with him. She knew anyway what Jake would say. He would say 'Oh, I knew I wouldn't be long, and I thought you wouldn't want to miss your jogging.' This, with variants, was the cost of her regular run. Fran thought it a fair price, on the whole.

'It's beautiful,' she said again, slowly, and then, as Jake seemed to have forgotten his bet, 'Who did you meet?'

'Clive. Your nephew.'

Fran knew who Clive was. The brief pause was not due to aunty absent-mindedness.

'Jakey, you didn't...' Once Jake had bought some cannabis from Clive. Not on the street, but in the house, Gwen's house, right under her sister-in-law's nose, practically, except Gwen never seemed to be looking. On that occasion Fran had broken her habit of reticence to reproach Jake.

'Nothing to worry about, darling. He was on his own, and I bought him a beer.'

Fran smiled at Jake in the mirror, stroking her amber, relieved. 'Gwen's always afraid he gets into bad company.'

'He was talking about going to look for his mother. Can you believe it, he's only just found out he was adopted? They never told him. I must say, Fran, that is seriously weird.'

Fran frowned at the pale woman in the mirror with the big yellow stone blazing at her neck. She felt suddenly tempted to snatch it off. 'Clive isn't adopted' she said.

'I always suspected as much.'

'Jake, Clive is not adopted. Don't you think I would know?'

'Families don't know everything, Fran. My brother's wives don't know about my sister.'

Fran hesitated, sidetracked briefly by this glimpse. She wanted to say, *That's different, because they weren't wives at the time.* But then she thought, neither do I. I know nothing of Jake's family or his family secrets. Why not? Then she thought, what do I know of Gwen's secrets, either? She felt bleak and dismayed.

'How did Clive find out? Did he say?'

'It came out last week, apparently, while Leonora was staying.'

'And Babette was, too.' Fran spoke wryly.

Jake shuddered histrionically and tipped the bubbling froth deftly into two glasses.

'Don't talk about that woman. You'll sour the champagne. You seem surprised about Clive.'

Fran filtered her feelings carefully. Here was sun and champagne, and a gift of glowing amber. Jake had not noticed any edge in her voice. Luckily. She said lightly 'I'm not so surprised you met Clive, anyway. He does live in Bath.'

'Not now. He walked out. He's living in a bender near King Arthur's Mound now. Cheers, darling.'

Fran lifted her glass and reciprocated cheerlessly. She smiled at Jake through the eye of the golden bubbles and resolved to visit Babette for a talk.

Leonora was dozing in front of the television when Fran called. The conservatory buzzed with idly circling flies drowned out by the droning of the Grand Prix. Babette, her arm still strapped in a sling which now looked distinctly grubby, appeared from the recesses of the bungalow as Fran stepped in. Fran remembered her last visit, when Polo sat in the kitchen examining his runes. Everything had seemed somehow tidier then. The irrational thought flipped into her mind that Babette had for some reason drugged her mother.

'Hi,' said Fran. She ran her hand under her hair, wiping the warm sweat from her neck and trying to find a suitable expression. A placatory smile sneaked hopefully into the corners of her mouth. After all, there was no need to quarrel with Babette. She just wanted to get to the bottom of this curious tale about Clive.

'The quilt seems to be nearly finished,' Fran said, nodding towards the billowing mound on the table and across the floor.

'It's not a quilt.'

'Oh. I mean, hanging. Only the backing to complete? The pictures all look done.'

'They are.'

'They're, um, really amazing. Is there any sort of... scale?'

Babette shook her head. 'Art is not like life,' she said. Fran examined the jets over East Timor and wondered how to come to the point.

'What on earth is Leonora watching?' she asked at length. The question was clearly unnecessary and Babette made no reply as the grinding sound of racing cars continued to overlay the sunny afternoon.

Fran filled the kettle. 'Tea?' she said, brightly. She did not usually preempt offers of hospitality in her mother's bungalow, but today everything seemed different.

Babette continued to watch Fran with her arms folded.

'Where's Jake? Doesn't he come visiting any more now?'

'Of course he does. I just popped out on my own to pick up some things at work, and decided to come on here.'

Babette's indifferent smile implied disbelief. Fran, aware of the evasion in her explanation, felt irritated. It was perfectly reasonable to decide to drop in at the bungalow without telling Jake. After all, he comes and goes too. They were both free agents. This was her family, and Fran wanted to be clear on the facts before she got into an argument with Jake. Not that they would argue, of course. If Jake was right, Fran would confirm it. And if he was mistaken, she would be tactful.

She smiled limply at Babette and poured water on the dark tea leaves. A pungent scent, slightly oriental, intensely aromatic, released itself into the atmosphere. Fran swirled the pot slowly.

Babette sat heavily, leaning her elbows on the table and cupping her chin in her hands. She said, still staring intently at Fran. 'Your precious Jake. Porcelain Jake – touch him, he'll break.'

It occurred to Fran that Babette was sounding a little crazy. She twanged the hot metal teapot sharply down, hoping to rouse her mother. She wanted to break this uneasy rapport that felt both hostile and conspiratorial. Abruptly she found words for her real mission at the bungalow.

'What's all this about Clive? Did you tell him he was adopted?'

Babette's head was tilted sideways now and her eyes were bright. She looked to Fran like an exotic bird of prey.

'Don't you think he has a right to know?'

Fran lifted the pot to pour. This was not so straightforward after all; it was beginning to feel like some curious moral maze.

'I don't think the issue of rights is that simple, Babette. You've rather begged the question of whether you had the right, as an outsider, to interfere at all.'

"Well, if 'insiders' aren't prepared to speak out, someone has to. By your ethics, no child would ever be rescued from abuse and taken into care.'

'Those are entirely different situations!' Fran splashed scalding tea on her hand and swore briefly. 'How can you equate protecting an abused child with throwing a bombshell like that at Clive? And how do you know, anyway, that it's true? Who told you in the first place? I never knew.'

'Gwen.'

Fran's hand was shaking. She put the teapot down. 'Gwen never told you that.'

'Not in so many words. She hinted. I told you before, Fran, silence can be very articulate. Gwen tells me things in her evasions.'

Déjà-vu, thought Fran. She remembered something Jake said about a sense of déjà-vu when Babette was around. She has an aura of psychic noise so intense she blurs the edges of reality, he had said.

'So. Nobody told you. But from Gwen's hints and evasions, you decided Gwen has a secret, and that her secret is Clive.'

'Leonora has confirmed it. And Neville. You forget I have done a counselling course,' said Babette smugly.

Tears strained at Fran's eyes. My mother, my brother. Secrets and lies.

'Why are you doing this, Babette? Ganging up with Gwen, excluding me?'

'Listen to yourself. You sound like a kid in the playground.'

Fran put her cup down and got up. The racing cars on the television whined on. She wandered to the window and said, with her back to Babette, 'But Gwen is absolutely not your sort of person.'

Babette gave a little grunting laugh. 'What would you know about Gwen's hidden depths? You're one of those optimists who always sees liquid left in the glass, even when it's all draining away. You always see the superficial in people – you ignore their inner turbulence. A slick, slipshod way to live, in my view.'

Fran turned back. She kept her voice calm. 'So it was an entirely moral decision, Babette, to tell your hostess's son he's not really her child at all?'

'Hostess? You dare to talk about my morality when your rules are bourgeois manners and Little Princess posturing. Make up your mind what I did wrong. Did I grass Gwen up, or forget to pass the Mint Thins?'

Fran winced, lacerated. All her life she had avoided rows, and now that she had been precipitated into the middle of one, she had no idea how to get out. *If I were you I wouldn't start from here* counselled a dry voice in her mind. Injustice welled into something close to anger. This, she thought, is the woman I have defended and now she turns on me.

Babette's last fierce words seemed to be resonating around her in a sudden silence. Fran realised abruptly that this was true. The television was quiet, the screen blank. Leonora with her fingers still firmly gripping the remote control now stood in the doorway peering at her daughter.

'Hello dear,' said Leonora.

Fran flushed with relief. She crossed into the living-room and greeted her mother with her usual light kiss on top of her head. Leonora's hair was dressed differently today, she noted, gathered up behind her head in a black velvet scrunch band. It was the way Fran had shown her mother at the Home.

She fetched the tray of tea and kneeled by her mother's chair.

'Leonora, do you remember that photo of Clive on the beach you used to say looked so like Neville when he was that age?'

'Of course I do. I have a picture of Neville taken at Tenby, on the summer of his seventh year.'

'So they did look alike as children?' Fran looked up to check that Babette was listening. 'That didn't surprise you?'

'Not at all. Caucasian children on a sandy beach inevitably look similar in a photograph taken on a sunny day.'

Babette laughed. Fran persisted.

'Can I see the photos?'

Leonora looked cunning. 'I have been having something of a turn-out. I doubt if I can put my hands on them at this moment.'

'They don't look very alike now. It's hard to see any family resemblance.'

Leonora looked noncommittal and did not respond. Fran took a deep breath. 'I mean, is my nephew really a blood relation?'

Leonora's expression of vague indifference intensified and her voice took on a reproving tone. 'Your brother asked me to regard Clive as my natural grandchild. That is what I have always done.'

They finished their tea and Fran looked at her watch and explained that she had to go. Babette, triumphant, followed her to the back door.

'Goodbye, then,' said Fran coolly. She had wanted to leave without a word to Babette but habit overcame her. Babette repeated the salutation smiling, mimicking her formal tone, and then said to Fran's departing back, 'Don't worry about Jake. Nothing happened.'

Fran stopped involuntarily. 'I'm not worried. Why should I?'

'No reason. Twins are often strange, aren't they.'

Babette's satisfied smile hung in Fran's head like the disembodied grin of a Cheshire cat as she drove home. Jake was in the garden.

Fran found a bottle of white wine in the fridge and poured a glass. She was still physically shaking from Babette's attack. It seemed utterly mysterious. Fran had sometimes been in arguments where her positivism was attacked as naive idealism – sometimes even by Jake – but Babette's savage critique stunned her. Fran could not conceive how her innocuous philosophy could provoke such clawing. All she wanted to do was find and follow her path by focussing on love. To concentrate on filling the canvas of her life with golden moments, keeping careful outlines around any turbulent passions, and painting every moment with clarity to create, and colour, the life she chose.

She drank her wine and looked up at her Klimt painting, her inspiration and icon. She thought about Babette's hanging, overloaded with angry polemic, grabbed from debris and random scraps. She poured another glass and took it out to Jake.

Why didn't you tell me your dead sister was your twin?

No. Silly to ask something like that while still upset. Perhaps Jake was already regretting telling Babette. Fran decided she would not let Babette spoil their day.

'What's the matter?'

It was nearly midnight. Fran and Jake were naked in the big bed. A warm night breeze ruffled the flowery curtains ever so slightly. Jake lay back, puzzled, as Fran turned her face away from his caresses.

Fran could no longer dissemble.

'Did you fuck Babette?'

Jake sat up again.

'I wouldn't mind if you had,' said Fran bravely. 'I'd just like to know.'

'You wouldn't mind?' His tone was flat yet angry, as though she had hurt him at some unreachably deep level. Fran tried to find his muted anger reassuring.

'I'm not jealous,' she said. She had aimed for light and reassuring, but her voice sounded tight, and like it was someone else's.

Jake opened the bedside drawer and withdrew a packet of Camel cigarettes, lighting one before he looked up. Almost tiredly, he said 'Love without jealousy is impossible.'

'I only meant...'

'Well I didn't.' he said shortly.

'It's the lie that would come between us, not the act,' Fran persisted. Her words were quiet, and her courage just about reached her lips before it faltered; her eyes would not look at him. 'Love shouldn't be possessive,' she persisted, 'I'd just like to think you'd tell me.'

'I wouldn't tell you,' said Jake. 'But I didn't.'

'You could tell me. It's the real you I love, Jake, not a sanitised idea of you.'

'So love the real liar.' said Jake, and he turned away.

Fran was bewildered. She was offering the purest, truest, love she had, and somehow it had become muddied.

'I told you Babette would come between us. Why can't you trust me,' said Jake bitterly.

Why should I, when you've just told me you would lie to me? thought Fran forlornly. She didn't say that.

'Fuck Babette,' said Jake angrily.

Fran laughed nervously. She didn't want their first row to be about Babette. But it was.

He called her cold and passionless and she cried. Love has nothing to do with jealousy, Fran said through her smeary tears. Love is about everything, Jake insisted – every human feeling. It's not just glitzy gold paintings, and jazz, and sunshine – it's sadness and loneliness too, and black despair. Jake dragged in the Klimt painting from the hall. 'What is it that's so important to you about this thing?' Jake said. 'It's got no real emotion, just ornate patterning and superficial charm.'

Fran stared at the black slits that sleet across the golden painting until her eyes were glazed with tears. The pain was terrible. Not the realisation that Jake saw their painting in quite another way from her, but something even worse. He had neither understood nor shared her feelings, and he had lied about it. Jake had lied to her about this quintessential symbol of their emotional twin-souling, and that seemed to Fran the worst betrayal of all.

But next morning they had forgiven each other; before the dawn they had found familiar ecstasy and Fran was glad, because their first row was over and Babette had not split them up. Babette was quite powerless after all.

21   Lost Boys

Gwen had been in turmoil all week. It was no new thing for Clive to quit the house for days on end, often ungraciously and abruptly. But this time was different. Something strange and unsettling appeared to have happened at the bungalow on Sunday. Clive had arrived back white-faced and shaking with emotion. He hurried upstairs to his room, collected belongings apparently at random, took his sleeping-bag and departed. Gwen, poised on the stepladder with a brushful of pimento one-coat satin finish, stared openmouthed at the commotion. Neville called from the settee, 'Where's the fire?' but Clive only growled something unintelligible and slammed out.

It was the unintelligible growl that frightened Gwen more even than the banged door and the snarl of the motorbike accelerating illegally fast up the street. It sounded something like 'real mother'. In fact, it sounded exactly like 'real mother'. And as dawn released her from a wretchedly sleepless night, Gwen knew that her son's words were not unintelligible at all. Clive had shouted 'Fuck you both. I'm going to find my real mother.'

And Clive had not yet returned. Gwen often told him he treated the house like a hotel and now she feared he had come to the end of his booking. Without her elderly mother-in-law, without her incapacitated friend, and with not even a recalcitrant teenage son to tend, Gwen's week had dragged. There was only Belinda now, and Belinda really did treat the house like a hotel, apart from paying no tariff of course. Gwen had taken to standing in front of the fridge looking mournfully within, as Clive often used to do, though unlike Clive she marvelled at the amount of food there available and unrequired. She flicked channels on the television, as she had so often begged him not to, trying somehow to simulate the feeling of vague distraction which she now knew as the scent of his presence, and missed achingly.

Clive had disowned her, and Gwen did not know why. She phoned Leonora but Clive was not there. She wanted to tell Babette her son had rejected her, but a lingering uncertainty over etiquette prevailed. How long a friendship is required before asking someone to listen to such a confession? How soon after injury inflicted on the listener? Should the plaster be off before she heaped more on Babette's shoulders? Gwen thought it should. Finally, in desperation she called Fran at work and asked if she could come for lunch, nothing fancy, just a nice salad. Fran arrived around twelve and found Gwen sitting on the stairs holding one of Clive's trainers and sniffling.

'Fran, how nice!' cried Gwen, wiping her peach-like cheeks of all tell-tale streaks, and she bustled her into the kitchen. 'How nice you could come – no, no problem. I just thought it would be nice to have one of our talks.'

'What talks?' said Fran. She was prowling around in a long lacy cardigan over one of her long-skirted frocks, smears of ochre charcoal along the ribbing of the cuffs.

Gwen washed the lettuce. Rose-rimmed sprays with rounded edges like tender oak leaves, tiny fronded sprays of green like crisp moss. 'Fresh this morning, from my friend who has an allotment,' Gwen said gaily but Fran ignored the provenance. 'What's going on, Gwen?'

Gwen placed the lettuce meticulously in the metal salad shaker and agitated it carefully over the sink. She laid each leaf on a clean cloth. She ate one absently as she told Fran her tale, which as far as Fran could decipher boiled down to the fact that Clive had claimed she was a fraud and then disappeared from her life.

'And the Peace Hanging has gone too. They are finishing off the backing at the bungalow.' Gwen spoke bleakly of her double bereavement.

Fran gave a gurgling, slightly manic, laugh. She said inanely, 'Bit of a double whammy, as raids go. A ragbag of scraps, and your son.'

'Sun?' Gwen sounded bemused. Her face behind the foundation seemed to be filling with something slow and seeping, like a paper towel self-saturating. Her eyes looked smeary. 'Oh, son.' Then, simply, 'Yes. That's what if feels like, Fran. My sun has gone. Neville used to say, he will come through, and I always thought, these teenage years are tiresome but one day he will talk to me again. He will hug me, like he used to when he was a tiny boy. I only wanted him to be happy. I wanted him to get his exams, and a job, because I thought then he would be happier. And now he's gone, and I can see how none of those things I nagged him about matter at all. And I can't understand how I ever thought differently. It's like one of those Magic Eye pictures. When you suddenly see something clear-edged and certain in the chaos, you wonder why you couldn't realise it before.'

This is the moment, Fran thought. This is where I have to say something caring and honest and compassionate, and show her I'm not hurt by her secrecy.

'I suppose it's the same for Clive,' she heard herself saying. 'Being told your mother isn't really your mother is something that won't go away.'

Gwen sat heavily on the breakfast bar stool, her mouth a haggard black hole of surprise and dismay. She began to pick at her pale elbows with a kind of fearful desperation. Fran noticed there were red abrasions and tiny blue bruises there already. She wondered if Gwen had any special tablets for this kind of situation and after a few moments as Gwen was still drawing noisy shallow breaths, she fetched a glass and filled it with tap water.

Gwen got up to empty the glass down the sink and refill it with Evian and Fran decided tablets would not after all be required.

Then Gwen said, 'But why would anyone tell him that?' and Fran realised with a lumpy feeling that her sister-in-law had not seen Babette's guiding hand in Clive's departure. Gwen seemed even more confused than Fran was. 'Why would anyone lie to him like that?' Gwen went on, and now Fran felt even more confused than Gwen clearly was.

'He said he was going to look for his real mother – Gwen, you've just told me that yourself. What did you think he meant?'

'Well I didn't know. That's why I phoned you –'

'Gwen, what's not true? How not true? Tell me, Gwen!'

Fran pulled the other stool close to Gwen and tried to take one of her hands. It was limp and trembled at her touch. 'Clive is my child,' she said. 'I am his mother. Why didn't he ask to see his birth certificate? I have it safe in my jewellery drawer.'

Bloody Babette, Fran thought. She probably saw it there, and that's what gave her the idea of mischief making. She's a Loki, a menace who tricks people into hurting other people, like that blind god who killed Baldur the beautiful son.

Gwen was still talking. 'If he had asked me about it all, I would have told him,' she whimpered, 'but he never did.'

'Asked you what about what all?' Fran demanded. She tried to ask kindly and softly, but it definitely came out like a demand, and Gwen looked up wretchedly, twisting her handkerchief. It's like drawing teeth in a blackout, Fran thought: no wonder Clive buggered off to get his answers somewhere else.

She tried again more gently. 'From what you've just said, Babette is either mistaken or else deliberately lied. If he is your natural son, why all the confusion?'

'Artificial insemination,' said Gwen limply. 'But a perfectly natural birth, I assure you. I had five stitches.'

And the donor? Fran almost whispered the question, but Gwen, picking absently at the damp lettuce leaves, needed no prompting now.

'Neville has a very low sperm count. He had various tests... they had to fiddle about a bit. To get things right. Very embarrassing for him, actually. And I was injected in the end. By quite a nice lady doctor, as I remember. But to be honest, I don't remember much. I've rather drawn a veil over all that. We both have, I think.'

'Is Neville Clive's father?' said Fran at last.

'Of course he is.'

'So why did he ask Leonora to regard Clive as his son?'

'Because he is,' said Gwen.

'Then, why all the mystery – why the secrecy? What's the problem? Gwen, what is the matter?'

Tears were rolling down Gwen's face now, unstoppable. They

seemed to seep from the saturated crevices all around her eyes, they rolled down her cheeks heavy and round like cascading pearls. Fran stared at Gwen's drenched exhausted face and thought *oh god, this is where I'm supposed to hug her*, and then found she was already leaning forward to do so. Gwen sat lumpily in her tableau of grief while Fran fondled her flaccid arms. She tried to rock her. Gwen was so unresisting they both nearly fell. They separated and straightened themselves, and Fran got up and filled the kettle and switched it on.

'It was after,' Gwen was whispering. Fran stood very still watching the little red light at the base of the kettle.

'What? What happened after, Gwen?'

'Nothing.'

Fran unhooked two mugs from the pine mug-rack and placed them by the kettle. It was beginning to hiss. Amazingly quick, these cordless.

'You don't have to say any more.'

'That's it, that's what happened. Nothing. I was celibate for seventeen years.'

Celibate. The kettle was nearly boiling now. Celibate was not actually a word that held terror for Fran. Quite a pretty word – like celandine. Something compact and starry and self-sufficient. Before Jake, Fran would often choose celibacy from the tempting array of life's possibilities. *Celibate* makes her feel almost nostalgic for days when her thighs were not constantly tingling, her labia not always slightly sticky, her mind not somehow distracted by confused longing.

'Celibate,' Fran repeated as she poured the boiling water onto coffee granules (decaff ersatz was all she could find and now was not the moment for enquiries or for rummaging). Hardly the worst thing in the world, though, is it, she thought.

Gwen was sniffling, pink-eyed. To her the word clearly carried no inner glow. It was a hidden shame, like syphilis. Fran had a wild impulse to say *No problem with the wet patch then?* She bit her lip and brought over the coffee and sat beside Gwen again.

Celibate. Such a silly word, like *celery* or *halibut*. Fran thought of the double-bedded room upstairs where her brother had sprawled and slept for seventeen years beside Gwen, thought of Gwen finishing her tasks and nightly trite chatter, screwing the tops on her jars of nourishing cream, settling beside him for another pristine night. *Rejected*, thinks Fran.

Rejected is a bad word. Like *dejected*, or *discarded*. Fran pictured Gwen night after night in her nightie back-to-back with his big warm body, and she mentally counted the hours of rejection Gwen had silently absorbed. Say seven each night, seven nights each week, forty-nine times fifty-two. Eight hundred and something. Times seventeen. Hours, that is. Gwen probably counted the minutes some nights.

Fran put her mug down and put her arm round Gwen again and this time took her weight more strongly and Gwen crumpled less clumsily against her. They stayed there for a while rocking together.

'You won't tell Jake,' said Gwen piteously.

Fran remembered Jake saying *What Gwen needs is a good shag.*

'No. I won't tell Jake. Actually, we had a tiny tiff last night.' It seemed unnecessary to say that Clive's disappearance had in a sense caused it, so Fran added quickly, 'Not serious but, you know, our first.'

Gwen nodded indifferently.

'He has told me where Clive is staying, though. He's at that bender village by King Arthur's Mound. I think some of the travellers went there after The Eviction.' Fran almost expected Gwen to leap up crossing her fingers as if hexing vampires at the mention of The Eviction, so she added quickly, 'because of their children doing so well at the local school.'

Gwen was already getting up and tidying her stool under the table. 'Can we go now?' she said.

'Well, I think you should talk to Neville first,' said Fran. 'And I ought to get back to work — never mind about lunch. I'll call you tonight.'

Fran got as far as her car before shame at her prevarication overtook her and she went back to find Gwen sitting exactly where she left her, surrounded by the limp lettuce leaves.

'OK, let's go now,' said Fran. 'At least we can find the place and suss it out.' She called Don to say she wouldn't be back till later that afternoon. She did not phone Jake.

They drove around the lanes near King Arthur's Mound for nearly an hour before they finally tracked down the bender village.

'That looks like it, over there,' said Fran. She pulled the Clio over to the side of the road and switched off the engine.

Gwen looked where Fran was pointing. Slightly higher than the hedge-line, several smooth blue roofs rounded like small biospheres were visible. 'There's a windmill, too. See, between the trees.'

Gwen took a deep breath.

'Why don't we walk down there and take a look,' Fran suggested, indicating a narrow but well-trodden path through the woods towards the field. Gwen was looking nervous, as if she might flag up the notion of such a venture requiring a man, but she did not.

They set off together along the path. Gwen was in light trousers and sensible shoes but Fran's floral frock had a long skirt. As she took her sister-in-law's hand to steady her over a rugged ivy root Fran felt for a surreal moment like Rosalind and Celia in the Forest of Arden.

'Have you thought what you'll say if you see him?' Fran asked as they picked their way along the dry mud route towards the blue roofs – 'don't get upset, Gwen, or you may do more harm than good.' Gwen said no, she did not know what she would say. 'Perhaps I won't need to say anything,' she said. 'I just want to be sure he is happy.'

What did Gwen expect to find at the bender community? A troglodyte village swarming with dirt-smeared squat figures picking lice from each other's matted hair and conversing in primitive grunts? Dancing dervishes with glinting rings in every orifice whirling to discordant jungle music while wind-powered psychedelic lights strobed the woodlands? Naked babies whispering in the reeds?

No. Of course not. Or, perhaps. A few naked babies perhaps. That would be quite sweet, really.

But the village was orderly, the blue globes glinting in the afternoon sunlight. They were quite big close up, arranged around a central circle of grass and connected by a network of paths. Each separate habitation was surrounded by small cultivated area of herbs and vegetables. Red blossom of runner beans glowed from a row of canes; purple flowering sage scented the air. No-one seemed to be around apart from a small child in a bri-nylon cardigan seated in the centre of the circle playing with a plastic tub of water.

'There must be someone caring for the child,' said Gwen looking around. She was hesitating now. The determination which had launched her into an anarchic wilderness had faltered at the realisation this was simply someone else's home.

'This central area is visible from all the doorways,' Fran pointed out. 'They probably all look out for it. There's probably people watching us now, wondering what we're doing. Hello?' she added cautiously, but no-one emerged.

'I can hear someone over there,' said Gwen, and she plodded on along the narrow path towards the woodland where, as they came over the rise, a large lake could be seen. Here, causing the sound of shouts and splashes Gwen had heard, the figures of three men were distinctly visible silhouetted against the sunlight. They were emerging from the water and all three seemed exhausted. Two were aiding the third who appeared particularly unsteady.

'In no state to go swimming,' Gwen commented as the central figure was clearly laughing as he was half-dragged, half-carried, back to the shallows of the lake. The women stopped at the muddy edge, shielding their eyes from the sun, as the three men continued to approach. Two of the men were young and fully dressed though shoeless; the bedraggled figure between them was older, portly and bleary in gaping boxer shorts.

'Good gracious Neville,' said Gwen.

The man stumbling and dangling between the younger men grinned happily. He flicked some debris from his mud-begrimed chest.

'My lovely wife,' said Neville, and then, as if introducing them to each other, 'My wonnerful wonnerful son.'

'I'm afraid Dad's lost his glasses,' said Clive. 'We tried to stop him but he was determined to go for a swim.'

Clive was soaked to the skin, his jeans drenched to the waist. He looked half scared and half excited. His companion, who showed no emotion other than slightly amused tolerance, appeared from his even-more-saturated appearance to have been the primary life-saver. Neville was far too burly for Clive to manage unaided.

With his head now completely shaven and his chest tattoos covered by a sopping wet teeshirt, Gwen hardly recognised the young man at first. But the aqua eyes and slow luscious smile were the same.

'Hello Polo,' said Gwen.

'Hello again,' said Polo, and as Clive looked puzzled he added, 'I'm not using that name now. I'm Hawthorn.'

'Oh. I'm sorry.'

'That's OK.'

'Your friend used to be your grandmother's gardener,' Fran clarified as Clive still looked unenlightened. And then, as someone had to say it, Fran did.

'Small world.' said Fran.

She felt that pleasantries should now extend to include acknowledgement of the fact that Polo/Hawthorn appeared to have just saved Neville's life so she helped the two youths lower him to the grass while murmuring appropriate appreciation.

'Came to see Clive. Been having a heart-to-heart,' her brother explained, waving in the general direction of his son. 'Fancied a swim.'

'We had a good chat,' Clive confirmed. 'About loads of things.'

'Myth of Sisyphus,' said Neville. He seemed to find it terribly funny.

'You're a jammy fucker, Clive,' said Hawthorn, 'I wish my mother would come searching for me.'

Gwen seemed to be taking a while to catch up with the flow of events. 'Small world,' she said faintly.

'We've done that, Mum,' said Clive. He clicked his tongue

with just a touch of familiar petulance. Gwen hugged him shamelessly.

Hawthorn announced he was going off to change. Neville located his slacks and pulled them on over his boxer shorts. They immediately began to blotch wetly.

'We'll have to go home,' said Gwen scoldingly. She took his arm. 'I was hoping to have a look round, too. Perhaps next time. Will you come back with us?' she said to Clive, 'For a few days, at least? To talk about your plans?'

Don't push it, Fran thought, but Clive said contentedly, 'I've got no fucking dry jeans, I suppose I'll have to.'

Neville was fairly easily persuaded to leave his car when Fran promised to bring him back to collect it later. Clive said to Hawthorn, 'I'll call in and see you, anyway.' They embraced, recoiled at each other's wetness, then laughed and embraced again. Neville slapped Hawthorn's' back and hugged him. Gwen shook his hand.

'Well, goodbye,' she said primly, while Fran said 'Thanks again,' and Neville said, 'Don't forget. Sisyphus.'

'He won't,' said Clive.

'What on earth was all that about, Neville?' said Gwen as they walked away.

'Sisyphus rolls his stone endlessly up the slope. These days – high-tech systems – essentially no need. Technology makes myths superfluous.'

'Well said, Dad. Especially with all those esses.'

They reached the Clio and Clive helped Fran slide Neville into the front passenger seat before climbing into the back beside his mother.

Fran told Jake about it all that evening. A hot night, though the weather forecast had threatened storms. The swifts were darting low. Flying ants invaded the room where they sat. Need some poison, said Jake. Fran did not reply. Her housework, like her mother's, tended to be guided by Buddhist principles. But she was perfectly happy – Fran remembered this later, most distinctly – that night as they discussed the gardener.

'He's a curious bloke. Quite charismatic, really. Nice looking.' Jake frowned, then altered his look to one of thoughtfulness. 'Have I met him?'

'I think you'd remember if you had. He saved Neville's life, there's no doubt about that, though I don't think Neville realises that yet. Combination of Carlsberg and cannabis, he probably thought he could walk on water.'

'And the rest. Illegal substances vital to parental bonding, are they?'

'Actually, I think that was down to the gardener too. The prodigal's return, I mean. It's more likely Clive would listen to him than to his parents. Gwen must have realised that, she seemed to have mellowed to him.'

'That's presumably because he abandoned the bungalow and so she's no longer terrified of Leonora becoming plasticine in his clutches.'

'Well, whatever, Gwen is obviously feeling less irrational about him since he left Mum's. She talks about him now as this kind of Lawrentian character, tending the earth and in tune with the seasons. She actually said Lawrentian. Most unGwenlike.'

Jake laughed meaningfully. Fran remembered her new empathy with Gwen.

'I knew what she meant,' she said serenely, 'It's nothing to do with suppressed yearning for a gamekeeper. She was suspicious of him before, in case he was trying to con Leonora into leaving him her stuff. And now she's seen him in his own setting, she knows he isn't.'

'Actually darling, that's quite as irrational as anything else Gwen has come up with. Even if he is rolling round in earth's diurnal course, with rocks and stones and trees, he's perfectly capable of flogging a bungalow.'

Fran collected the supper plates and put them in the sink. Jake poured himself another glass of wine and topped her half-finished glass. He watched her standing at the window, using the shadowy reflection as a mirror as she fiddled with some falling tendrils of hair. He waited until she finished before reaching out to pull the clip gently away and watch the tumbling hair swing out tawny and toffee-mallow across her warm shoulders.

In the long moment that tugged between them Jake thought about Fran's warm body beneath the flimsy fabric and Fran thought about her inheritance. She didn't want to, but Jake had started it.

'I don't think he is materialistic. These people have a sense of living, of being on their land, inhabiting their place. We have so much to learn from them. Town people get no real sense of their roots and culture. No, listen, Jakey, 'city life' used to mean smart and sophisticated, now it's seen as slick and superficial. Or else something degraded – 'urban blight.' These people have reclaimed the land and the air, and the pace that life should be.'

'*These people* are actually middle class hippies who've bought a bit of land from the council. They are probably very nice chaps but I don't think they epitomise the heritage from the past, the qualitative present, and the sustainable future.'

'I thought they were Convoy people?'

'Fran, your bourgeois romanticism is delightful. It's a co-operative venture. Like the Co-op.'

Fran did not like being called bourgeois, however delightful. She said uncertainly, 'Well they do have New Age travellers staying there.'

'I'm sure they do. Travellers travel around, by definition. The world is just a place to walk about in.' Jake was smiling with the amused satisfaction of a player who holds all the best cards. He loves it when I don't know things, Fran thought. Perhaps he's missing Cassie.

'There's no splendour about living in the country,' Jake was saying now, and Fran looked up, dismayed.

'Don't you like the cottage?'

'That's not what I mean. We're on mains for sewerage and water, we've got electricity, central heating, cars, cable TV. This is not country living, thank god. We have to open the curtains to know what season we're in. Would you really want the squalor of real country living?'

It occurred to Fran that what Jake had been missing all week was not Cassie but London.

The city was his element. Like a silkie shedding its seal skin, able only to dance for a while on the land before it must dive back into the airless sea, Jake needed to drive back to North London. His lungs needed the heady mix of pollutants, he needed the noise and the cross-cultural mix of ideas.

'You need a breath of stale air, from the sound of it,' she said lightly. 'Too much scent of new-mown grass and birdsong here.'

He laughed, conceding. 'You're a clever girl. I do need the city.'

'Full of traffic fumes.'

'Yes. And voices – ideas – diversity. There's not much diversity about a hollyhock.'

But I grew them from seed, thought Fran forlornly.

Babette took Gwen's call later that night. She said 'Oh,' a couple of times and then, 'Oh, well, that's alright then.'

'What was that all about?' said Leonora peevishly as Babette hung up. She was still crocheting, swathed now in a voluminous shroud of musty coloured wool, her fingers twisting and flicking like a fisherwoman whose whole life had been spent at the shore mending nets.

'Gwen. Mother's worries, children's whims,' says Babette. 'Family stuff.'

Leonora digested the summary. 'Ironic,' she said, 'All the freedom I gave Fran, and she only wanted us to be ordinary.'

'Freedom,' Babette mused breathily, then she sang *Freedom's just another word for nothing left to lose,* and Leonora added stridently 'Nothing will come of nothing, speak again.' It was quite like charades for a heady moment. Then Babette became weepy.

'Freedom – what an illusion. I gave up my child for that.'

'So did I,' said Leonora.

'But you said Fran –'

'Not Fran. Neville. My little boy. Boarding school at seven, and I've never kissed him since.' And Leonora bent her head and wept for the tiny plump boy with quivering cheeks whom she had left enfolded by a long brown corridor which smelled of

Dettol and cabbage and echoed with the shrill panic of cheerful children.

Babette walked to the window.

'This heat's getting me down,' she said. 'It's so close. We must be near thunder.'

But it was Sunday before the storm broke.

22   Accusation

So everything was alright again; everyone in their proper places and the pattern of Fran's life once more bright and clear. They had come through.

'I have to admit, it's a relief that Leonora has found someone to look after her, especially someone with, um, caring experience,' Fran said.

Fran was talking not to Jake but to Don Glossop. Strictly speaking this was one of her holidays, but Don had requested her, in her Impressing-the-Clients hat, to give some Design Input on a new series of Little Books of Big Thoughts. 'I've known Babette for a while,' Fran continued to explain. 'I used to work with her before I took this job. I don't think you've met her though.'

'Yes, we did. I saw her at that Art Society exhibition. Of course I remember your gorgeous friend.'

'Babette?'

Fran's light-chat voice had a startled edge. Another surprise. Of course, Babette has a sweet face, when she's not looking sceptical or sulky, but gorgeous? Bountiful, certainly; buttocks like the Venus of Willendorf and bosoms to smother a suckling babe. Babette can look amazing when her fiery hair swirls and curls around as though defending her vast personal space, but gorgeous? in her lumpy leggings with her Mister-Pickwick belly?

Apparently yes, for Don nodded. 'Babette, that's the name. A feast of a woman.'

'Yes,' said Fran. She thought of all the times she had assured Jake that his jealousy was absurd because she was simply not Don's type, and she felt vindicated and obscurely disappointed.

'I never really felt loved when I was a child,' Fran had unexpectedly found herself telling Don after the Big Thoughts client had departed suitably impressed and they could both remove their metaphorical hats and share out the rest of the champagne.

'People talk about their first memories and they're all about some kind of connection – someone who loved them. I don't have that. I can't talk to Jake about it because he pours out loads of stuff about how much *he* loves me, now, which is very nice but he's not listening. And I'm not really close to Babette. She never believed anything sad or bad could really happen to me – she said I was like the little princess in that story by Frances Hodgson Burnett – you know? She thinks she's a pauper and then finds out she's a rich heiress – and it turns out there were millions and millions of diamonds in the mines!'

Don said he was not familiar with the work but he took her point.

'She reckons you'll come out of everything smelling of roses because you're a babe?' he summarised. Fran blushed and thought of Jake and wondered if she had guessed already that Don saw her as a babe. The admission felt deliciously close to conspiratorial. Deliciously? No, of course not. Dangerously close, that's what it felt like. Fran pulled her gratified smile back to a prim smirk.

'But your mother didn't pay you much attention?' Don steered them back helpfully, clicking unobtrusively for another bottle of champagne, and Fran agreed gratefully. 'She wasn't horrible or anything, just indifferent. Always busy doing things for other people. Which was wonderful of her, of course, but it did leave me feeling I was less valuable and important to her than – well, anything, really. Ireland, Greenham, Antarctica. I can't even remember all the things she campaigned about. She pushed me off on some friends of hers in the country for a while too, when I was really young and, having no father, I suppose I believed from early on that no one really wanted me. And then Jake... just adored me. And I wanted to be wanted.'

'He can't be the first.' Don untwisted the slender wire and swirled the pale liquid into Fran's glass. She reached out with her fingers to indicate when he should cease the cascade but slowly and too late.

'No, well, perhaps not,' Fran conceded, sipping. 'But I used to be a bit frosty with admirers. I suppose I didn't believe they wanted the real me. Whatever that is. I never let them get close in case they rejected me too. And then Jake – he loves me, really loves me.'

'And the problem, in this case, would be...?'

'Well, that's it. I mean, it's that. I'm not used to feeling loved. I'm waiting for some great crisis – something terrible to smash it all up. A terrible storm – a tsunami. I can't shake the feeling of, suppose he decides he doesn't love me after all, suppose he rejects me. Suppose I'm simply not lovable. That's the fear.'

Don had not spent the last two hours discussing the upcoming production of Big Thoughts for nothing. 'You have nothing to fear but fear itself,' he said helpfully, topping up her glass unnecessarily. 'Confront it!'

'How? Split up because that's what I'm afraid of?'

'Nu-uh. That's not your fear. You can do endings. It's relationships you're afraid of.'

Fran put down her empty glass and picked up the serviette she had been absentmindedly pleating. She unravelled it slowly, scattering wholemeal crumbs on the white cloth.

'I don't think –' she began slowly.

'Give your inner child a hug,' Don quoted helpfully. 'Go and see your mother, before it's too late.'

'Too late for what?'

'The key to the future is in the door of the past,' Don continued sagely. 'Present moments march unstoppably like ants. Are ants unstoppable? I would imagine some kind of glue spray would probably do the job.'

They seemed to have drifted into safer waters. 'Can I go home now?' Fran said, and Don suggested a taxi. 'You can pick up the car on your evening jog.' he said, and Fran, noting the number of empty champagne bottles on the trolley, agreed.

'A man came round looking for you,' Jake greeted Fran as she arrived home. 'He wanted to wait. He's in the garden.'

Her visitor, a small man with a shaven head like a slightly furry duck egg, turned out to be Rupert. Fran's first thought was that he was very different from Babette's description, and then she realised Babette had never described him. For some reason she had pictured a tall man with staring eyes, rather like the man who sat each evening on the bench close to the factory. Someone slightly manic and volatile. This apologetically smiling man seemed essentially gentle.

'I'm really sorry to bother you,' he said, stepping back from the lemon balm he had been sniffing, 'but I've been trying, and failing, to get in touch with Babette. We've got to sort out where she wants to be staying. The house has already been reallocated for me and Milly.'

'Milly being – ?' Fran faltered. Rupert opened his wallet to show a Polaroid photograph. Fran, half-expecting a black Labrador, half-fearing an anaconda, found herself looking at the quizzical smile of a very pretty Japanese girl. 'Babette's been bombarding the answerphone the whole time I was away,' he said, 'I'm seriously worried about the balance of her mind.'

'But Babette said... I'm sorry if this is embarrassing, Rupert, but I think you should know that Babette told us that she left after losing a baby.' Fran decided not to mention the abortion rows Babette described. Their few moments' acquaintance seemed insufficient to accuse him of demanding the murder of his child.

Fran watched a line of marching red ants with concentrated attention, hoping that what she had said would be enough to forestall any awkward surmise about reunion. When she looked up, Rupert was pulling a sad reflective grimace.

'I'm not totally surprised. She's got a thing about lost boys and babies. She told me she'd had a baby that died when it was five months old, accidentally drowning in the bath.'

'Oh God! Poor Babette. What a terrible thing!'

'Well, that's what I thought. She told me all about it when I first moved in, and I felt quite protective of her. I think that was almost what started our relationship, I felt sort of privileged that she chose to share that with me. But I found out later she made it all up. The baby wasn't five months old at all, it was a five-month foetus. It was a miscarriage.'

You've told so many lies none of us knows what to believe, Babette. And now we don't really care, either. Fran rehearsed her speech as she jogged to collect her car and drive over to the bungalow with Rupert's message. She was frustrated to find Leonora in a particularly lively mood, so her challenge to Babette had to be delayed until her mother remembered a favourite gardening programme and left the kitchen abruptly.

'Actually, it was really you I wanted to see, Babette,' said Fran. 'Rupert came round this afternoon.'

Babette nodded coolly. 'I suppose he told you how we quarrelled about my dead baby.'

No, he said you quarrelled about the lies you told him about it.

Fran did not say that. She said, 'Rupert gave me a letter for you. It's the one you sent back – he asked me to persuade you to read it, and I really think you should.'

'What's it say, then?'

'Well, it's to you – he didn't tell me exactly, of course. But I know he needs to talk to you about the rental – he's offering to take on your share, actually – he just wants to get your separation on a sensible footing.'

'Oh, a sensible footing! Not like a play-house with roses round the door, then, where there's no room for real emotions.'

'Babette, I'm sorry you feel bitter, but I honestly don't understand why.'

'I know,' said Babette. The way she said it made Fran shiver. As though that was the worst part. As though not understanding was the only really unforgivable thing.

'Why didn't you tell me the truth about the baby?' Fran said into the fragile space between them.

'Because Joby was disabled. I thought you would say it was for the best.'

'You don't know that I would have said that. Because of course I wouldn't have, I would have understood – I've always stood by you. I've tried to support you –'

'Yeah? Then why are we talking about you, instead of me?'

Fran fumbled with her car keys. 'Anyway,' she said, 'I've given you the letter. I promised Rupert I would.'

Babette tore the letter slowly across. Her eyes were still fixed on Fran.

'The trouble with you, Fran, is you've never really suffered. You don't know what real pain. is. Your idea of being hurt by someone you love would be if they didn't agree with you about some bloody painting.'

A pink petal of anger flared on Fran's pale cheek. She bit her lip and said nothing.

'Why do you let her upset you?' Jake said that night.

'It was upsetting what she said about the baby. I don't know what to think now. We used to be really friendly and I never knew she'd had a miscarriage.'

'She's winding you up, Fran. Forget her.'

'But why does she keep pretending she's had a baby when she hasn't – making out that she's a mother when she isn't?'

'Because she's a screwed-up bitch. I've told you that before.'

'And I know she got that Clive thing all wrong, but Gwen does confide in her, even family stuff they've never told me.'

'Why should they tell you? Would you report to Gwen if we were trying for a baby?'

Fran was briefly distracted by the hypothesis, then admitted, 'Probably not. But I wouldn't discuss it with Babette, either. Although I suppose she'd claim to see through my translucent silence in her usual myopic way.'

Fran tried to sound breezy and satirical, but she felt hurt and threatened by Babette's grip on her family. It occurred to her that this angry antipathy between Babette and herself was nothing to do with their experiential relationship, it was driven by some deeper and more primitive connection.

She said slowly 'I think this is about children. Babette's jealous of me because Clive's my nephew – she's hostile to you because of Cassie. This is about babies.'

'Probably you're right,' Jake agreed. 'Fecundity.' He savoured the word deliciously and nuzzled her shoulder. 'Mad cow,' he murmured.

'Maybe we should seriously consider whether she's a fit companion for Leonora, Jakey.'

'She's fine there. Your mother likes her.'

'I used to like her. I used to think she was really nice,' Fran mourned.

'You could say that about anyone before you get to know them.'

Fran laughed but she was slightly hurt. Surely Jake didn't include her in this universal cynicism? His belated tolerance of Babette seemed somewhat cynical too. *Forget Babette* Jake urged again, and Fran decided to obey and to enjoy the serene and sunny days now that she and Jake were safely alone again.

Saturday afternoon. It was still hot. 'We must be close to take-off,' said Jake. He meant the refrigerator, thrumming frenetically in the kitchen. Fran kept her fridge on full cold, so wine bottles emerged swathed in a chill veil turning instantly into diadems and the salad was icy crisp. She left the window open so sun and summer scents invaded; the washed terracotta floor baked dry in minutes and the heavy air was soundless, the stream quiet, soaked to a sliver by the sun.

Sometimes, these sun-soaked days, Jake suggested they might spend the weekend in London – see an exhibition, or a play, or meet his friends. But they always stayed at the cottage. The big bed below the window waited for them, satin covered. Irresistible.

Fran lay on a beach-mat in the back garden reading. She wore nothing but her scanty cutoffs and a big brimmed sun-hat. Succulent saxophone notes dribbled from the CD player on the back windowsill. On the tray, nearby, lay the debris of coffee cups and plates with pecan crumbs. A shadow straddled her, long and gothic, then compact as Jake squatted.

Carefully Jake lifted the shady hat and disengaged the abalone comb from Fran's tawny hair and let the tresses tumble slowly onto her shoulders. Like a golden waterfall, said Jake. His hand cupped her chin. His hand smelled slightly apple-y from the shower gel. Fran breathed the warmth of his skin and closed her eyes.

'What are you reading'

'*How to make love to a negro*. By Dany Laferrière – I think it's his first novel.'

'Sounds interesting.'

'Mm. It is.'

Jake reached across to take the book. Anticipating, she surrendered. Leaned back. Listened to Miles Davis in the sun. She knew Jake would scan briefly, avidly, and soon he would start to read aloud to her. Erotic outrageous extracts from another time and place. And then they would make love. Cerulean sky. Golden saxophone notes sliding. The whole garden an erogenous zone. No wonder Fran didn't want to go to London for the weekend; no wonder Jake couldn't be bothered to urge it.

Afternoon was lingering into dusk. Summer loving in the soft grass will merge into winter loving by the log fire, thought Fran. Babette has gone, Cassie has gone; the challenging times are over. We have won through.

The phone rang.

Jake lifted the receiver and said, 'Yeah?' and there was a longish kind of pause before he put the phone down again.

Sometimes emotions do not ebb, they shear. There is a dark but definite line transgressed in nightmares and in madness. Fran looked up and saw somehow, in the tranquility of the twilit room, that Jake had crossed it now.

'Selene?' said Fran. Jake nodded.

'She says Cassie has been sexually abused.'

'Oh Jake no!' How terrible – who by?'

'Me' said Jake.

23   Sour Times

The weather had done that anthropomorphic thing that weather sometimes does in times of crisis. By next day a storm had swept the garden and there was a small flood beneath the back door. The cottage smelled dank. Pallid rain-sodden roses hung dolorous around the window and the lavender stalks dribbled steadily.

'Rain,' said Fran. 'Still, I suppose we need it. The hanging baskets were hopeless.'

She had not cried properly since Jake put down the phone.

'What's happened? Why is Selene accusing you?' she had said then, and as Jake did not reply, 'Call her back, Jake. Let me talk to her.'

'No,' said Jake.

'I want to know what's going on.'

'She says that Cassie told her I exposed myself to her. '

Fran heard herself giggling, a gulp of slightly hysterical laughter that spilled into her reply.

'She's just remembering what you said, when we were in the bathroom that last night. But I was there, Jakey. Tell her I was there too.'

'She knows. She says you abused her as well.'

Now Fran's giggle was definitely hysterical but she clung to it as if that sound alone could stop her drowning in the thin air. Jake was not laughing.

'She's mad,' said Fran at last.

'She's calling Social Services, that's how mad she is. They will of course notify the Police.'

'What am I supposed to have done?'

'Touched her pubis. According to Cassie, Selene says.'

'Jake, I helped her to wash. She's a little girl. I was looking after her. Oh, this is crazy – I'm going to call Selene.'

'Don't,' said Jake.

'But it was completely innocent. We did nothing...' Fran's mouth was dry. She remembered Cassie's bold bright voice *What's that*, and Jake's response *I don't want anyone's daughter exposed to.* And then the phone had rung, and she had answered it.

Fran thought, this is horrible. It's impossible. Then she thought, suppose it is true. Suppose he did do something. Then she thought, I know nothing about Jake, really, at all.

Fran remembered the night perfectly. Or did she? *What's that?* Was Cassie's voice merely confident and curious, or was it more coquettish, knowing? And Jake's quick reply. Was that panic? *I don't want anyone exposing themself to my daughter.* Why did he think of that? Why then? Had Cassie ever followed Jake into the bathroom during the day? What happened while she was out at work? What did Jake say then?

In one day, Jake had become a man she barely recognised. He was in turns self-pitying, recriminatory, irritable, and simply bleak. Fran did not know how to react. She listened, she found herself exhausted; she remembered that she too was accused and had no energy left to deal with her own pain and indignation. To Fran it was logical to talk to Selene.

'Can't I simply ring her? Or go and see her?'

She did not understand why Jake demurred.

Jake demurred because he was very nearly out of control and feared to pass any initiative, even the initiative of pain, to another person. But Fran was fearful now.

'Why won't you let me talk to Selene? Why did she leave you and take Cassie away?'

It was only a question.

Perhaps it was a question Jake should have answered long ago. But Fran never wanted to know before. Jake looked at her as if at some precious edifice smashed. Fran saw the fragments, did not see her own clumsy movement. Who had done this to them? Perhaps it was Jake.

Jake poured himself a drink and walked to the window.

Jake's arms were firm and brown. His blue sleeves were rolled to the elbows and his cotton shirt was open at the neck. His tie – yes, today for some curious self-protecting reason Jake had chosen to wear a tie, silk, green and gold – was loosened. He leaned at the window in a half-protective stance. He looked to Fran, as always, breathtakingly beautiful.

'Selene left because I hit her,' said Jake. He turned his luscious kissable face towards her, his dark eyes insouciant blue. 'Is that what you think? Of course I didn't, Fran; don't you know me at all?'

Fran felt ugly and mean and angry. Her head hurt.

'I'll have to go,' she said, in a tiresome fretful voice. 'I have some stuff to see to, at work.'

'Don't go,' said Jake.

'I'll be back soon.'

Fran drove over to Leonora's bungalow and found her mother in the kitchen. Babette was outside collecting tomatoes. Beyond the fine drizzle her figure, vast in a kimono and with a bulky arm-sling, was clearly visible through the greenhouse windows, raiding the loaded stems. The tomato plants were keeling considerably and some had slumped completely since the departure of Polo. Babette's silhouette looked different today. Someone had clearly helped her with her hair, which was piled on top of her head like a rumbustious cottage loaf.

Fran greeted her mother with her usual minimalist embrace and Leonora, after a shrewd glance, put down the local paper she had been reading. The mental health hostel was still headlining, Fran noted abstractedly: DO YOU WANT THIS MAN WATCHING YOU? The figure in the photograph looked thinly familiar.

'Something has occurred,' observed Leonora.

Fran nodded.

'Something seriously weird. We had this hysterical call from Jake's ex-wife.'

Fran's account was calm although her voice was slightly shrill. Leonora listened carefully as she peeled a pear with a tiny mother-of-pearl-handled fruit knife. She peeled slowly, immaculately. Vitamins lie beneath the skin, chemical spray on the surface. Leonora separated the wholesome from the injurious deftly. Tiny slivers of translucent pear skin fell fine as baby's fingernails on the willow-pattern saucer.

Leonora listened. Leonora tidied her pile of snail-trail slender pear droppings and wiped her knife. Then she wiped her fingers. Then she wiped her lips. Her mouth was stained with ochre lipstick and craquelured with age. Then she spoke.

'It is untrue, of course. Jake would do no such thing,' said Leonora decisively.

Fran gave a little moaning sound of relief.

'When I had a little boy, I kissed his genitalia daily,' her mother continued in a more reflective tone. Fran looked across to the marital photograph of Neville in its prop-up frame and wondered if he ever relived this distant ceremony. 'But times have changed and Jake is a man of his time. He may lack abstract morality but he does not lack contemporary style.'

'But what shall I do?'

Leonora clasped her daughter's wrist briefly. Her bangles glittered as they clacked together.

'Talk to my Mrs Ant,' advised Leonora. 'Dear little body. Such a treasure.' and while Fran wondered wretchedly what on earth her mother was talking about now, Leonora called out shrilly, 'Annie Ant!' and a small bespectacled person appeared in the doorway with a retractable tape-measure and a quizzical expression.

'Mandy,' said Fran, recognising her immediately.

'I call them Ant and B' said Leonora. 'They look after me between them, the ant and the bee.' She gave a chortle and gestured to the portion of tape erect in Mandy's hand. 'Measuring me up for a commode, I expect.'

'It's your socket height, Mum,' Mandy scolded soothingly. 'And what's up now?'

Mandy perched solicitously on a stool as Fran repeated her tale. 'We had this hysterical call from Jake's ex-wife,' she began, and then as Mandy continued to nod her narrative crumbled to a mosaic of wails and denials.

'Children don't usually lie,' said Mandy, looking troubled. 'Are you suggesting this is False Memory Syndrome?'

'I'm not accusing anyone of anything,' said Fran, 'I'm saying, I'm innocent, Jake is innocent. We never did anything like that. At all.'

'Of course not. But we can see what the Mum is worrying about. Repressing memories of abuse can cause enormous problems in later life. Eating disorders. Multiple personalities. To name but a few.'

Fran said nothing. In the face of this resumé, innocence began to seem a wispy, fragile, sort of attribute.

The door from the back garden swung open with the sound of a sharp kick. Suddenly the air was full of the sharp tang of fresh tomatoes and the pungent smell of Body Shop. Suddenly the space was full of Babette. Fran looked up, full of misery and trepidation.

'What's up?' said Babette. Her dark eyes strobed Fran's face.

'We had this hysterical call from Jake's ex-wife,' Fran began docilely, and then she started to snivel. Suddenly Fran's face was full of bosom as Babette hugged her. The air was full of fractured explanations – *possible unfortunate misunderstanding, serious allegation, naturally very upsetting*, from Mandy, and *ludicrous charge, I would stake my life on that, what's left of it*, from Leonora. Fran crouched in the consolation of Babette's hug. Babette pushed the strands of Fran's hair behind her ears and they swayed together in silence as Fran's weeping story ceased. The comfort of women, thought Fran. She blew her nose. Babette put the kettle on.

'There's an easy explanation,' said Babette.'You two bonk away all over the cottage. Oh, come on, you know you do. She could easily have seen you at it.'

'But we didn't,' said Fran agitatedly, while Mandy frowned and looked as though she wanted to say she could see what Mum was worrying about, again. 'Honestly, Babette, you're wrong about that. Having Cassie staying with us changed everything. What could be more important than protecting a child?'

Fran spoke from her heart, and Mandy nodded. 'Was this a very acrimonious break-up, do you know?' she asked.

I hit her, boasted Jake in Fran's mind. *I hit her*, he sneered. *I hit her*, he confessed. *Of course I didn't Fran, don't you know me at all?*

'I don't think anyone is consciously lying,' said Fran. 'It's a misunderstanding. Selene has got it all wrong – I think I know the time she's talking about, and she's twisted a perfectly ordinary bath-time into something sinister.'

'Well, just keep saying that, then,' Babette advised, and Mandy said that Mum would of course be counselled but unless there was an At Risk issue, she might be advised that Police interviews could magnify the episode for the little girl. 'Everyone will tell her to think carefully about the best interests of the child,' she said, almost hopefully, before going off to continue her measurements.

The kettle boiled and Babette made a pot of coffee. 'The horrible thing is,' said Fran, accepting the mug and curling her fingers tensely round it, 'I keep having waves of panic and... well, you know, I just keep thinking about it.'

'Yeah, well, Jake is a shit,' said Babette 'but not a shit like that.'

Fran accepted the consolation of Jake's supporters. A shit, and amoral but stylish. Not an abuser.

Babette stroked Fran's quivering arm and made sympathetic little noises in the back of her throat. 'Welcome to the real world, Fran,' she said. 'It's full of pain.'

I've always known that, Fran thought. *Do you think I could grow up in the long shadow of fatherlessness with a mother like Leonora, who cared about everyone in the world more than her daughter, and not know that?* She nodded and held on to Babette's hand. 'Fathers and daughters – it's a big thing to me,' she confided. 'I never knew mine.'

Fran blew her nose again, refused a coffee refill, and gathered herself to go. Babette walked with her to the car.

'Your Dad was a bit of a dish,' she told Fran, 'I've seen a picture. Your mother keeps his photograph in the bureau.'

'I didn't know she had one,' Fran said. She wondered whether to feel hurt that once again Babette's finger was on a pulse that she had failed to find, then remembered that gross gaffe about

Clive. Babette likes to pretend she knows things, thought Fran. She's a bit sad that way.

As she got into her car Fran said, 'I'm glad we're friends again. I hated all that tension when you left.'

'You started it,' Babette said boisterously. Fran didn't want to quarrel again so she said nothing.

'You dumped me for Mister Testosterone, you didn't care what happened to me,' Babette continued with something of her old aggrieved tone. 'I could have been stuck up a tree for all you knew.'

A vision of Babette swarming up the Wollery rope ladder with carrier bags of shopping overlaid the mournful images in Fran's mind and she managed a small self-conscious laugh. 'I couldn't really believe you were in the tree house. I didn't know what to believe.'

'No. You never do. Lucky I have other friends. And I milked this a bit.' Babette waved her beslinged arm conspiratorially in farewell.

Fran heard Selene's voice on the answerphone as she arrived back home. She picked up the receiver and handed it wordlessly to Jake. She heard him say dryly, 'Yes, I've given her best interests a great deal of thought too.' And then, 'And is that what Cassie actually said?' And after a while he hung up.

'I'm off the hook,' said Jake.

'Do you mean she believes us?'

Jake did not mirror her smile. 'She's not bringing charges, that's all. Fuck knows what she believes.'

He went into the bedroom. Fran followed him, longing for some shared expression of relief. Jake was lying on top of the white coverlet, fully dressed, staring up at the ceiling. Fran sat on the side of the bed and wondered what to say. She tried to avoid looking at the grime where his shoes touched the pale satin.

'That's good,' said Fran. Jake's face was flaccid, his eyes bruised and anguished. She licked the comforting salt of her silent tears.

'So I guess it's all over, but it doesn't feel like it. I never thought anything could come between us like this.'

It was the next day and Fran was talking not with Jake but with Don Glossop. She had woken alone and gone downstairs to find Jake finishing off last night's final bottle of wine in the kitchen. He had ignored her suggestion of coffee. 'I suppose you have things to do again today,' he said in a bleak sardonic voice and Fran decided that she had.

She drove into work and sat at her desk with prickling eyes until Don Glossop arrived to say cheerily, 'Not much of a holiday! Can't you wait to get back to us?'

Which is when Fran replied irrelevantly 'I never thought anything could come between us like this,' and her hot eyes started to melt into smouldering tears.

Don fetched a box of tissues and held it towards her.

'You don't have to talk about it, whatever it is,' he reassured her, and Fran who had arrived feeling the grime of her grief was legibly, literally, written across her face, realised that words still needed to be found. They should have been words of clarity and relief, thankful words, the sort of words used in prayers of gratitude.

Fran took a clutch of tissues and said, 'Everything's ok but it feels like it isn't and never will be now.'

Don sat by her. 'Why?'

'Oh I don't know. It's us. I just don't know us anymore.'

Don moved her mouse and sat on the desk beside her.

'Tell me,' he coaxed.

'We had this hysterical call from Jake's ex-wife,' Fran started, concluding her summary still without raising her eyes from her desk: 'So it should be all over. But Jake is still depressed.'

She took another tissue and wiped her face, then looked up, with what she hoped was a brave, rueful smile.

'I suppose it's because his self-esteem is hurt. He is a man who needs to think well of himself.'

'Most men are,' suggested Don Glossop helpfully.

'Why wouldn't he let me talk to Selene? I wonder if I should phone her.'

Don pursed his lips. 'He might not like you talking behind

his back.'

'But that's paranoid – why would he see it that way?'

'Most men would.' said Don.

He looked at her as if he wished he could think of something else helpful to say. Fran realised that the consolation of confiding in him had metamorphosed into dismay at her own disloyalty. She hadn't even told Jake about talking to Leonora and Babette, and now she'd told Don as well. Jake would see this as total betrayal. She wondered whether, if she said that, Don would tell her that most men would, when he said something that struck her as totally bizarre.

'I think Jake should go and see your Mum and have a talk with her.'

'Don, my mother never sees things the way other people do. She has outrageous morals and furthermore Babette is there and Babette thinks he's a shit. Even though she doesn't believe he's an abuser.'

'Nevertheless,' said Don. 'She trusts him, you don't. He needs to talk. You two aren't. Your mother might help you start.'

But Fran did not want Jake to talk to Leonora. She didn't want him to know that she had appealed to the judgment of Leonora before believing him or that she had wept in Babette's arms. She most especially did not want Jake to know she had consulted Don Glossop and that a family conference was Don's idea. Now that would definitely infuriate him. Plus he would become irrationally jealous.

She said wretchedly, 'I just want it all to go away. The thing about Cassie is over, it's OK. Nothing's going to happen. Why is he behaving like this? Is he feeling guilty?'

'Most men –' Don began, and then got off the table and stood looking out of the window. 'Fran, perhaps he's feeling a shade let down by your mistrust.'

'Me?' Fran said astounded. A fierce vigorous voice rather like Babette's muttered from deep within her *That's right, make it my fault. That's the man thing to do isn't it?*

'I don't think this is anything to do with me,' said Fran instead. She thought about yesterday at the bungalow and yearned for the comfort of women.

'Take some time off,' advised Don, still with his back to her. 'Go home, Fran. Talk to the guy.' He sounds almost sorry for Jake, Fran thought grimly.

'I will,' she said. 'I'll just check the hard-back run, before I go.'

Fran went down to the factory floor and picked an *Encyclopaedia of Mythology* off the line as finished copies snaked along to the packing area on their mobile runway like luggage from some planet of books awaiting baggage claim. She flipped through the glossy pages looking idly for Sisyphus and saw *the legend of Proserpine*. Fran remembered something Jake told her once about their Kiss painting. 'It's Pluto and Proserpine,' he had said, 'remember the story? How Pluto's desire for Proserpine brings death to the earth because he steals her away to live with him in Hell. Look at the ivy in the man's hair.'

Fran did remember the story. 'It's only Winter, not Death,' she had said. She was pretty sure Jake was wrong about Hell, too. Proserpine was dragged down into the underworld, but she came back. Her mother's love saved her and brought the earth back to life. Jake disagreed. Something went wrong, he said. He couldn't remember what, and they could find no account of the story in Fran's books at the cottage. There was only a Swinburne anthology with a poetic fragment from *The Garden of Proserpine*:

And Love grown faint and fretful
Sighs, and with eyes regretful,
Weeps that no loves endure.

Now as Fran stood beside the conveyor belt and the encyclopaedias of mythology slowly sidled past, she read that Pluto was another name for Hades, King of the underworld, and Proserpine was Persephone, his wife. But the man with ivy leaves in his hair was Dionysus, god of wine and lust and fecundity. Fran flipped the book closed and tipped it into the inspection bin.

Jake was asleep on the settee when she returned home. Fran considered waking him but decided instead to go for a run. The rain had freshened the air and she took a longer route than usual, as far as the ruined castle where rooks circled high above the ravaged walls. Her mother had always told her that rooks flying high was a sign of good weather coming. But they always fly high, Fran thought as she ran past, so it's not really a sign of anything at all.

'How was work?' Jake asked when she returned. Sourly and without curiosity, she thought. 'Did you find anything important to do?'

Fran told him about the myths and legends, and the colour plate of Dionysus. Now was not a good time to risk Jake's jealousy. She gazed out of the window at the deepening dusk of the garden as she chatted, watching the roses glimmering with that curious luminosity of white flowers in darkening evening air.

Fran did not realise that Jake lived daily with jealousy. Those unmentioned chats, those unattributed jokes, all scorched livid weals in Jake's mind. He knew, well before Fran did, with whom she would find solace. To hear her sunny noncommittal summary of her working day was no reassurance to Jake.

That night she wandered round the cottage, unable to sleep. She looked out at the blackness of the garden and thought how city nights were never so dark. The blurred glow of massed human habitation overtakes the stars; a dense bruise-red is the nearest to black the sky ever gets. She fetched a drink of water and paused in the shadowy hallway to look at their Kiss painting, noticing for the first time how the woman's pale fingers are pulling frantically at the man's hands, her face icy and resistant.

At the bungalow Leonora and Babette were discussing orgasms.

'D'you ever use a dildo?' enquired Babette.

'I bought one on mail order, but I can't be bothered with it. I suspect a hairspray can would be as effective – the slim travel-size. I have never tried a vibrator. I believe that is considered the Rolls Royce.'

Babette was dismissive. 'You don't need penetration to have a good time.'

'Have you tried a banana?' Leonora enquired. Babette's scorn deepened.

'All vaginal penetration is a kind of male invasion. It's a man-thing, to make us believe you have to go blundering into the body the way they go. The best orgasms are clitoral.' She spoke the definitive word piously, uncrossing her legs and shifting her thighs slightly apart. A sea of Indian cotton swelled and settled with the gentle sound of tiny bells. The tiny inset mirrors glinted like dolphin backs arching under moonlight. Babette placed her hand tenderly on top of her central contour, moulding the mound between her thighs like a child making mud pies. Leonora lifted her close-work spectacles and watched intently as Babette shook it a little, gently, like loosening a rabbit jelly.

'Clitoral,' Babette repeated, rolling the word butterily around her mouth. 'You don't need a banana for that, or a carrot, or a dildo, or even a particularly long finger.' Babette spoke with a researcher's certainty.

'How long do you find you need?'

'Finger?'

'No, how long in time? For the full effect?'

Babette looked down thoughtfully at her rumpled hummock and gave it a few twirls. 'Depends. If you're moist already, a few minutes. If you're just thinking, uh-oh, haven't had a cum for a week, better get cracking before my little horn atrophies, that can take a while. Don't you do this, then?'

Leonora looked scandalised and removed her glasses. 'I have made a lifelong practice of maintaining my body in healthy exercise. Of course I do. Francesca's father introduced me to my clitoris – a place never visited by Neville's father – nor previously, oddly enough, by me. I didn't know I had one. We weren't told, in those days, and nor was there the encouragement to explore. So I am grateful to that man. He gave me Francilla and he showed me how to pleasure myself. As he left me soon after, these are both agreeable souvenirs.'

'So why the hankering for carrots?'

Leonora laughed throatily. 'Occasionally my dear, there are perverse memories in this stubborn old body. The trace memory of deep touch. A p-'

'Don't say the p-word,' Babette advised, removing her massaging hold to hex Leonora with crossed fingers.

'A pleasant thrill, that comes from the thought of someone else's wanting. The smell of needy skin. The touch of another's passion. Being caressed to satisfaction is something I can do perfectly well myself. But being wanted – ahh. The pure pleasure of possessive passion. That is the secret sorrow every old woman knows.'

'Tell me about it,' said Babette. 'Think I don't know? Being big means spending all your youth wondering if anyone will ever want you. Your family jokes about your size and your friends never mention it. I know all that stuff.'

Leonora was unimpressed. 'You are still young, and with youth there is always hope. There are plenty of people who love flesh. What you are talking about is ordinary social insecurity. What I am talking about is the vanishing of ripeness. The day when you look at yourself in the mirror and see that the vibrance is gone. There is no oozing sap, only a dried twig that once trembled with blossom. Take it from me, my dear, once you pass seventy, life throws a chiffon scarf around your throat and when you try to remove it you find that it is, in fact, your throat. One of Nature's jokes. Another is chin hair. Your pubic hair wilts like frost-nipped parsley, your eyebrows pluck themselves into isolate strands, your lashes disappear leaving your eyes naked as grass snakes, your parting widens like a motorway with every shampoo until there's more hair in the sewage than on your scalp, and Nature thinks, I know what will entertain her, I'll give her a beard. A little prickly one, like the case of an unripe conker. I don't mean to put you off ageing in any way,' Leonora added, as Babette seemed temporarily silenced by this catalogue of predictions, 'but why do you think old women retreat into their memories? Living in the past is not senility, it is the quest for vanished vibrance. We are groping for the flickering pulse of our essential selves.'

'But – hell's piss, Leonora, you're not like that – you don't dwell on the past. You're still very much in the present.'

Leonora raised her eyebrows, which were sprigged intermittently with white although her hennaed hair gleamed vibrantly. Her face was an inscrutable mask. 'I have not yet quite submitted. I know dementia is hovering, but I intend to leave the party before we are introduced.'

Babette looked for a moment as if she might argue, but instead she said, 'Well we'd better get this baby backed now, and decide how we're going to get it transported.'

I know that it might sound …more than a little crazy… murmured *Savage Garden* from the precariously-balanced transistor on the bureau as the women surveyed the implacable mounds of fabric on the floor. *There's just no rhyme or reason … Only the sense of completion…*

'It's going to cost an awful lot,' Babette said eventually. 'D'you think it would be more effective staying here, as promotion for the Cause?"

Leonora contemplated this seismic withdrawal.

'Promotion for which cause?' she asked eventually.

Babette shrugged. 'There's bound to be one soon. Another war, f'rinstance.'

There was another plangent pause.

'One hopes Mr. Blair will not involve us in a war,' Leonora said eventually and Babette agreed it was unlikely.

'I could see if the Home would like it, for the entrance hall,' she suggested, 'though I gather the place is kind-of collapsing fund-wise, and may be taken over by someone or something soon. I haven't been following, to be honest, but I do know it's something to do with funding.'

'It always is,' said Leonora sagely, with the wisdom of the very old and no longer involved in decision-making.

The sun was dangling like a blob of ketchup over Bath, and Babette pulled the patio doors wide open so that she and Leonora, lured like rabbits by a scent of lettuce, could both step across the Hanging and achieve the back garden. They crossed the grass together towards the sunset.

'I intend to get my timing right at last,' said Leonora. 'I have lived my whole life out of step – in the wrong time for my deepest desires. I was in my thirties when jive came along – forty before the sixties started to swing. Do you know why I abandoned Greenham Common? Arthritis.' She gave a bitter laugh.

They had reached the brink of the canal beside the willow. 'I dream of climbing trees at road protests, but what can I do while I'm awake?' she said grimly. 'The only reality I have now is my dreams. Waking life is vapid. Time passes and I don't recall what I have said, or done, or why. I sometimes feel I am making merely guest appearances in my own life's party.'

A slim, gaily-painted, narrowboat was floating by. A woman emerged from the cabin and shook a bag of rubbish over the rail, then seeing the Leonora and Babette she said 'Pardon,' and disappeared. Babette lumbered to the canal brim trying to catch the wet trash and hurl it after the barge. 'How the hell did she get onto this stretch – it's not on any of the hire routes, and the crusties know better,' she ranted, '– that junk's not even biodegradable,'

'Everything degrades and disperses in time,' observed Leonora as Babette returned grumbling.

They made their way back to the house. Babette settled the Hanging as docilely as she could but it still seemed to want most of the room so she perched on top of it while Leonora took the available chair.

'Blimey, what's that for, displacement therapy?' Babette

wanted to know, as Leonora retrieved her crochet bag and settled to work on the doily shape which was already large enough for a shawl and now seemed to have ambitions of becoming a shroud.

Leonora looked up with a slight smile but chose an alternative topic in her response. 'Why did you tell Gwen the baby was five months old?' she asked, almost idly.

Babette covered her eyes with her hand as if the memory might choose this moment to slip quietly away and leave her alone. After a few moments she answered quietly. 'Rupert asked me that. All he could say was, 'Why lie?' and talk about false pathos for a baby that never existed. And he couldn't see that that's why I told him the way I did. I knew if he thought Joby was 'only a miscarriage' he wouldn't understand the agony of losing him. He would think it somehow mattered less because I hadn't held him, lifted him, bathed him. To me it mattered more. He was Joby, and I never even touched him. I wanted Rupert to understand the pain, and it was the only way I could get through to him. And for a little while he held on to a tiny bit of grief for me. Then he found out, and he resented that bit of sorrow he spared, before he knew he needn't have bothered.'

'Perhaps he was disappointed you didn't trust him.'

'Why should I trust him? Everyone told me it was a blessing. They said because the foetus was disabled it had aborted itself. Funny way of looking at it, isn't it? 'Oh I'll have a shit life so I'll just flush myself out right now.' Cut out the painful middle bit, of living – we could all do that. People kept saying to me in different ways, *it's for the best*. As if I would have cared. My child would have had a life. He might not be able to save the world but at least he wouldn't be part of the problem. I'd rather he grew up disabled than a politician, or a policeman. Or an estate agent. Or a soldier. Or a fucking teacher, like bloody Rupert.'

The list of the guilty subsided. Leonora said obscurely 'I have made the right choice,' and then lapsed into silence.

After a while she dozed.

When she woke Babette was beside her bureau, looking at something she had taken out of the top drawer. At the sound of Leonora's sudden rousing breath Babette pushed it back and closed the drawer. She smiled with artless candour. 'I was looking for your will, actually' she said.

'My will or my wont,' said Leonora with a shrewish look. 'Will you won't you will you won't you join the dance.' She stood and lifted her skirt and hobbled briefly in an improvised gavotte. Babette watched impassively.

'Open the bottom drawer,' said Leonora, steadying herself. 'I have something to show you and you shall have it if you like it.' Babette obeyed, and Leonora leaned down and began to rummage into clouds of pale tissue paper within. Surges of rustling paper billowed like a misty Japanese mountain-scape. When these veiling membranes were parted Leonora lifted out, comatose in her arms like a slumbering woman, an evening dress with a long full train. It was pearl-grey taffeta and elaborately fringed and beaded. Wiring in the bust and bustle enabled it to spring to a body shape of exaggerated femininity. Babette kneeled down to examine the dense silky fringes more closely.

'This was yours?'

Leonora raised her sparse eyebrows expressively. 'No indeed. Weddings in my day were more austere. Post-war shortages, you know.' (Babette did not know, actually; she had abandoned History before Options.)

'This was my grandmother's,' Leonora continued. She lifted the decorated panels high like wounded wings.

'Wow,' said Babette sincerely. 'It's fabulous.'

Leonora nodded. 'It is my final relic. I have a policy of disposal, as you may have noticed. I aim to clear the decks before I die.'

'You've years yet,' Babette scoffed. Leonora looked at her sharply.

'I certainly hope not. I consider myself in injury time already. I shall be exceedingly glad of the final whistle.'

Babette stopped stroking the fragile fabric and laid the dress reverently on the table where it lay splayed like a wounded bride. She picked out a cherry from the fruit bowl, popped it in her mouth and spat the stone reflectively towards the fireplace. 'Why me? I'd never squeeze into it.'

'For your creative embroidery. It will rip.'

'Don't be daft. What a thing to do to an heirloom. It would fit Fran.'

'Fran has enough distracting beauty to worry about,' said Leonora after a pause.

They both regarded the swooning shape of the dress for a few moments, perhaps separately envisaging Fran serenely attired in its lavish contours. Leonora continued with the aspect of their conversation she felt most significant.

'Death has an unfairly bad press. People assume suicide must be from the nadir of depression. It was always my ambition to design my demise at my personal peak, though I fear I am a little too late for that. Still, I should like to retain initiative.'

'You can get help, if you're thinking of euthanasia.'

'Official routes are always cumbersome. The way to avoid distressing one's relatives is to contrive an accident.'

'They'd still be distressed, Leonora. If not downright dismayed. Accidental death is just as upsetting as the real thing.'

'After a certain age, I doubt it. *A good innings* is the accepted phrase. And if the technique is neat and speedy, there are further comforting clichés. *She wouldn't have known anything about it,* they say.'

'Which rules out cutting your throat or slitting your wrists,' said Babette after a thoughtful pause.

'Definitely.'

'I'm glad of that. I'd hate to find you in a bloodbath, Leonora.'

'I speak theoretically, of course. Oblivion is best.'

'Obviously. How, oblivion?'

'To cease upon the midnight with no pain.'

'Tricky to achieve. Synchronising with the stroke of twelve.'

'Midnight is not literal, Babette. Art is not like life. As you yourself have remarked.'

Leonora folded the dress back into its nest of tissue. 'Do take it, dear. Otherwise I shall have to give it to Gwen for her wretched Heart shop and it will disintegrate in the dry-cleaning.'

Babette shrugged and helped Leonora wrestle the dress back into its box.

'I take it you've settled your will,' she suggested, with a lingering look of enquiry. Leonora nodded vaguely. Now that the matter of the frock was settled, she seemed content to let her mind wander.

'Neville was an odd little boy,' she said unexpectedly. 'He always seemed to be wearing the wrong shoes. Whatever the other boys were doing, it seemed he couldn't join in because his shoes were wrong. He'd forget to take plimsolls so he couldn't do games – or he'd forget to change back and arrive home soaked and shivering with his boots in the school locker so he couldn't play with the others in the snow. When I think of Neville as a little boy, a disembodied and exasperated voice always seems to float above him saying *Where are your shoes?*'

'We've all got those voices,' said Babette. 'Mine's a ferocious whisper: *Hold your tummy in.*' After a moment she asked, 'What's Fran's?'

'Fran's looks gave her every advantage. I suppose that was her curse.'

'She doesn't even remember her father.'

Leonora snorted. 'Well, that's hardly a problem. I should have thought that you, dear, would be aware of that.'

'I used to be,' Babette agreed. 'I used to think men were a waste of space. But I'm not so sure now. I'd like to talk to one occasionally – I'd even like one of my own. Not for every day – just special occasions.'

Leonora pursed her lips sceptically. 'Any man? Even one belonging to someone else?'

'Oh, come on Leonora, they don't 'belong' to other people! You can't say "hey that man's mine", like "that's my pint, I've had a mouthful of it already". They belong to themselves. We all do.'

Babette tucked the wedding frock box under her chair and took another fistful of cherries. 'I could have eaten Jake for breakfast, you know,' she said. 'Or an early lunch, maybe. Jake's a late riser. And he'd have eaten me back, bite for bite. But we didn't. I even left the bloody cottage. She never gave me any credit for that.'

'She trusted you.'

'Well, she shouldn't have,' said Babette, 'Anyway, that's not trust, that's naivety.'

It was almost dark. The luminosity of these evenings was on the wane, dulling, as though summer was sullenly subsiding. From the main road the street light, already on, was just visible through the leafy trees.

Babette leaned forward and said quietly, 'You should tell Fran.'

Leonora jerked as if rousing from reverie. 'What about?'

'How do I know?' Babette said, exasperatedly. 'I can't get it out of her, because you've never told her. Whatever it is she doesn't know about her father.'

'She's never asked,' Leonora said primly.

'Any bloody kid deserves to know where they bloody came from!'

Leonora looked cunning. 'The present moment is all we can know' she said. 'Like a sip of coffee, the next one exists only in your imagination, the last one only in your memory.'

'Zen twaddle' said Babette. 'If the last sip burned my mouth, my lip stays sore.'

Leonora assumed an air of confused indignation. 'Are you suggesting I have somehow scorched my daughter?'

But Babette was bored now. 'Just tell her,' she said, yawning.

'She won't like it.'

Babette got up to draw the curtains closed.

'I saw blackberries today,' said Leonora abruptly. She made the observation sound ominous.

'Yeah. It's called autumn.' said Babette, after another potent pause. 'So, about this will. Who's getting the bungalow?'

25   The Scream

Jake was beginning to feel that everything was conspiring against him. The last thing he needed was some idiot slowing down at the roundabout so he'd rear-ended him, and now as well as all the insurance kerfuffle, the Porsche was out of action and he had to take the train to London. And he was late, again, with his art deconstruction column.

Jake looked into the window of the *Pret a Manger* in Bath as he munched his croissant, a late brunch to while away the time before the London train. A vestigial reflection of his face, interrupted oddly by the glittering glassy outlines of bottles in the fridge, stared back at him. It looked strained and unkempt. He put his hands up briefly to finger-comb his hair and left them in position to continue staring at his self-image for a few moments.

In his dream last night he had been walking streets he didn't know and he had the sense of a hooded figure following him, maybe Fran. There was no-one else around on these endless streets and he grew suddenly exhausted with his isolation and stopped to turn and confront his follower. He couldn't clearly see the face in the cowl but it wasn't Fran. It was his sister.

The dream had stayed with him all day. Now Jake rested his notebook on his lap and wrote his piece without bothering to research further, quickly but clearly so he could fax it off without copy-typing and printing.

In 1893 a Norwegian painter walking in Oslo noted a strange sky and stopped by a fjord to make notes about the intense, near-audible, force he sensed, which he transcribed into a painting that has become famous throughout the world. It's called, in Norway, Skriket – Shriek. You know it as The Scream. You know it from reproductions, on cards, mugs, tea towels, posters, shopping bags: it is as ubiquitous as Mickey Mouse. Soon probably there will be dolls, finger-puppets, and lampshade stands all featuring this gargoyle figure. Why? Why does this crude, terrible, mask of terror and despair grip us so unforgettably that we try to trivialise it into parody and artefacts? It is because Munch gives us a glimpse of the unspeakable: our own existential angst?

Nearly a century later, Pablo Picasso aged 90 and close to death, painted a series of self-portraits in the space of a few days: they are all monstrous but the most terrible of all is a thin face stricken with horror, the terrified eyes engorged and an eerie red beyond the grey skull-like head. Remind you of anything?

Many painters, and other creatives, have come close to that feeling of utter despair, a fury and disgust at being alive on a planet which is septic and rotten to its core. What are Shakespeare's themes? Madness and death – Richard II calling for a mirror to stare at his distraught face as he recognises he no longer has any purpose in life. We live lives 'Where but to think is to be full of sorrow / And leaden-eyed despair." That's Keats, celebrating his own route to death. Sadness is a luxury, despair is a soft-centre chocolate as poets pussyfoot around with words for the unspeakable. But beyond all we know and fear lies something far worse – unimaginable yet certain. Painters try to show it. Munch tried. But maybe real agony of existence is not visible at all, maybe it's just an endless, near-secret sound… a shriek."

Jake gathered up his pages without re-reading them, binned his sandwich wrapper and coffee carton, and headed for the door. As he headed down Princes Street he reflected that he had said nothing about the artist, not even that he had a sister who died, and Munch never got over it.

26   The Meaning of Life

At the cottage, Clive was leaning in the kitchen doorway talking to Fran about *The Meaning of Life*.

'It's quite good' he said 'but I think *Life of Brian* is better. What do you think?'

'It's sweet of you, Clive,' said Fran, 'and it's lovely to see you, of course. And of course we both love Monty Python, usually. But I don't know if either of us really feels like a funny video tonight.'

'I thought it might cheer you up,' said Clive. 'You are my favourite aunt, you know.' He looked at her anxiously through circular golden sunglasses.

'Jake might want to watch it,' Fran suggested, trying hard not to disappoint. 'Jakey?' But Jake wasn't listening. That seemed to be his principal hobby these days.

Fran turned back to Clive and smiled auntishly, conciliating. Clive seemed extraordinarily young today, she thought. More like a kitten than a teenager, even in his Doc Martins, with his slim jeans and spiky lashes, his baby-soft wry smile.

'Come in, anyway,' she said, 'have a drink. A beer? Will it be alright, riding that?' Clive had arrived intriguingly on Babette's Honda. Fran decided she couldn't be bothered to ask but Clive noticed her embryonic curiosity and explained, 'I'm borrowing it. I'm going to get my test and be a dispatch rider.'

'On a moped?' queried Fran, bewildered.

Her nephew's expression deepened into a more familiar irritation but he answered kindly. 'Dad's getting me a motorbike. Mum says it's OK. Pizza Palace wants riders, I'll start with them.'

Fran sat down feeling shaky. At any other time she would have rejoiced to hear Clive talking about parental support and personal goals – indeed to hear him talking about his plans at all, for Clive was not often articulate. Today her mind felt clouded.

Something seemed to be buzzing in her brain like the indolent fly which was circling the kitchen. She fetched a bottle of lager from the fridge and watched Clive open it expertly on the side of the table. Sun smeared the windows and dust particles swam in the shafts of sunlight.

'You're back at home, then,' Fran said listlessly after a while, and Clive said cheerfully through the bottleneck, 'Mostly.'

'Right,' said Fran vaguely. She was thinking about Jake, moaning in his sleep. It sounded a bit like Cassie, but it was not. *Jessie*, Jake had muttered. Fran heard him distinctly. *Jessie*.

Of course Jake couldn't be expected to be champagne-popping elated as the black cloud of Selene's accusation scudded away. But Fran had hoped that life would at least return to normal, normal being a passionate intensity of languorous loving. It had not.

Jake seemed to Fran like a man almost disabled by grief. It was as if he had stumbled into a world of atrocity where nothing is cherished and innocence is destroyed, and it had shocked him so far from his previous complacency that he had no idea now where he was. In this dreadful place, anger and guilt swirled inconsolably, irreparably, into despair, and Jake seemed to have lost track of his most normal routines. He took messages on the phone and forgot them. He wrote notes and forgot what they meant. Jake stared at inconsequential things and could find no sense in any of them.

Fran tried to understand his inertia. 'It's understandable,' she urged, 'after a trauma, like that, to feel upset – to be emotional and even a little irrational.' Her definitions were no consolation to Jake, just thin words describing an abyss.

'Why don't you see a doctor?' Fran urged as Jake remained at the cottage. He had not exactly decided against going back to London, he had simply failed to find the energy. Yes, he did have some work on, he was not sure of the deadline. Perhaps he would go tomorrow. Fran, who had used her time at home since the phone call to clean the cottage and tidy the garden, regarded his procrastination with silent panic.

Jake said he would work from the cottage. But he had lost some paperwork with important designs. He looked everywhere.

Fran looked in the bin-bag of stuff for the recycling bank and there it was, in with some old Sunday papers. 'Perhaps I put it there,' she said bravely. They both knew she had not.

He had not shaved. In the past Jake sometimes omitted shaving for a day or two, knowing that the dangerous, darkly-textured, look sparked excitement. Somehow this time it was not the same. He looked messy, with his frightened-child, sunken, eyes. Fran did not know what to do.

'I would never do anything like that to Cassie,' said Jake. 'I wouldn't have done it for all the tea in China.'

'I know that' said Fran. 'Even Selene knows that now. Jake, no-one is accusing you.'

'Not for all the tea in China,' said Jake.

The bizarre bribe echoed around Fran's mind. She thought wildly of tea forests, Lapsang lakes, and Earl Grey mountains. She wanted to laugh. Trillions of leaf-loaded rickshaws. Chinese junks tea-jammed.

'Why not get some help, Jake? I mean just practical, physical help. Doctors can prescribe for depression. I have a woman doctor, she would understand.'

Jake agreed, limply, to an appointment. He came back saying the doctor simply sat stroking her legs looking like she was wondering whether to have them sugared again and offered a prescription for sleeping pills.

'Perhaps if you went to London, then,' said Fran. Perhaps, she thought, then I could look forward to your return. Perhaps those were always the best times. Waiting and longing. The glitzy romance of distance, not this awful contiguity.

Their lovemaking was not going well. I can see why it's called humping, Fran thought uncomfortably, hoping her pubic ridge wouldn't fracture. Her lips felt bruised and purplish, like withered plums, refusing succulence. She was no longer enjoying any of Jake's touches. His massaging fingers hurt her. His breath was fetid and his poking tongue tasted slimily of yesterday. She didn't trust that his urgent kiss wanted her; it seemed to want something beyond her that she did not know how to give. All the magic days and nights had vanished into a darkly crowded space that was merely lewd and yearning.

They seemed to be quarrelling about everything.

'Those people at the bender place were on the news programme,' Fran said, adding, 'the ones you said were merely middle-class hippies. They seem to be really nice.'

'I didn't,' said Jake without looking up.

'Jake, you did. I remember when I came back from fetching Clive – '

'I said *middle-class*. I didn't say *merely*. It's you that sees *middle-class* as a judgment on integrity. Middle-class is simply a socioeconomic factor, you don't have to get all self-denigrating and paranoid about it.'

And then there was Babette's hanging. Or was it the thought of Babette herself making Jake look so surly and bleak. All Fran said was –

'What?'

'Jake, why don't you listen to me? I said that Babette is thinking of taking the hanging to Bosnia. There's going to be an international exhibition somewhere in Sarajevo, now that the war is over.'

'Of course, a hanging. Just what Bosnians need, now that the war is over,' Jake sniped, 'Babette bounding over with a bin-bag full of embroidery.'

Was there any point in reminding Jake that this was not what he said before? That he had talked about the creative energy of the project, and the subliminal power of such messages for peace.

'This summer has shown us we still have a lot to discuss – it's a good thing we didn't decide to have a baby,' Fran said, trying to sound rueful rather than enraged. Jake looked up astounded. 'A baby? Why on earth should you say that?'

'You suggested it –'

'I did not.'

'Jake, you did. You said we might need the spare room for a nursery.'

'Oh for heaven's sake. That's only saying we may need the room – like saying we might want an extra study.'

No it isn't, thought Fran. It isn't the least like that.

Croissant crumbs on crumbled bedcovers. No longer sultry specks of sybaritism, these days more like littering leaves.

'Summer is nearly over,' said Fran sadly. She licked her finger and pressed it on one of the brown pastry flakes and sucked the fragments. Jake said nothing.

'Jake, it's all over. I don't know why you are taking this so badly. Selene made a mistake. It was all sorted in a couple of days.'

Jake shook from his reverie and pressed his burned-down cigarette into the ashtray.

'I know. I don't know. It feels like a bereavement.'

The heavy word lay between them. Cautiously Fran said, 'What was your twin called?' and Jake said, 'My sister was called Jessica.'

We were all twins in the womb, thought Fran. We spend a lifetime searching for our other half. Jake is no different.

'I'll just go out, then,' said Fran. 'For a run'.

Fran ran her usual route. The man in the palomino-pale coat was sitting on the bench again. 'Hey,' he called out. She faltered, her breath fluttering in her chest.

'I love fans,' said the man. 'Do you? Do you love fans?'

'Yes,' Fran shouted back absurdly, gasping with relief as if at some curious, incomprehensible, reprieve.

Fran walked down the long gravel path from the printing factory. Her sandals scrunched quietly in the empty air. The afternoon shift had gone; the night shift was in. Fran had stayed late at work. There were some important things she wanted to check. Eventually she could think of nothing else to do so she set off for home.

Fran walked slowly, her hands in the pockets of her butterscotch cotton jacket, the long skirt of her tiny-flower patterned dress clinging. She tweaked a tiny sprig of conifer from the dense hedge as she walked, crushing it in her hand to release the intense and piney fragrance.

In her peripheral vision she could see a man sitting on the bench beside the neat lawn at the side of the lonely road on the edge of the small town. It was not the usual figure. This man leaned forward, staring, morose, jeans dirty, light jacket crumpled, dark hair messy, smoking.

'Jake,' said Fran surprised. 'What are you doing here?'

Jake said, 'Waiting for you.' He threw the cigarette away.

Fran hesitated. 'Here?' she said cautiously.

'I want to talk to you,' said Jake.

'Why here?'

For some reason this felt frightening. Why? The visibility was good, the road was close and, behind her, there was at least fifty yards of driveway before the curve of the high hedge screened them from the view of the factory windows. Anyone travelling the road would observe them, anyone coming down the driveway would witness this encounter. But there wasn't anyone on the drive and no cars on the road.

'Why here?' She meant, why are you staring. She did not want to say that.

'You won't talk in the cottage. You go out.'

'I have to work.'

'You have to work. You have to run. I never see you.'

Jake had stood up: he had moved towards Fran, he was holding her wrist.

Of course I didn't, Fran, don't you know me at all?

Most attacks on women are made by men whom they know. Domestic violence has no class barriers, assault is indifferent to socioeconomic status. The highest percentage of murders are domestic. Have you ever thought about that? Fran had. *Fran, don't you know me at all?*

Mental illness affects one in ten. Fran knew that too. She knew she mustn't consider herself vulnerable, because a victim can provoke attack. But who is a victim? How many people in ten are that?

Jake moved close. He was not twisting her wrist and he held no weapon. Jake was speaking.

'I can't stay here,' Jake was saying. 'There's no point. I'm going back to London. I won't be coming back.'

Fran heard within her a curious thin gasping howl, as if the air itself was gagging her. Not coming back, not coming back. She only wanted respite, not this giddying infinite forever space between them. She wanted Jake the way he was, she wanted their times of separation brief and sweet, defining and outlining their togetherness; she wanted his going away to make their weekends once more like glittering prizes. Not this, this was not what she meant at all.

'I'll come home' she wailed. 'I'll talk – we can talk'

'The cottage isn't home' said Jake. 'It's never felt like home. That place was always for you, not for me.'

Fran sobbed. Their things, their lovely things. The change of address cards sent so recently, so gaily, to all their friends. The hanging baskets, dripping with lobelia since the rain. It could not be possible.

'But the cottage,' she wailed.

'Torch it,' said Jake.

Fran screamed thinly.

'It means nothing now.'

'Don't go like this. Let's talk, Jake. Jakey. Please, let's talk. Let's go to the pub – talk over a drink.' Fran was frantic, but she was cunning too. Jake would never drink and drive. If she could persuade him to drink with her, he would not leave her.

Jake pulled her to him so tenderly, so carefully. His caress was without passion. She tensed, pressing against him wantonly, but his touch did not respond.

'I'm sorry,' said Jake. 'For a while it was magical.'

He released her; he turned and walked away.

Fran gasped and crumpled to her knees. Her starry-petalled skirt flowered the grass-blades as she swayed and howled. Jake walked away without looking back, though Fran called his name repeatedly in anguish and despair. Fran was remembering, too late, that the meaning of life is only connection.

Gwen's diary had altered beyond anthropological credibility as summer progressed. No longer a halting linear journey of her querulous groping through listless days, it was now a tapestry of thoughts and dreams, full of snippets and quips, fragments of poems, pertinent comments from reviews, radio soundbites that made her smile – a colourful collage of words.

There was some dialogue, too.

'I talked to Clive after The Rescue. I asked him outright why he went off like that. He said, 'It wasn't the adoption, it was the secrecy.' I have no idea where he got that idea from. However, since there was no adoption there was no secrecy either, and I pointed this out to him. Clive said he knows that now, but it felt like secrecy. And funnily enough I think I know what he means. I have tried for years to construct a person I can be comfortable living within, a person called Mum or Dear, but it doesn't seem to happen that way round. It seems you can only make your own edges from the inside, by trying to explain feelings even if you don't know what they are. Even when this is quite painful. I think this is the only way some feelings can find their own name. Fran says everyone is ultimately unknowable – she got that from some Art book I think – but it seems to me now that we have to try. Because that's how we love.

I know nothing about Neville's work. I do regret that now. And there are other things we should talk about.

Clive said to me, 'I came into the room and it felt like you two just zipped up the air around you so there was no space for me to be.' I said, 'When, Clive?', and he said 'Always.' Oh, I felt so sad. I kissed his brow and said, 'You are the apple of our eyes, Clive. Always were, always will be.'

Gwen was pleased with the poignant honesty of her writing, and felt she had chosen the right place to conclude this cameo. Clive had in fact dodged her kiss and said 'You don't like apples,

Mum,' but he managed to make these responses gentle enough to entertain them both. Gwen was content to leave it at that as the taxi driver tooted outside. This was the final day for the collage, and Gwen had been invited for a last-stitch celebration.

Leonora and Babette were talking about death again when Gwen arrived. 'Can I have this, when you're dead?' she heard Babette demanding from the living-room, and Leonora from the kitchen called back, 'Take it now, dear, whatever it is.' In this instance it was only an embroidery hoop, but that was not really the point, Gwen felt. Deflecting ignoble thoughts of property distribution, Gwen focussed on the issue of premature plans as a challenge to good taste.

'You've got years in you yet,' she scolded. 'I do hate to hear you talk about passing.'

'You need have no worries on that score,' Leonora reassured her, 'I never use that risible synonym.' "She passed" – what absurd affectation! Passed what, one might ask? Her bus-stop? The tomato ketchup? A turd? Do say what you mean, dear. Although why you should have any aversion to my referencing my demise, I have no idea. If I don't mind dying I don't see why you should object.'

(*It's very disconcerting*, Gwen confided to her husband later, via her diary, *My headmistress always said it was bad manners to talk about death, and as for demanding items after* ... Gwen paused, suddenly unsure where her husband stood on the vexed question of alternative terminology. The phrase 'shuffle off this mortal coil' came suddenly to her, and Gwen was pretty sure this was Shakespeare but it was rather flowery, and probably not the point. Gwen crossed out *after* and wrote firmly *this is not polite*. She had never been encouraged to mention her mother's death by either her father or her teachers, and surely they couldn't all be wrong.)

Abandoning such thoughts, Gwen had joined Leonora and Babette in poring over the crochet squares now piled onto the dining table for tacking into final shape. It was still not clear whether they had enough, or too many, crocheted squares for the purpose of backing the fabric frontage of the Hanging – or even if the resultant artefact would ever actually hang anywhere. Babette had taken to saying breezily, 'Sufficient unto the day!' when these practicalities seemed to hover rather too closely for comfort.

'Amazing to think so many different women once knitted with these wools. What life they must have seen, what stories they could tell,' she said now, stroking the multicoloured pieces: sensuous saffron merging with chilly mint, bordered with a ruby braid Leonora had tagged boiled loganberry.

'Yarns from yarns,' Leonora quipped. She gave her short unladylike laugh.

By the end of that day the Hanging was complete. Gwen felt almost sad. Babette produced Chardonnay and cakes to conclude her ceremony and Gwen hesitated, patting her midriff. Babette waved the box at her encouragingly. 'Cake's not a hanging offence – it's a hanging celebration. This one is calling you. Gwe-en!'

Being addressed by Babette in the persona of a sobbing puff pastry was a compelling experience and Gwen capitulated. Leonora accepted wine but wafted the cakes away. She wandered across to her bureau and began rummaging vaguely.

'What are you after?' Babette called through a spray of pastry flakes. To Gwen she said, 'She's got all sorts in those drawers.'

'I have made a new will,' said Leonora. 'It requires two witnesses.' She closed the drawer and looked candidly at her daughter in law. 'Those mental health people need a hostel.'

Gwen was alarmed. 'Here? Is that wise?'

Babette was not alarmed. She was downright rude. 'The whole point of a halfway hostel is that it's halfway, not stuck out in the sticks. Integrated. There's only ducks here. How does that integrate anyone? They'd go bonkers.'

'As I understand the term mental illness, this contingency is already covered,' Leonora said with a touch of her old asperity. Babette rolled her eyes histrionically.

'What would they do for entertainment? Walk up and down the tow path and watch each other fall in?'

'It could be sold,' said Leonora stubbornly.

'I thought you were leaving it to me. You hinted as much.'

'I am leaving it to you, dear. But you can sell it to them at a fair price. Then everyone will benefit.'

Babette laughed raucously. 'Leonora, you're hilarious. You can't seriously leave me your house, you've only known me five minutes plus I'm your carer! The courts would over-rule anything you wrote in two seconds and the tabloids would start a witch-hunt. No thanks, thank you very much.'

'I have no objections for myself,' Gwen added helpfully, 'but I do know a beneficiary can't sign as witness to a will.'

'All Property is theft, anyway,' said Babette. Neville arrived to collect Gwen at that moment and the will was withdrawn unexplored and unexplained.

'We've been talking about that p-word,' said Babette mischievously. He blushed and Gwen said quickly, 'Politics.' 'Pastries,' corrected Babette sugarily.

Leonora assumed that air of distant dignity she seemed to trail these days. 'Probate,' she said serenely. 'I need to sort out my affairs before I am too far past my peak.'

'Pique?' queried Neville puzzled. He remained at the door, gesturing towards the nest of fabric beyond to indicate his reluctance to tread on its folds, and Gwen abandoned her mini-meringue and picked her way docilely to join him.

On the way home in the car Neville told Gwen. 'I'm a bit bothered about Babette.'

'But Babette is a perfect companion,' said Gwen. 'She takes Leonora's eccentricities in her stride. And of course as a woman she can cope.' Gwen uttered the verb expressively, with a moué of her lips and wafting hand movements which obscurely yet effectively conveyed the kind of small private debacles she had in mind for which a woman's coping hand might be required.

Neville concentrated his attention on the road ahead. 'I don't like it,' he said. 'That boy was a fad – he was obviously not going to stay long. Babette is different, dear. Babette is looking for somewhere to live. She'll make herself a fixture, mark my words. The place will be impossible to sell with a sitting tenant.'

Gwen remembered Leonora saying *I shall not leave my house*

to either of my children and how sad and thwarted she had felt. It seemed a long time ago.

'We have a very nice house, Neville,' she quavered. 'And I suppose it is up to your mother who she chooses to inherit.'

'It's not, actually. My father left everything in trust to me. Leonora has been living on the interest. The bungalow comes to me automatically.'

Gwen's mouth made a soft O of astonishment. She was too dumbfounded to speak as Neville brought the Volvo to a halt outside the garage and reached out of the wound-down window to point the new remote control at it. The mended door rose slowly. Neville watched it with an intent expression of childlike pleasure and appeared unaware of the effect his disclosure was having on his wife.

'And Fran?' asked Gwen later, as she brought in the supper trays.

'What about Fran?'

'If everything comes to you, what will Fran get?'

'Well, Mum's personal effects I suppose. Jewellery?'

'Neville, it's costume!'

'She must have some other stuff. Clothes, or fans. Or something.'

'It would barely take a morning's sorting at the Heart Shop. There's nothing worth pondering. Poor Fran.'

A wasp had landed in Neville's creme brûlée. He lifted it out carefully with his spoon and laid it on the tray, saying as he did so, 'Fran will be all right.'

'Isn't it strange, Neville? I always thought Fran was the favoured child.'

'She is,' said Neville. 'Inheritance is not necessarily anything to do with preference dear. My father was old-school, he believed in primogeniture.'

Gwen digested the information. She was tempted to say, Poor Fran, again but it seemed there was no reason. It was not a question of spurning, it was simply one of those official things.

The wasp was still on the spoon, struggling as it paddled in the dark syrup.

'Shall you squelch it, Neville?'

'Not much point. It's nearly the end of the summer. It will die soon anyway.' Gwen let it lie. They took their coffee into the garden.

But Gwen couldn't help feeling sorry for Fran now she knew that all she would inherit was Leonora's personal effects. Personal effects meant clutter, and Gwen knew about the clutter of mothers. Although her own mother had of course left her before she had the opportunity to make an inventory, Gwen had learned much from the women who come into the Heart Shop. Women her age, mostly, lugging black bags that smelled of mingled eau de cologne and dry cleaning fluid. *Mostly clutter, I'm afraid*, they would say bravely, and Gwen replied brightly *Not to worry, it all gets put to use*. And it does: Gwen knew the routine so well she could have followed it in her sleep. The good clothes are pressed and put on size-numbered hangers with tiny tags, the furs are wrapped in polythene ready for Russia; the folded fabrics and tablecloths with matching napkins go on the shelves and the clip earrings go in a basket on the counter. The tins of buttons are carefully tipped into the button tray (where do all these buttons come from? Can anyone's lifetime be long enough to wear enough garments to spawn all these buttons?) Everything is put to use. Even the unpicked zips, their frays of nipped thread still ragged along the rims, and the used elastic neatly wrapped round strips of card from the back of Basildon Bond letter-pads (each with a slit at the side to tuck the loose end through and keep it tidy, stop it from unravelling and tangling. Can't have tangled elastic, that's no good to anyone, no use at all. They knew about that, these mothers) – even these have a place in the Heart shop, down in the floor-bin with the leftover bits of fabric from curtains and coverings.

Gwen's colleague Marilyn loathed the black bags. 'I'm glad old habits are changing,' Marilyn said. 'After all, it's not obligatory. Our generation won't be leaving collections of safety pins and balls of wool from unravelled jumpers, will we? I shan't be sorry. Smelly stuff. This place would do better with the catalogue seconds, I'm always telling them that.'

'Rather shoddy stuff, though,' Gwen had said. 'Those black bags have hidden depths. That last one had a cashmere cardigan.' Marilyn smirked. She had bought that herself, for five pounds. 'Cheap 'n cheerful, I always say,' she replied, truthfully, because she did. But that is not the point, thought Gwen. Providing cheap clothing is only part of it. The Heart Shop is as important to the donors as to the customers. Taking all these drab accumulated bits and bobs at a time when mourning relations teetered on the brink of thinking, *Is that it then? Is that all a life amounts to? A trunkful of toiletry gift boxes and a tinful of buttons?* We absorb these things, Gwen wished she could explain, and thus we absorb a part of their grief. It's a healing thing, recycling in the way Nature does when flowers die and leaves fall and winter comes, before everything is reborn next spring. She wanted to say this to Marilyn but her colleague was not one for sentiment. Gwen's clumsily budding philosophy embarrassed her. 'We're just running a charity,' Marilyn would say boisterously at such moments, 'it's not a therapy centre you know.' Gwen disagreed, profoundly but silently.

Now Gwen stood with Neville beside their fountain watching the melodious silvery water flow. She was thinking about Leonora's effects. Minimal really, by any standards. She recalled Babette's curiosity about the bureau, juxtaposed oddly with her belligerent opposition to Leonora's proposals.

'I don't imagine Babette will do anything unworthy,' said Gwen after a long thoughtful silence. 'She is quite idealistic, you know. Her Hanging is after all dedicated to world peace.'

'Well, we all want that,' Neville said noncommittally.

Even those of us whose income is dependent on developing computer programs for the MOD? Gwen was hardly aware she had uttered the words. Only the look of astonishment on Neville's face confirmed the fluttering echo of her enquiry in the still air.

'Someone has to do it, dear,' said Neville. 'If our company didn't, another one would.'

Gwen stooped and picked a daisy from the verdant lawn.

'Defence is the best form of deterrent,' Neville said.

'And attack is the best form of defence,' Gwen heard this other Gwen say, and then, not snippily but almost grimly, as if she really wanted to know, 'So where does that leave us?'

That was the moment I decided to go to Bosnia with the Art for Peace women. Gwen wrote. *Babette tells me they are happy to include the Hanging among their installations. She met with them in Bath outside the Pump Room earlier this week. She spread it on the pavement beside the pillars and people stopped to marvel, several threw pounds and one woman asked if there was a petition to sign. Babette was much enthused by the response.* ('There was an amazing busker there too,' Babette had told Gwen, 'a unicyclist with an absolutely brilliant act.') *I can picture us now, travelling together with the other Arts Forum women, talking together as our Peace Bus takes us through the ill-lit, war-torn, streets of Sarajevo. It will be such a privilege take our work, compiled from all our hopes and fears and passions, handing it on like a baton of hope.* Perhaps not a baton. Perhaps like a splendidly coloured banner of support that might lead to deliverance.

Babette called for a coffee next morning and Gwen decided to ask about accompanying her to Bosnia then. In for a penny in for a pound, she thought recklessly, and introduced the subject of travel by telling Babette a little about her visit to the bender village. She would have said more had not Babette interrupted early in the narrative, at the point when, after a delicate pause, Gwen mentioned Clive's friend.

'Friend?' said Babette roguishly. 'What sort of friend?'

Gwen recalled the simple affection of the boys hugging each other at the lake.

'Just a friend. Hawthorn, he calls himself. Neville says it's something to do with being an Eco Warrior. Isn't it funny, when they are being so grown-up and sensible about the future of the planet and then they give themselves these silly animalistic names like Badger and Fox, as if it's only a game.'

In fact Gwen was not feeling at all funny or silly; she was finding it a perfect escape clause from any awkward memories to intrude on this fortuitous meeting. No longer a dragon boy – in fact, another person entirely: a saviour, of her husband and her child, and maybe her marriage too.

Babette was unexpectedly thoughtful. She said, 'Hawthorn isn't animalistic. It isn't even silly.' Then she said, 'Actually I took that name for a while. My partner's name was Hawthorn.' Then she said, 'My son's name is Tom Hawthorn.'

Then she said 'He is twenty three, now.'

Then she left the room. Moments later Gwen heard her moped accelerating down the road.

28   What do Busy People do all Day?

Neville was in the restroom, resting, with his mobile sitting quietly on his lap like a patient spaniel. It rang and Neville roused to respond. He listened, and then said 'I'm a bit tied up right now' and closed it up.

Neville stood up and regarded himself in the big wall mirror. 'Tied up,' he said thoughtfully, aloud. 'Tied down. Buttoned up. Collared.' He pulled off his tie and unfastened the top button on his shirt. 'Loosen up,' Neville advised his mirror image.

Words, thought Neville. *Odd things. Hard to make them say what you mean. They seem to say what they want to, whether you like it or not.*

Leonora, now, never seems to bother much with making sense. She chooses words she fancies, whatever they mean. Neville suspected his mother often adjusted her opinion in order to flourish some flamboyant soundbite. Leonora, unlike many of the elderly, does not lament the degradation of modern speech; she listens to the world around her as keenly as an anthropologist might to some strange tribesman. Or perhaps that should be the other way round. Jake uses words casually, entertainingly, bullyingly. He is shallow and worldly, but he can sound wise. Or maybe that's the other way around too. Babette though vulgar is only occasionally boring. Fran is... endlessly evasive.

Neville's rumination omitted his wife. Perhaps he did not listen enough to have a representative sample. He mused instead on Clive, who seemed almost allergic to conversation, and thought how like the boy he was at that age. At this age too. So perhaps that's another thing that goes either way around. Is there a word for things that are incompatible yet somehow end up the same?

Neville quit the restroom and returned to his own area. He highlighted the day's emails and deleted them. He picked up a memo from his in-tray – a fax of a printout of an email. The subject, ringed in fluorescent orange with evidence of exasperation, was CONTAMINATION PREDICTIONS – PROJECT K. The message read *Can We Go Ahead?* For nearly a week cloned forms of this enquiry had arrived on Neville's desk. Now he slid a CD into his computer and watched a world map spread across the screen in high resolution detail. Neville shifted the mouse around Eastern Europe in a rummaging kind of fashion, clicking occasionally at random. He targeted Serbia with a cavalier flick of his finger and watched myriad tiny skulls whizz across the screen as the extent of his devastation was calculated. He had taken out the capital, unwittingly but effectively, so he got a thumbs-up sign.

'An Austrian Army Awfully Arrayed Boldly By Battery Bombarded Belgrade,' Neville recited absentmindedly as he sat clicking on illustrated projections of mutant outcome. He watched the estimated percentage of malformed children and ruined habitat grow as a red pulsing line spread across the screen to indicate wind-carried damage and rain-contaminated rivers. The line stopped just east of Trieste. Thumbs up showed as the programme offered him his final choices. Re-run this scenario? Select another target? End?

Neville picked up his desk phone and keyed an internal number. 'The answer is no,' he said, mildly. Neville's voice was always mild. 'A definite no.'

'The MOD is very interested. They've suggested we tender.' The voice at the other end sounded peevish.

'Abster, read my lips,' said Neville, and Abster probably could in the open-plan arena, barring lofty yuccas intervening. 'En-oh. No way José.' Still mild but now jubilant, Neville concluded his long, silent, quandary.

There was a short pause. 'I may take this further?' said the invisible Abster.

'Right-ho.' said Neville. He hung up and sat for a moment watching the screensaver. 'Tender,' murmured Neville. 'Gentle touch, touchy, ticklish. *Tender is the night*,' he crooned quietly, and decided to take an early lunch. Perhaps go for a swim. Or maybe the other way around.

The women were still busy with their hanging when Neville arrived at the bungalow later that afternoon to see if his wife might like a nice night out. Supper at a restaurant perhaps. He still felt elated but also slightly unsteady, and found it comfortingly reassuring, as he knew he would, to see his wife plying her needle pacifically while Babette, wielding pinking shears, was holding forth on politics.

Neville slid into the room as Babette was concluding her tirade. 'Tony Blair, actually, is not a true socialist, he's an opportunist, and the way he's kowtowing to America will drag us into a war sooner or later.'

'But Leonora admires him so much,' Gwen began, and found herself immediately in recoil as both Fran and Neville said in unison, 'Tony Benn!'

Neville patted his wife's hand. 'Both in the Labour party, dear,' he said appeasingly. 'Easy mistake.'

Babette stepped in to assist in the politicising of Gwen: 'Tony Benn is the unofficial leader of the true Left wing of the party. He's bloody old now but he's got more integrity in his little finger than Blair has in his entire fraudulent body.'

'But there's not going to be a war again, is there?' Why would Babette talk about being dragged into war, Gwen wondered, when there's been peaceful co-operation everywhere for years now.

Apparently she had wondered this aloud, for Neville was now telling her there had never, ever, been a time in human history without war. He sounded like a sad headteacher, the sort who genuinely means it when he says, 'I had hoped not to see you in detention again.' (Clive had had one like that.)

'Just this year, for instance, there was the Afghan Civil war – that's still going, a Civil War in Nepal, another in Sierra Leone – we got involved in that, by the way – plus Al Qaeda in Yemen, a coup in Ecuador, the Eritrean War of Independence – that's still going on – Russian bombings and battles in Chechnya, a massacre in India, a massacre in Columbia – oh, more, much more – you put your finger on the globe, my dear, and you won't be far from conflict. The armaments industry is the busiest and most lucrative in the world.'

Neville stopped. He had suddenly noticed the women's eyes were fixed on him like startled does transfixed by the sudden appearance of a stag. It occurred to him that he had never been one to bring his work home, so to speak, and possibly none of his family had realised what was involved when working on a project for the Ministry of Defence. From force of habit his hand slipped into his jacket pocket for a comforting roll of wine gums, but then he remembered his big news and withdrew it.

'Babette, can you spare my wife for this evening? There's something I have to talk to her about.'

29   Late Calling

Leonora was in her boudoir. Carefully she applied depilatory cream to her upper lip and used her tweezers on two or three stubborn bristles under her chin. She smelled under her arms and sprayed with *White Musk*. She unscrewed her lipstick tube with a slightly shaky hand and drew a determined Cupid's bow of russet across her lips. She picked up a tissue, kissed it, then peered at the mouth in the mirror. Red stains leaked into the tiny lines above her lips, thin as spider's blood. She sighed. She examined her teeth carefully, as a vet might, and finally pulled back her fine saffron-coloured hair into a black velvet scrunch band on top of her head. Leonora pulled her eyes sideways with her fingers to push the years away. She released the stretched flesh; it sagged perceptibly. She put her tongue out at the old woman in the mirror.

'I have never had any respect for age,' Leonora explained, but her reflection looked unamused.

A shuddering, shaking, banging noise abruptly overlaid the music on the radio. She turned her head slightly on one side like an alerted parrot. She switched off John Peel and the noise came again. Someone was banging on the back door. Babette, perhaps, having forgotten her key.

Leonora shuffled to the back door and flung it open. No-one was there.

Now the same kind of impatient thudding came from the patio doors.

She tracked through to the main living area. A dark outline stood beyond the curtain. She pulled the cord laboriously and the curtain yielded.

Leonora recognised the figure and opened the door.

'It wasn't locked,' she said as Jake stepped in.

'Well, it should be. I might have been a marauder.'

'Is that what you came to tell me?'

Jake laughed; no he didn't. Maybe he thought he had laughed, but his face was bleak and frightened like a child's.

'I've left Fran.'

'Probably,' said Leonora unhelpfully. She closed the curtain and sat down.

Jake scowled, prowling the room with sullen restlessness. He fidgeted with a fan spread out in display on the bureau. He sighed with a kind of self-conscious reticence.

'Sit,' said Leonora.

Jake sat, dropping ungraciously like a sprawling teenager.

It was becoming apparent to both of them that Leonora's motley collection of seating was not intended for a full-sized man like Jake. Or perhaps it was Jake's emotions which needed the extra room, perhaps they had engorged his subtle energy and spilled into physical dimensions, for Neville never seemed to have this problem. Neville managed somehow, mostly, perching on the tips of seats or standing judiciously in doorways. There seemed to be nowhere for Jake to be. His long legs slithered, scuffing the floor. He slouched, and scowled.

'Do settle,' Leonora instructed. He stopped prowling and sat down beside her on the settee.

'Mothers and daughters,' said Jake enigmatically. 'She never forgave me.'

Leonora waited. In some obscure way it was clear to her that Jake was not talking about her daughter, nor even his wife. After a few moments he clarified. 'She simply never forgave me for surviving, after Jessica died.'

Leonora sighed. It appeared her bedtime would be even later than she had anticipated.

She rose and strolled towards the patio window. For a woman of her age recovering from a sprained ankle she moved with remarkable grace. Her hair, in this new style devised by Fran, had an elegant Regency look which was kind to its wispiness. The foxy red tint had faded as late sun streamed silvery through frail escaping tendrils. Jake watched the gauzy stream of smoke veil slowly around her.

'Mothers err,' said Leonora.

Leonora's dressing-gown was a long robe in tones of blood and bronze. It was made entirely from patchwork, the old-fashioned hexagonal kind, in different fabrics; shot taffeta next to soft-sheened velvet, printed peony-pattern next to plain rust red. As the Peace Hanging was still occupying a large corner of the room in a similar cavalcade of disparate colouring, the cumulative effect seemed to Jake a curious confirmation that the entire fabric of his life was unravelling into fragments.

Leonora turned her gaze fully on him.

'What is it you want from me, Jake?' she asked. 'I can't intercede and I can't give you absolution.'

She reseated herself and took a cigarette. Jake, as if on autopilot, produced his lighter. Leonora's hand quivered; he steadied it until the flame had taken.

Her paper-pale face was etched with the weariness of the passing of years. Jake remembered the crisscrossing of oystercatcher claws in soft sand seen on an early childhood holiday and it occurred to him that Leonora's wrinkles were the song lines of a journey. Her life's long travel was etched delicately across her face like the imprint of fine lace.

Now Jake stared at the hand he still held. Tiny dark marks like speckles on a thrush's egg patterned the skin, blue veins trailing across like quartz lines in pale sandstone. He felt her brittle nails and kissed the soft tips of her fingers.

'Do you think I chose Fran just to be the lost sister I've been seeking all my life?' Jake said.

Leonora removed her hand gently. 'I am not a counsellor,' she said, 'and I am not your mother. If you take my hand, you take it as a man holds a woman.'

There was more of reproof than coquetry about her tone but Jake took her hand again and stroked the age-drizzled fingers.

The folds of Leonora's throat quivered slightly like a petal-pale chiffon scarf as she inhaled. Her eyes were fiercely bright.

'This is extraordinary,' said Jake.

Leonora waited.

'I never realised how beautiful old flesh is.' Jake kneeled in front of Leonora like an acolyte. Obscurely he remembered the portraits by Francesco Vanni of kneeling monks and acolytes and a tiny, intrusive, part of his mind wondered if he now understood enough about this inexplicable posture of adoration to use it for his next column.

Leonora laid her cigarette in the ashtray and leaned back. 'And what will you do with this newfound understanding?' she enquired.

Jake lifted his hand slowly to touch her face and trace the outline of her crinkled lips, fingering the mouth that had stored seventy years of secrets. He felt within her kaftan and fingered her nipples. No he didn't, he remained quiescent, imagining this, as tree shadows shifted against the moonlit window where the curtains had not fully closed since he blundered in. He gazed at her steadily. Leonora raised her fragile eyebrows and said, kindly but with an unmistakable edge that may have had a tinge of exasperation, 'Do get up dear, this is all very lovely but rather uncomfortable.'

Jake stood obediently. He fetched a tapestry footstool with a drooping fringe from the other side of the room and settled it beside her, still watching her intently.

Leonora said, 'Do say what you've come for, Jake. We can't go floating around like this all night. You seem to be having a trying time, but prowling like this isn't really helping either of us.'

So very Leonora, Jake thought tenderly, though slightly stung that his intense rapport was so unreciprocated. Her tone was sharp, yet so absolutely apt he found himself wanting to weep. Impossible to think that this ancient crone is actually mother to delicate, dazzling Fran, Jake thought. That sort of thing happens only in gothic legends.

Leonora's robe had slid partly open revealing the soft, long, dark aureoles of her breasts. Jake imagined scooping them into his hand, squeezing the tiny buds of soft tissue gently, steering a nipple carefully into his lips and nuzzling it. Romulus suckling from the wolf, he thought. Leonora noticed his stare and pulled the robe across irritably.

'I really think you should tell me whatever it is you came to say, and then go,' she said, 'Pour yourself a whisky if it will help, and one for me, but for god's sake get on with it. I haven't got all night for this kind of thing.'

Jake obeyed her instruction, and brought the decanter over too.

Leonora smoked and sipped as Jake talked. She stroked his hair a little as he wept. She looked, briefly, at the photograph he showed her, and nodded gently as he told her how important that fading polaroid was to him. She listened to his grief and his anger at feeling blamed. She nodded as he reached a small but certain intention to talk with his mother when he returned to London. She heard the two-a.m. chime of one of the clocks – the noisiest one – set by Babette during the time she needed repeated medication and then forgotten about. She noticed a moth, caught under the lampshade, struggling with tiny frantic wingbeats to escape. Leonora listened without moving, wondering whether any rescue action from her was required, but after a while the room was quiet again. The moth must have achieved release.

30   Abdication

Fran telephoned her mother that night.

Since their confrontation in the lane Jake had been calm and purposeful; he had packed the car carefully with most of his stuff and spoken little. Fran stopped crying and pleading. Just before he left Jake had told her, 'I'll be back on Sunday for those boxes. The stuff in the bag is junk, you can throw it.' And then he had driven away.

The boxes were full of his work and the bag contained mostly papers and some old clothes. Fran picked out a shirt and pressed it to her face; it smelled of fabric softener and empty longing.

'I'm getting rid of the cottage,' Fran told her mother on the phone. 'I can't bear it here.'

'What a good idea,' Leonora said calmly. 'I always felt it was something of a Wendy house. Unsuitable for real life.'

You'd know about desirable residences, perched on the edge of a canal with a self-combusting kitchen, thought Fran savagely. Aloud she said, 'Can I come and stay at the bungalow?'

'I don't think that's a such good idea,' said her mother. 'It would be impractical for us both. If you are selling, you should not leave your property vacant, and I don't want another visitor. Babette suffices. We would be prowling around like the witches in Macbeth.'

Fran gave a hysterical laugh. 'You'd rather have Babette than your own daughter.'

'Francilla, have you been drinking?'

'No!'

'Well perhaps you should,' advised Leonora. Fran hung up.

'That was a bit hard,' said Babette ruefully. Leonora had no extension so Babette had to stand close beside her to listen in.

'Flitting from house to house is a distraction, not a solution,' said Leonora.

'I meant on me,' Babette said. 'She'll blame me for this, you know.'

Fran took Jake's papers to the paper bank and his bottles to the bottle bank. Perhaps I'm on auto-pilot, she thought; my heart may be breaking, but we must save the planet. His clothes she salvaged. Too good to throw away; Gwen would like those for the Heart shop. Fran added other items to the bag of donations: souvenirs of days with Jake, mementos of trips, artefacts he had bought for the cottage. There's so much here I didn't choose, and I don't even actually like, Fran realised. The place was beginning to have a stripped look. There was more space in the rooms without the cluttering icons of their contiguity. Fran unhooked the Klimt painting and added that to the jettisoned pile. *I'll be back on Sunday*. She wanted Jake to understand he had clawed out her heart.

She found Babette at Gwen's having coffee when she arrived with her donations. Gwen was explaining to Babette that she didn't quite understand how early retirement worked, and yes it was rather sudden, but it was obviously a good thing because Neville had become a New Man. Not that sort of New Man who wants to do things women do, obviously, but he did seem, well, generally more cheerful. And the pension was generous too – and a bonus, just for signing a non-disclosure deal.

'I suppose my mother told you Jake's left me,' Fran said when she could get a word in, adding quickly, 'I don't want to talk about it.'

Gwen assented promptly and Fran felt obscurely disappointed that neither of them attempted to coax further disclosures from her. They now seemed completely wrapped up in some plan of their own. Babette was smiling like a Cheshire cat and talking about meeting Clive's friend Tom Hawthorn.

'Clive's going to tell him to phone the bungalow,' Gwen thrilled, 'Such a nice boy.' She was tweaking tendrils of hair and almost blushing. 'He's been a very good influence on Clive.'

Babette shuddered histrionically.

'What an appalling thought. My son has turned out to be a

Good Influence.' She didn't look appalled; she looked radiantly happy. Fran tried to rally to their euphoria but she was not in the mood to applaud Midsummer-Nights-Dream-type reunions. She was not actually in a mood to applaud anything at all.

'What's up, Auntie? Is it Ms Monthly?' coaxed Clive charmingly.

'No,' said Fran shortly, uncharmed. She noted disapprovingly that Tom's good influence was resulting in flashes of wit in Clive, and decided she preferred him sullenly mute.

Clive had rescued the Klimt from the bag. 'I've always liked this,' he said. 'Can I have it?'

'I wouldn't have thought it was your sort of thing at all,' said Fran.

'Yeah. It's like one of those magic-eye pictures, the more you look the more you see. It would make a great jigsaw.'

'It would be difficult,' Gwen said, examining it, 'with those complex patterns.'

'I like them difficult. You could do the patterned bits first.'

'The proper way is to do the edges first.'

Fran got up grimly. Babette gulped her coffee and dislodged herself from the breakfast bar.

'You're right to dump him, Fran. Jake's a shit. I told you that.'

Without warning she swooped and hugged her. Warning bells rang for Fran. *Trust is vanity.* 'Ask him what he was doing round at the bungalow the day before yesterday,' said Babette. 'I could hear him, talking to Leonora. Muttering about something!'

'I knew you weren't listening,' Fran said, 'all this excruciating debate about jigsaws. I can't ask him anything – I told you, he's gone.'

Now that Jake had gone Fran knew utterly that his love was the most important thing in her life. Losing it was unimaginable pain. The worst part, worse even than the rapacious ragged void of loneliness, was knowing that she had let this happen. There was no quintessential moment of choice, only a long clumsy turning away. Like a bad dying.

Fran spent the evening alone looking out from the bedroom

window at the lane below where Jake had driven away. The tangle of roses that hung around the window frame softened and the glass became translucent as unspilled tears blurred her eyes. She waited for the headlights of Jake's car, for Jake warm and vivid beside her, telling her *I couldn't go*, and this time she would promise him, again and again *I know we can make it together.*

Fran woke alone from a dream that Jake no longer loved her. Wide awake and trembling and alone she remembered that Jake no longer loved her. Her eyes were strangely dry and her jaw felt walnut hard. Perhaps that's from silent screaming, she thought. She crossed to the window and watched the hot night sky, longing for the consoling laceration of tears. Acid tears, to dissolve me, Fran thought; why can't I cry? She slept again and woke alone achingly to the day, her body disbelieving, drenched in sorrow like a strawberry rolled in sugar, with sorrow lying all around like softly fallen snow, like feathers from gutted birds. For some it took a war or the loss of a child to push them into the chaos of despair. Fran needed only a night of lonely self-reproach. It was a small walk from an unimportant place but she got there just the same.

I'll come back for that on Sunday, Jake had said. Fran clung to the words; her gritty grief shaped them into a seed of hope. Jake was coming back. He would return to the cottage her own Jake again; slamming the car door and seconds later holding her tightly with tigerish murmurs of love, like the last time he came home, like every time, and the last two weeks would be simply erased.

Fran walked from room to room but Jake's echo was in every one of them. She went out into the garden. Martins darted in the pearl grey sky and Fran remembered Jake saying *I'm sure there's a nest in the eaves.* I am at the edge of what is bearable, thought Fran.

She heard the sound of a car and then a door closing and her whole body shook knowing that this was Jake arriving. Fran gasped. So sensational was the recognition of his proximity she had for a moment forgotten to breathe. She went back into the house. Jake was standing in the hall. For a reckless instant she believed he had come back to her.

Jake took the second box out to the car.

'D'you want a coffee before you go?' Fran asked politely and he nodded. He followed her into the kitchen. Fran watched her reflection in the shiny kettle. I will say nothing, she decided. I will not speak unless he does.

'We could try again somewhere else,' she heard her voice plead. 'In a city – we could move to London.'

Jake's voice, behind her, was gentle. 'It doesn't matter where you are, you can't solder an abyss, Fran,' he said. 'We go the way our life-lines go, that's all.'

'I know,' said Fran. 'By the way. What were you doing round at the bungalow the day before yesterday?'

She was ready to believe whatever he said, ready to ignore Babette.

'I'm sorry, Fran, but it really doesn't make any difference to you and me,' said Jake.

She was ready to disbelieve whatever Jake said, ready to believe Babette.

'I just want the truth,' said Fran.

'Have you asked your mother?' said Jake.

'What? Asked my bloody mother what?'

'Whatever you want to know. I don't do confessions.'

Fran stared at the kettle. It had boiled now so she poured water on the coffee. *So Jake has fucked Babette.* She depressed the cafetière. *Even my mother knows.* She poured two cups. *And he probably did all the time she was staying here, too.* She gave one to Jake.

Was she better than me? Unaskable, unknowable, unbearable. There was no way to ask, no look to accompany the question, no place on earth to hear the answer. There was no way to forgive Jake unless he said *of course not, it was a terrible mistake*; no way to believe him if he did.

'Was she better than me?'

Jake was not tempted by comparative evaluation. He said 'Your mother is wonderful. She's so distant from my understanding I feel I'm on the edge of another time and space, like touching, oh I don't know, a dragon's egg. It's not entirely sexual, but it is erotically arousing.'

Jake was leaning back almost tiredly, not looking at Fran as he spoke. He did not see the look of utter incomprehension on her face.

His shirt was open at the neck and she watched the smooth bronzy line of his throat slightly scented with sweat, his lowered lashes a dark fringe concealing those azure eyes. He looks like an actor, she thought. Perhaps he is speaking lines intended for someone else. *Your mother... is erotically arousing.* What kind of gross and monstrous reproach was that? Big beads of tears rolled like tumbling pearls from her eyes. She felt no muscle twitch as they released, only the burning as they etched her cheeks. Fran searched for a corresponding sense of weeping grief but her mind felt numb and empty. Maybe this is how they do it in the movies, thought Fran.

Jake spoke again.

'I honestly don't think this is helping, Fran. Whatever I say, it's up to you to decide how you feel.'

Fran nodded. I could have told you that, she thought with furious contempt. You could have asked forgiveness, you could have said you still loved me.

She said icily, 'You tell me this as though it's simply unimportant. A lie might have saved our relationship, but you couldn't be bothered.'

Jake looked up. 'Once' he said 'I would have done that. That was before Cassie.'

His daughter's name came lingeringly through the warm air, the sibilants gentle in Jake's soft voice although his tone was soaked in sadness. Fran realised what that name meant to him now: neither the little girl he'd left nor the real child, neither love nor responsibility, simply the accusation that had destroyed their world. When Jake said 'Cassie' he meant the terrible abyss, the week when trust and love were wiped away. Jake meant the time he stared into the deep pool of his essential self and saw only dislocated images in twisting water. Jake had been alone in dark places where Fran was afraid to follow. They both knew it.

Now, miserably, Fran understood. This was not her punishment from Jake. It was something that had always been there, the jostling husk around the erotic passion, as the gasping lovers discover the pain of parting is no less than the pain of clinging together. Fran thought of the painting she had tried to trash, which Clive had carefully retrieved. She wished the ivory face of the girl was still on the wall in front of her so she could smash it again and again until the frame and the glass were splintered and the canvas broken into shreds. After Jake had gone, she stayed watching the empty space on the wall, blinking from time to time to release insistent stinging tears.

Fran drove over to the bungalow that night. She let herself in the unlocked conservatory doors and drew the curtains back so the light of the full moon illuminated the room. She prowled around outlines transformed by sheen and shadow. At the bureau she knelt and quietly opened the small top drawer and found her fingers resting on a slim wallet. As she withdrew it, a something slipped out from within and Fran, catching it, found herself holding a small photograph, not much bigger than a parcel postage stamp. There was a folded envelope too, bulky enough to contain a letter, so Fran pocketed that and turned her attention to the photo. Probably cut from a photo-booth strip, the sort you get from a machine in a post office for your passport or, more likely, at the seaside messing about with your friends. This face wasn't messing about though: it had a steady, shy smile, and thoughtful, long-lashed, eyes.

A slight noise startled her. Leonora was standing in the doorway.

Her mother was wearing her ornate dressing-gown and watching her curiously. They seemed to have somehow passed through the moment of challenging enquiry on both sides, so Fran just held up the photograph.

'Babette told me there was a picture. I wanted to find it.'

'Well, you had better look at it, then.'

Leonora switched on the side light, and Fran looked down at the picture.

Paul, thought Fran. *Uncle Paul.*

Babette gets everything wrong, that's not my father. I must have been about four when he turned up. He brought me a doll.

The unexpected memory smarted her eyes and for a moment she felt dizzy.

He came to stay and then I was packed off to that so-called independent school run by a friend of Leonora's in a ramshackle house in Hereford, and when I came back he was gone.

Leonora was still quietly watching her and waiting.

Fran said, 'I remember him, he stayed for a while when I was little. He gave me a doll.'

Leonora said nothing. She swallowed, as if digesting some ill-tasting but necessary medicine, and continued to regard her daughter.

Fran said, 'And you took it away. You sent me off to that stupid so-called boarding school when I was only four, the one with the dogs. I hated every minute. I was the youngest there, by far, and they all ignored me, and I learned nothing. Nothing!'

Leonora seemed ready now to join her in reminiscence.

'Well you managed to pass your 11+, so no point in being bitter now, dear, as you've done very well since. Self-teaching is the best way.'

'Oh yes, I was good at that. I learned that I was on my own, because my mother didn't care a jot about me.'

'That is rather unfair, Francilla. Neville had thrived at boarding school. I saw no reason why you should not.'

'Neville went to an actual real school – a posh one paid for by his grandparents – they took him abroad in the holidays and everything!' Fran hadn't intended to get embroiled in a row about school days, but it was beyond exasperating that her mother still considered it had been a good move to abandon her for three years in an unruly houseful of hippies with a do-it-yourself curriculum and a kitchen full of dogs who slept in the saucepan cupboards.

Leonora was managing to look astounded, as though an experimental mixed-age rural commune somehow equated the high-ranking institution which Neville's grandparents had funded in return for anonymity about the fact his father was a curate. She looked for a moment as if she might say more on the topic but Fran was now dripping with tears and wailing chokily, 'I don't even know what happened to the doll.'

Leonora patted her daughter and Frans sobs redoubled chokingly. Leonora stopped patting and waited till her daughter had stopped coughing before speaking again.

'Paul was sick, my dear. I was afraid your doll might be contaminated. Which is also why you had so few clothes when you first went to stay with my very kind friend.'

Fran's sobs subsided entirely. It sounded at that moment as though Paul might have had cholera, which made her rather like the little girl in the *Secret Garden*, who managed to come out alright in the end – or maybe irritatingly perfect Sara Crewe in that story by Frances Hodges Burnett. Relief that her mother might be on the brink of an important confession struggled with exasperation that they still seemed to be looped into a tangle of evasions.

'Fuck Paul. I think you need to just tell me who my father was, Mum. It's about fucking time, isn't it?'

Leonora looked almost alarmed. 'You don't usually use that word,' she observed, and Fran felt like saying *Fuck fuck fuck* but then realised that this was not the word that had caught Leonora's attention.

'Mum Mum Mum,' said Fran crossly and collapsed once again in tears.

Would Leonora reach out to cradle her daughter in her arms, rocking her slowly, wordlessly, until the lifelong hurt dissolved and simply flowed away?

No. Leonora had many talents and strengths and skills but hugging her daughter was not one of them. She patted her child quietly on the shoulder and deftly removed the photograph from her hand and replaced it in the wallet. Fran watched silently as her mother's fingers lingered on the cover for a moment as if feeling something different about the weight or the thickness, but apparently not, as it was returned it to the shelf without further exploration or query.

Fran's desire to cry had ebbed, overwhelmed by a more urgent need to simply walk away, but as the bureau front closed she discovered she had been uttering a long guttural moan which became a howl of anger.

'I don't understand you. I don't understand why you never talked to me about anything that mattered! All those stupid displacement activities like protest marches, all those posturings and missions and causes, and now you've hooked up with Babette so you can carry on with your save-the-world antics and you won't let me near you, not even to stay in your house, and you won't tell me anything that matters.'

Fran was aware that screaming like a banshee at her mother's life choices was in its own way something of an answer to the question as to why she hadn't been included in more of these, and she was expecting at least some put-down that would make her ashamed of her tantrum, but Leonora was now making a definite attempt to enfold her.

Fran stopped howling and adjusted her mother's stick so it wasn't resting on her foot but otherwise made no resistance as Leonora clasped her. She could hear the clock ticking in the kitchen. It seemed to be ticking for a long time.

Eventually Leonora spoke again.

'Oh for Gods' sake let's have a drink. I have a Muscadet already open.'

Fran said she was driving, and Babette would probably help out with the wine if it was a problem, and could she please, please have the photo?

Leonora nodded slowly and judiciously, 'Of course,' she said. 'You may consider it yours, after I'm gone.'

Fran nodded. It wasn't much, but it would do.

Outside, the cool night air seemed to calm her instantly. Instead of going straight back to her car, Fran walked down the narrow back path that led to the canal bank. She took off her sandals and stood in the quietness of the garden feeling the grass cool and damp around her ankles. The moon shifted lower behind the willow trees.

You're the dancing queen, Fran hummed. *Oh, see that girl, watch that scene. We are the dancing queens....*

She was glad, though surprised, that her mother had not apparently noticed the absence of the envelope which had provided the main thickness of the wallet which now held only a small photograph of that man who had brought her the doll that her mother took from her when she sent her away.

The man who was not her father.

Fran stood beside the river until her eyesight adjusted to the dusky air. She withdrew the stolen letter from her pocket and unfolded it. The mid-August harvest moon was full and her mother's handwriting was firm and clearly legible. Fran could hear the slush of shallow water near the bank and an occasional melodic bird song that might have been a nightingale as she read the document that was her mother's pre-empted legacy.

Fran finished reading the letter and slipped off her sandals to step carefully into the shallow edge of the water. She stood in the cool flow listening to the flowing water catching on the dark rocks.

Then she read the letter again, until a cloud passed across the moon and it was too dark to see – almost, in fact, too dark to make her way up the bank and across the garden to retrieve her car.

Fran sat in her car breathing deeply into that trace memory that had eluded her. The recollection of a man's arms around her, holding her tight, lifting her up to the air and covering her face with kisses when she was a tiny child and hardly knew where her own body ended and the outside world began.

Fran had found out at last why her father left her. Her mother had given her something of value after all. She had given Fran back her long-forgotten first memory, and it was love.

32   Ruined Maids

Jake had picked suicide for his theme of the month.

"*Shakespeare's characters have inspired many paintings, the most well-known of them probably being Ophelia as painted by John Everett Millais in 1852. The pre-Raphaelite brotherhood, of which Millais was a key figure along with the much finer artist Dante Gabriel Rossetti…*' Jake paused and deleted the respectful reference to Rossetti. Rossetti had helped Lizzie Siddal, he had tried to love her, and it had all turned sour. Not really relevant here.

"*Here, Ophelia lies supplicant, still as lovely in her death scene as she was in life: white flowers, symbols of purity, adorn the bank and nothing of her has been despoiled. There was, in fact, quite a spate of paintings of drowned women in England at that time. The decade between 1850 and 1860 produced no fewer than four morbid examples: Frederick Watts (Found Drowned); Dante Gabriel Rossetti (Found); Augustus Egg (Misfortune, Prayer, and Despair) and Abraham Soloman (Drowned! drowned!). The inference in each case would be clear to the Victorian viewer: these were women who had 'erred' – the euphemism for succumbing to sexual advances from a man – and had thrown themselves into water in despair since their lives were no longer worth living. They had fallen to the level of the sluts and whores who were contained in the 'foul ward' of the workhouse. Such was the generally held view of that era. And despite Millais' glamorous interpretation, when the painting was first exhibited it was considered even by his admirers to be inappropriate: Ruskin wondered why Millais could not paint 'pure nature'. The model by the way was the notorious Elizabeth Siddal, a titian-haired artists model much used, in every sense of the word, by all of the brotherhood painters, and a fine painter in her own right.*"

Jake wondered whether to delete 'in every sense of the word' but decided as he'd already mentioned Victorian values he may as well leave it in.

And how far have we moved from Victorian values? Jake wondered as he faxed the piece. We don't cover table-legs but we still have a Mary-Whitehouse dominated broadcasting corporation. Still hypocritical, too – you can't write *fuck* in an article, yet you can't sit on a train without seeing tits flashed at you from some bloke's copy of *The Sun*. How absurdly slow social evolution is, he thought with exasperation – we thought the '60s would overturn all those cumbersome social rules and moral values, but the Establishment got over its shock and steadied its grip. *The Little Red Book* and the trial of Oz are sentimental history now and *The Sun* will mingle mammaries with the tripe they call news till there's no trees left to make paper.

33　Not Waving

Leonora sat on the bank of the canal popping pills. She was washing her medication down with madeira, which might seem a strange choice for a sunny day but she kept it in the fridge and added plenty of ice. The tablets were plastic in bright colours and when Leonora had carefully separated the red side from the green to shake the contents into her glass she tossed them into the canal where they floated briefly like tiny marker buoys. 'Bye-bye my biodegradable buddies' said Leonora as they submitted to the weedy waters and sluggishly submerged.

Eventually her glass slipped and rolled down the last inches of the bank Leonora was so close to the edge she could almost touch it as it slid into the water. In fact she did: in fact, she reached after the glass and slipped into the canal just as sweetly. There was no panic as the splash subsided, no shout at all, just a whisper from Leonora's lips of that P word that Jake helped her to remember. *Passion*, murmured Leonora.

Babette found it hard to cry as she told the family, over and over again, about finding Leonora in the canal. 'I just kept thinking, 'How young she looks', all the wrinkles washed away and her skin somehow smoothed by the water. If I didn't know how old she was I'd have said she was in the prime of her life. Absolutely at her peak.'

The most poignant thing for Gwen was that she had been right all along. The bungalow was a death-trap, after all. Even Babette's vigilance could not protect Leonora from the canal. Not that she blamed Babette, of course; she could hardly be expected to provide round-the-clock care and who could have guessed Leonora would go wandering beside the weeping willows while Babette was on the telephone.

'She had a good innings,' Neville said.

'Bin bags,' thought Gwen, as they drove back home at the end of the day designated for honouring Leonora's leaving, 'it all comes to that. A life bagged up in plastic sacks.'

It was too hot for her black suit when they set off for the crematorium so Gwen wore a cotton dress with Broderie anglaise trim and a pleased flush, since Neville had told her she looked very fetching. He had opted for a light sports jacket. Clive was already out at the bungalow helping Babette with the buffet. *Thankfully, there has been little for me to do,* Gwen wrote. *Babette seems to have everything in hand. Mandy did ask me if we were thinking of suing over her medication. I said that would be a matter for her children and neither of them seem keen. At least she wouldn't have known anything about it.*

Babette simply beamed the whole afternoon and seemed incapable of a funereal expression. I almost wondered whether she had let Leonora slip in on purpose but she had nothing to gain. She was looking extraordinarily (Gwen paused, temporarily bereft of descriptive terminology, torn between *glamorous* and *grotesque,* eventually penning both)– *clad in some kind of antique flounced frock substantially let out at the seams.*

Fran seemed in something of a daze. I mentioned this to Neville but he said he thought this sometimes happened at funerals, especially to daughters of the deceased. Gwen put a little screamer after *deceased* to show she appreciated that this was one of Neville's little witticisms.

We were a small assembly at the crematorium. Jake was there – whatever his differences with Fran he seemed genuinely sad and switched off his Nikon for the service. He sent some wonderful flowers and the coffin was completely smothered.

Neville had asked Babette to go through Leonora's address book and invite every surviving friend but she said there wasn't one. I said, 'No friends?' and Babette said, 'No address book.' It seems Leonora had jettisoned her past.

The only mourner outside the small group of family and close friends was Denzil from the Home who had heard the news from Mandy and elected himself to represent, as he put it, her many admirers. He brought a posy of notelets, including an illegible one from Madge and a wry, probably truthful, acknowledgement from Mrs Milsom that 'we will not readily see her like again.'

Babette of course selected the readings. Secular was only to be expected, though under the circumstances a poem about not waving but drowning was a trifle étrange. But also... What was the word? Not pungent – *poignant. The music seemed rather a mysterious choice too. Babette said she felt reggae was more tasteful, though compared to what remained a mystery. Then Babette brought out the buffet, which was all piled onto a table which her son Hawthorn had carried out from the house.* Gwen had experienced a somewhat difficult adjustment since the Day of the Rescue, when she realised that the youth who had saved her husband's life was also her own life's biggest secret, but referring to him as "Babette's son Hawthorn" gave a helpful distance. And anyway, as Gwen had been assured throughout her life whenever she had been troubled by anything, no point in brooding.

Fran had wanted to slip off quietly before the buffet when she realised Jake would be staying too, but her car was needed in the cavalcade for lifts. She stood in the garden watching Jake holding Cassie's hand. He was wearing a dark collarless suit in some soft material and looked effortlessly elegant despite the heat. She heard Babette say, 'Selene doesn't mind?' and watched as Jake shook his head. 'Storm in a teacup,' he said. Fran was too astounded to know whether she felt relieved or exasperated. She stepped towards him and kissed into the air near his face, saying, 'You're looking well.' Breezily, she hoped.

'I wanted to express my condolences,' Jake said. 'Leonora was always very special to me.'

Fran laughed, 'Yes, I know,' she said.

'Solitary and passionate. I think what I fell in love with was the Leonora in you.'

'I see. Lonely and lewd.'

'Not at all. Your mother was the most amazing person I ever met. She saw her life as a journey, and she savoured every step of it. You'll be like her, Fran.'

'Will I? I'm not staying here, anyway.'

'Where do you plan to go?' This was Neville, who had been hovering. There seemed to be something he wanted to say.

Fran shrugged. 'I don't care. Anywhere. I'll use my inheritance to travel.'

Neville chewed his lip. This was about the only mannerism the siblings shared. He said, 'How much do you think you will need?'

'Whatever I get. There must be something.'

'Ants!' Gwen exclaimed, 'heading for the honeyed scones!' and she flapped at them with a napkin. Clive intervened to divert the lead ant and re-route the platoon to safety. 'Did you know,' he enquired ingenuously, 'that individual ants are actually totally anarchic? Gran told me.'

'What's a narkick?' Cassie asked without looking up from the rosebush where she was busy shredding the peachy blossoms.

'What on earth are you doing?' Clive demanded in lieu of further definition.

'I'm making nests for ladybirds.'

'Ladybirds don't need nests,' Clive told her. 'They fly away.'

'They need something to fly away from,' said Cassie sagely.

Fran turned away.

'Cassie seems happy,' she said, and Jake said 'Yeah, she's fine. I thought it would be good to bring her along.' Fran could think of no appropriate comment so she said 'Are you going back to London tonight?'

'No, I'm going to stay with my mother for a few days. We're planning a remembrance garden for Jessica next year.'

'Oh. That's nice.'

'Yes, we think so. For her birthday, as it would have been. A sort of present from us both.'

I could have suggested that, thought Fran forlornly. She imagined herself kneeling on a flower-filled bank as Jake told her, *you inspired this, darling, with your healing love.*

Fran took a helping of strawberries.

'From the garden,' Babette said. 'Picked this morning – amazing how many berries I found, right at the end of their season.'

'Leonora would have been thrilled,' said Gwen sentimentally.

'Really?' Fran said with an odd little giggle. 'I doubt if Mum would have cared at all.'

At the end of the afternoon Babette handed the bungalow keys over to Neville.

'Where will you live now?' he asked, pocketing them carefully.

'School term starts next week,' said Babette with mystifying indifference and a mouthful of meringue. Gwen swept the last of the soiled doilies into the rubbish bag and enquired delicately, 'Will there be any difficulty with your accommodation?'

'Oh, I'll shift around I expect,' Babette answered easily. 'Milly Tanaka is moving out so I might take her rooms, for a start.'

Gwen seemed satisfied. 'Pity about Bosnia,' she said to Fran *sotto voce*, 'but naturally Babette wants to stay in this area to get to know Tom.'

'Can't he go to Bosnia too?' Fran's enquiry was more flippant than investigative but Gwen answered quite seriously. 'Oh no, he's just been appointed Community Liaison Officer for the Half Way House project.' She gave Clive's friend Tom Hawthorn a look of inordinate pride. He was swinging Cassie up into the air and down again and, as she clung to him laughing, Jake called across sharply, 'Cassie, remember what I told you.'

'I'm not on a lap,' said Cassie indignantly. 'I'm in the air.'

Tom Hawthorn replaced Cassie gracefully on the grass and Jake said quietly, 'Well, be careful, for everyone's sake.'

'Plenty of time to decide where to live,' Babette said. 'Procrastination, that's my philosophy. Insufficient procrastination has always been my undoing. I shall try to be less impulsive.' She turned to Fran. 'You off?' she said. 'I'll walk you to the gate.'

As they walked up the path after Fran's farewells, Babette said 'She'd stopped her morning recital, you know.'

Fran was puzzled. 'I didn't know Leonora ever used to sing.'

'She didn't sing, she'd just recite stuff, quietly, in her room. Names – people and places, that sort of thing. She started it after she lost her photos in the flood.'

Fran was even more baffled now.

'What flood? The canal has never flooded since we've lived here.'

'The washing machine flood.' Babette's illustrative gesture at the recollection suggested a torrent Horatius himself might have feared to wrestle with. 'Let's just say, it was all getting difficult for her.'

Fran felt the familiar flash of guilt but Babette's added noncommittally 'All water under the bridge, really.'

Out of sight of the dwindling party on the river bank below, Babette gave Fran one of her hugs. 'I'm proud of you today,' she said.

'I don't know why. I didn't use any courage, just the usual avoidance tactics.'

'Well, at least you know the tactics. That's a start.'

'But I don't really feel anything. Jake's rejection left me sort of numb,' Fran confessed. Jake's tactile possessiveness had convinced her he would never reject her, and now he had. Still lingering at the gate, she said, 'I know I should have done something different, but I still don't know what I should have done.'

'Oh darling, you don't, do you?' said Babette and Fran nestled again in her hug.

'I should have talked, I suppose,' she said moistly after a while, 'but I didn't know what to say.'

'No-one does,' said Babette, wiping her face with a flounce

of vintage bridal gown. 'You find the right words by trying them out, that's the only way I know. It's like being lost in a forest. You can't find the path till you start blundering through the trees.'

Fran contemplated the scenario and managed a wry smile. 'That's not exactly the way I wanted to live my life. But I suppose you're right. Do you think a therapist would help?'

'No. Why?'

'Well, they're specialists in finding paths out of emotional forests, aren't they?'

'Yeah, but why go to a cartographer when all you need's a compass and a torch?'

Fran sighed. 'I wish I didn't need anything to get me out of a dark place. I'd rather not be starting from here at all. But here is where I am.'

'Here is where we all are, ducks,' said Babette, but gently, as they disengaged. Just as Fran turned away, she fumbled under her skirt panels and produced a brown envelope, saying conspiratorially, 'I found this. Thought you'd like it.'

'What is it?'

'Your inheritance, I think,' said Babette.

Fran peered within and saw the small black-and-white portrait from the Passport Photograph machine. She thanked Babette and took the envelope.

After they parted Fran sat in her car contemplating the picture of the beautiful man who died, whose name she never knew until last week, whose image was the only photograph her mother kept. Leonora had withheld so much from her, and Babette had taken so much of the little that was left of their connection, but this at least was hers, and would stay her secret. Let them all think she was miserably mourning a maternal passing or miffed because she lacked any inheritance; she was happy to stay apart from the palaver of bereavement. Once, she thought, I would have told Babette everything – would have even shown her Leonora's letter. Those naive times have gone, they left when Jake dumped me. I need time alone now, with my parents. Both of them.

She put the picture back in the envelope and picked up the letter that she had stolen on the last night of her mother's life, to read it once again.

My dearest darling Francilla,
~~Please~~ forgive me for failing to tell you everything you have, I know,
wanted to know. The truth is, I have always feared and avoided
intimacy, even —perhaps especially— with those I dearly love. My
beloved Paul was, of course, your father. We met on a holiday job
grape-picking. I was a mature student and considerably older than
him but we both decided to drop out of our courses and stay on, living
together. Why, I don't know — it seemed romantic but there were
no jobs once the tourist season ended and by the time I discovered
I was pregnant, Paul had found he was not so much bisexual as
homosexual. We parted friends but it was nearly five years before
we met again. He turned up at my place in St Ives knowing he was
sick — this is a hard part to write because he hadn't realised what
it was. He fell in love with you, Franny, but I was worried about
infection — two of his friends had died from this dreadful illness, so
although we didn't know the name of it then, or even realise then
how it was passed on, I feared for you. I couldn't keep you near him
— I even disposed of the doll he brought you, which was of course
with hindsight quite needless. As I say, we didn't know. I didn't mind
risking my life but I wanted you safe, and I wanted Paul to be loved
until he died. Which was two years later, and I was able to fetch you
home.

Francilla, my darling girl, you were such a beautiful child, and
so sweet-natured, never provocative, a little princess, and I knew you
would be a clever, beautiful woman. Don't give up on love yet — you
will always be beloved.

And then there were an awful lot of xxxes

And then there was a final line, after Leonora's scrawled
signature, which she had almost scratched out, or maybe
underlined in a shaky hand.

You were the love of his life

As with all the other times she had re-read the letter that was her
only inheritance from her mother, Fran felt a forlorn exasperation
mingled with her relief and happiness. It was only this time she

noticed a small addition scrawled in tiny letters, sideways, on the back of the page. The handwriting appeared to be written in biro not fountain pen, which might account for its oddly discordant look.

Fran read: Your father's father was an ambassador in Italy during the 1950s, he lived in Rome. She folded the letter, and the secret location again disappeared.

Why Leonora would have suddenly decided to impart this one, fragile, detail of her inheritance, Fran had no idea, but it glowed like the light under the door of a secret passage. She already knew that she had her father's surname. Her mother could not have given her anything more precious.

35   Next Day

Leonora had jettisoned her past. Gwen re-read her words and added *It is almost uncanny, all that clutter and none of it personal effects. Not even a photograph. We sent many family snaps over the years but none have survived. There was really nothing to dispose of. Even the ducks have gone.*

She felt somehow that the story was unfinished and wondered whether it mattered at all that the question of deliberate intent had not, somehow, cropped up. The D word, as Gwen mentally termed dementia, had been mentioned more than once when her care was discussed, always in the abstract and never conclusively. It now seemed to Gwen that Leonora, who had abandoned every project she ever started as soon as it began to bore her, was also extremely likely, after a couple of falls and one too many episodes of forgetfulness, to throw in the towel regretlessly. Should she confide this thought to her diary? For Gwen, now aware she was writing for two, had begun to suffer a basic authorial anxiety: how much does the reader already understand, and how much needs to be explained? Frankly, Gwen's inner author reminded her, if you have thought of it, Neville has. It was a curious way to commune but it had certainly enriched their relationship and Gwen was not quite sure how to move their precious new rapport to another level.

Gwen put down her pen. Neville was touching her head, carefully, uncertainly. He pushed his fingers into her glossy bob and rubbed gently on the lumpy nodules behind her ears.

'That head massage thing you like', he said. 'Is it here?'

'Yes,' said Gwen. She closed her eyes. Neville's hand moved caressingly across her temples and he finger-walked with soft pressure across the top of her head. In a minute, she thought, I shall say *Neville we should talk.*

Minutes passed.

It occurred to Gwen that perhaps they were.

Fran is sitting on the floor of her living-room, now carpeted with Babette's collage, looking around her at the paintings propped at floor level waiting for packing. Babette comes in with supper for them both on a tray.

'Macaroni cheese!' she announces. 'Nursery food, comforting now there's such an Autumn nip in the air. The wind's rattling that back door like a machine gun.'

'I know,' Fran says, taking her plate, 'I think the whole place needs quite a lot of repairs. I was surprised how much Neville paid me for it, but he was positive this sort of property is rising in value.' Neville seemed more positive about everything these days. Giving up his job had lifted lugubrious years from him; Fran barely recognised the vibrant couple in the Caribbean holiday photo Gwen sent her.

'And of course, there's really good internet signal round here, which helps a lot,' Fran adds, 'I think that's when the anti-mast protests in the village collapsed – people started realising the added-value to property from ruining the landscape.' She wiggles her fingers during the last three words to show where quote marks were needed to point out the ironies of local concern, and Babette nods.

'Yeah, middle class values are pretty flaky. Still, you seem to be coming through ok.' She looks around approvingly at the series of new paintings Fran has prepared for her exhibition. They are dark and thickly painted, with vestigial shapes that might be children crying thinly beyond a black membrane in a dense forest.

'Excellent,' Babette says. 'They're beginning to look a lot like life.'

'Well, I dunno about that, but Don's keen, and he's sponsoring the Gallery. Isn't it strange, Babette, the way last year turned out.

You getting that Head of Care job at the new Halfway Hostel –
which wouldn't even have happened if Tom hadn't done such a
good job reassuring all those local people –'

'I know! Cushty or what? And that only got funding because
of that bloke who used to sit on the bench killing himself,'
Babette adds, though still smirking with maternal pride.

Fran nods. 'Sad, wasn't it. Icarus, Jake used to call him.
He took him ciggies sometimes, and they chatted.' She notes
Babette's look of stupefaction and adds, 'You know, in that
painting of him falling to his death, and nobody noticing –'

'I know who Icarus is,' Babette interrupts, 'I just didn't know
Jake ever talked to that man.'

There is a conversation there, perhaps, but Fran is reluctant to
embark on it right now. She moves on seamlessly.

'Yes, it was awful – but it did highlight a need, didn't it? And
then everything sort of fitted together. Synchronicity. Or, what's
that other word, the one with a p – serendipity!'

'Yeah, we're just lucky, really. We're in a good place – this part
of the world is pretty well sorted.' Babette waves an expansive
arm, slopping cut-price Spanish wine slightly – 'Well, it is
now they've got rid of the smouldering piles of dead cows, and
we won't be seeing anything as horrible like that again in our
lifetime, with all the advances in meds and stuff.'

Fran nods. 'Yes, this is a good time to be alive. And we're
lucky to live down south, too, with less poverty or cultural
tribalism.' Noticing Babette is miming bafflement, she adds, 'I
mean, I realise it's not particularly mixed-race out here, not like
Bristol, but there isn't a them-and-us feeling about incomers, is
there?'

Babette concurs dubiously. 'Apart from the blow-ins pushing
up house prices, so local kids can't afford to stay and carry on
their family trades – plus there's no money in farming unless you
leave half your fields empty for set-aside payouts. Which isn't
really the way to feed a community.'

'But it works,' Fran says. 'It seems to, somehow, anyway.'

Babette shrugs, splashing Chardonnay across the Hanging.
She rubs it into the fabric, saying cheerily, 'Oh well, doubt if

we'll be doing anything with this, now, anyway. It was fun, but quite naive – a kind of affectation really, to think that because we're living in a country at peace we have the right to scold other countries about their wars. It's nothing to do with us, really.'

'Neville is still anxious about the Middle East,' Fran said, but cautiously because she really didn't want anything to wobble their rapport – not now, with the difficult days all behind them.

'Yeah,' Babette conceded, '– because he was educated in the old ways, when leaders started wars to throw their weight around. Weapons have got too deadly now – it's not just like sending off a few thousand working class lads to die in trenches, or even a couple of hundred Bomber Harrises. I'm as cynical as the next person, but I honestly can't see anything serious starting in our lifetime, can you?'

Fran strokes the silken embroidered peace lilies as she concedes. 'It was a great idea, a peace banner – a mantra, as well as a protest. But I guess we've all moved on.'

'Yeah. Even your paintings have gone a bit goth, haven't they?'

Fran had not considered her new work as 'goth'. She smiles sleekly and, to avoid discussion, murmurs, 'Let's just call it experiential learning.'

Babette shrugs. 'Well, whatever – and ta for letting me stay on here till my flat's ready at the hostel. Gwen said I could house-sit at theirs while they're on holiday, but Clive needs a bit of space for the band.'

'Stay here as long as you like,' Fran says, taking a forkful of supper.

Babette, with a mouthful of pasta, raises her fork appreciatively and, when able to speak again, says, 'Actually I was hoping your dad's family would still be living over there and they would embrace you in their Italian arms, all jangling with expensive bangles… *Cara! Cara!*'

She puts down her plate to create an impassioned demonstration and Fran snorts with laughter.

'Babette that's ridiculous! They were English anyway, and would have been very proper, I'm sure, even if they'd stayed. But nobody could remember my grandfather so he obviously wasn't very important. It was just lovely that they were all so… nice. Everyone I talked to. And then I got that interview on the local arts programme, once I'd brushed up on my very primitive Italian, and that was what led to the chance to exhibit when I got back… It was such a good thing to make that trip.'

'And when you take the exhibition to London, will you see Jake?'

'Well, Cassie, certainly. I had a sweet card from her with lots of kisses. That childish handwriting is irresistible, isn't it? Jake… maybe. We are in touch, you know, on Friends Reunited, but I don't know about meeting up. He says he'd like to, but… the world is full of men. I'm just going to… trust life.'

Fran smiles and offers out her hands to the air to show she knows that this might sound absurd, and that she realises that life is a swirling, sometimes brutal, flux of experience without finite line or form, and that it has neither frame nor fixative.

Babette spots a blob of sauce on the Hanging and wipes it up with her finger. 'You do know that he – Jake – was the love of your life,' she informs Fran in between finger-licks.

'No, Babette. My children will be the love of my life.'

This time Fran speaks with unaffected certainty. That's one thing I've learnt, she thinks. Leonora was mistaken. Your children are your children.

It seems strange, though, to be sitting on these tragic strafed streets talking about love and babies. But life goes on. And life is not like art.

Crysse Morrison describes her writing as a patchwork portfolio: her published work ranges from novels, short stories, and poetry to articles on writing, photography, running, and basically anything she was interested in at the time, from an interview with Linda McCartney, to educational books, games, and computer programs. *The Times* wrote of  her debut novel *Frozen Summer* (Hodder & Stoughton) 'Morrison is a superb storyteller', and Luke Wright found her first poetry collection *Crumbs from a Spinning World* (Burning Eye) 'sharp as a serpent's tooth and a lot funnier.' She has also written several stage plays produced in Bristol and elsewhere, a play for radio, co-ran a Children's Theatre company, and reviews theatre productions for *Plays International*.

Crysse grew up in South London and after gaining a Masters degree from Trinity College Dublin lived for a while in Northern Ireland, which later inspired her novel *The Price of Bread* (Hobnob Press, 2020). After returning to England she developed her career as a lecturer, eventually focusing on leading creative writing groups in many locations in the UK – even Centre Parcs – and around the world from Chile to Cambodia, including France, Spain, Italy, and Skyros, among other Greek islands. A selection of her short stories was published in 2021 as *Déjà Lu* (Hobnob Press) and Crysse maintains her strong interest in spoken word poetry, currently collaborating with Hazel Stewart as *Live & Lippy*.

Crysse has two sons who both work in media, and four grandchildren, and now lives in Frome, Somerset.